"I guess we've avoided it long enough."

Zak moved to the kitchen table. "Come and take a look at the survey."

"I sure hope you're wrong about this," Tess told him, "because if you're not, Gib's going to be the devil to live with."

Zak moved behind her, his chest lightly brushing her shoulder, his warm breath ruffling her hair. "This is where one corner stake is located—" he pointed to a spot near the south end of the property "—and this is the other." His finger stopped precisely on their Adam-and-Eve tree.

Tess's heart quickened. "But that has always been on Timber West land," she cried. "Gib will never accept this!"

She stepped toward the door. "I've got to get back," she said desperately, knowing that if she didn't move away from him now, she might reach out—and lose herself in his arms. And that, she decided, would be even more disastrous!

ABOUT THE AUTHOR

Patricia Edwards got the idea for *Sweet Promised Land* while on a photo assignment for a magazine. The subject was a father-daughter logging team. The setting, too, was based on reality; Patricia lives in a log house on thirty acres of woodland in Newberg, Oregon, with her wolf-dog, Sheena.

Patricia began writing several years ago as a means to sell her photographs, but now photography has taken a back seat to fiction. This is her first novel for Harlequin.

Sweet Promised Land

PATRICIA EDWARDS

Harlequin Books

TORONTO • NEW YORK • LONDON
AMSTERDAM • PARIS • SYDNEY • HAMBURG
STOCKHOLM • ATHENS • TOKYO • MILAN

To my mother, who encouraged an overactive child
to sit still and write a story, introducing me to the
world of fiction; to my close friend, Barbara, who
listened with a critical ear; and most of all, to my
own hero, Ed, who persuaded me to take an
abandoned manuscript off the shelf and bring it
back to life

Published April 1991

ISBN 0-373-70446-1

SWEET PROMISED LAND

CHAPTER ONE

Tess O'Reilly pulled her Jeep off the red-dirt logging road into a clearing, skidding to a halt in front of the trailer that would be her office. She climbed down and paused, her dark eyes resting on the timeworn buildings. It had been six years since she'd seen the logging camp. Nothing much had changed, yet it seemed different somehow. The silvery boards on the cookshack appeared more weathered, the fir trees behind the bunkhouse higher, the carpet of moss on the roof of the woodshed thicker.

Even old Harvey looked older. She stared at the International Harvester truck with TIMBER WEST LOGGING hand-painted across its door. It was still parked beside the water tower where it had been when she'd left, but now weeds reached through the grille and thrust from under a hood that remained ajar. She smiled at its crooked mouth. Harvey, as her dad had named his truck, was the first piece of equipment Gib O'Reilly had ever bought. Loaded high with cut wood, the old truck had brought them many a belly laugh as it belched and bucked over the rough logging roads. The sight of old Harvey brought happy memories.

Tess watched the men ambling to the cookshack. They, too, were different, unfamiliar, except for old

Ezra Radley, the little camp cook who scurried around the pack, a sack of flour slung over his shoulder. She couldn't hold back another smile as she watched his short quick movements. There had always been a special place in her heart for Ezzie.

As the last of the men funneled into the small building, she settled her hard hat over her thick dark hair, slipped on her denim jacket and strode toward the cookshack. At the entrance she paused, listening to the boisterous chatter coming from inside. Then she drew a long breath and swept open the door.

The guffaws and bellows of the men tapered into silence as eyes raked her, scanning the tousled hair framing her delicate face, the plaid shirt tucked into fitted jeans, the soft curve of her breasts.

She parked her hands on her hips and studied the gawking faces. "I'm Tess O'Reilly," she said. "I'll be taking over for my father." She waited, and when she got no response, she continued. "I want to get the equipment moved to the north plateau near the ridge this afternoon and start cutting pole timber on Monday."

A man with hair the color of wet sand stood and squared his shoulders. "Gib doesn't log that area this time of year."

Tess met his challenging eyes. "And your name is?"

"Broderick. Curt Broderick."

"You operate the dozer, right?" Tess said.

Curt Broderick looked down at the surprised faces of the men, straightened and replied, "Uh, that's right."

"Okay, Curt. Gib's not running this operation now—I am—and we *will* be cutting pole timber near the ridge."

Although she knew the man was right—they didn't usually log that area until the spring rains stopped—this year she and her father had decided to cut the pole timber for much-needed operating capital while the price was high. Otherwise, come tax time, Timber West was apt to fold. And one thing Tess had decided when she offered to take over her father's failing business was to set Timber West back on a firm financial foundation.

Curt shifted his weight. "We won't be doing anything until we get a tire for the skidder," he said, a satisfied smile twisting the corner of his mouth.

Tess looked directly at him. "Just get the rest of the equipment moved—I'll worry about the skidder tire." She was more than a little annoyed that the tire hadn't arrived. Determined that her first day would run smoothly, she'd arranged for the huge tire to be delivered earlier in the week. She'd deal with the tire jobber in Bakers Creek later, after she'd finished with the men. "Any other problems?" she asked, scanning their faces before allowing her eyes to rest on Curt Broderick again.

Curt stared at her with undisguised cynicism. Tess held his gaze. She'd worked crews of men before, and she'd learned early that spotting the troublemakers and confronting them first on a one-to-one basis often earned their respect. Curt Broderick, she suspected, was a man who needed individual attention. "Curt?"

she asked. "Any other problems?" She quietly waited for his response.

His eyes bored into her, then he shook his head. "No, just the tire."

"All right then," she said, turning from Curt, "which one of you is Jed Swenson?" She looked over the faces in the crowd, searching for the man her father had described to her as woods boss. When she got no response, she again looked at Curt. "Didn't Swenson see the notice posted about this meeting?"

Curt scratched his chin. "Well, yes. Maybe you can find him in the bunkhouse."

Muffled laughter spread, then died.

Tess propped her hands on her hips. "I don't intend to go looking for Swenson in the bunkhouse. You tell him to be in my office at suppertime."

Curt's lips spread into a rueful smile. "I will if I can find him."

"What do you mean, if you can find him? He *is* woods boss here, isn't he?" Suppressed chuckles rustled through the group. "I see," Tess said, crossing her arms and looking solemnly at the men. She studied their amused faces. "If you don't find Swenson, we'll start moving equipment without him."

A voice rose from the back of the room. "Gib doesn't work us past noon."

Tess stared at the man goading her, aware of more subdued snickers. "What's your name?"

"Dempsey."

"Mr. Dempsey, if you find the hours too long, perhaps a rest would be appropriate."

"Rest?"

"Away from here. Where the hours aren't so long."

Dempsey glanced around, then cleared his throat and mumbled, "Well, sometimes Gib does work us longer."

"I know how Gib O'Reilly runs this camp," Tess said, her ebony eyes flashing. "I also know he keeps logs on the dock—and they don't get there by people quitting at noon."

Dempsey flushed but said nothing as the men nudged him in the ribs and swatted him on the back.

Tess noted the man's heightened color and smiled inwardly. That one would be no problem. She raised her chin and looked from face to face. "Now, does anyone else have any questions?"

A voice bellowed. "You married?" Laughter erupted.

Tess stared at the man who had spoken, and a hush fell over the room. She repeated soberly, "Any questions about the job." Heads swung from side to side, and she continued, "Then in twenty minutes we'll start moving equipment up to the north ridge. Dempsey, I want you to gather the saws and take them in the pickup. Herring? Is Herring here?"

"Right here."

"Okay, Herring," she said. "You bring the tools, grease units and gas tanks in the small service truck. Curt, you move the Cat. And if anyone sees Swenson, tell him I'll expect him in my office."

"Good luck," called someone in the crowd.

Tess ignored the remark, removed her hard hat and turned toward the bar. "Ezzie," she called to the wiry little man behind the plank counter, "give the boys a round of beer—and one for me, too." She looked at the men and smiled. "Twenty minutes boys, then back to work—and you can call me TJ."

While Ezzie shoved bottles of beer into outstretched hands, Tess climbed onto a stool and watched. As the men moved from the counter, Ezzie made his way toward her, his cloth swirling along the worn but polished bar top. He slid a beer in front of her. Tess's eyes moved from the leathery fingers gripping the bottle to the whiskered face. Ezzie grinned. "Welcome back, TJ."

Tess smiled at him. "I guess I'm really home," she said. "I haven't been called that since I left this place."

Ezzie studied her for a moment, his bright eyes beaming from beneath bushy gray brows. He smoothed his whiskers. "You know, there's something I've always wondered but didn't dare ask about when you were a young whippersnapper, you being so spunky and all."

Tess tipped her head. "Well, I'm not as formidable as I was at fourteen. Go ahead and ask."

Ezzie hesitated, then ventured, "What does the *J* stand for?"

Tess shifted on her stool. "You've touched a very sensitive spot," she said, "but if you've waited this long to ask, and you promise never to tell anyone..."

"My lips are sealed," Ezzie said, leaning forward, his eyes wide with anticipation.

Tess moved closer, glanced around, then whispered, "It doesn't stand for anything."

Ezzie's lips parted and he stood straight. "Nothing? Then, what's your middle name?"

"Now you really have touched a sore spot," she said.

"We've come this far, TJ. You're not going to let me down now, are you?"

Tess sighed. "Okay, Ez, but this time you have to swear—on this bar top."

Ezzie's face broke into a wide grin. He raised his right hand and placed the left one on the bar. "May I never have another drop to drink if I tell."

"Okay, then." Tess grabbed the tip of his beard, pulled him close and whispered, "Veronica."

"Veronica!"

"Ezzie!"

"Sorry," he said in a hushed voice. "What's wrong with Veronica?"

Tess looked at him. "You're kidding!" she replied. "I have an image to uphold here. And anyway, TV would sound kind of silly, don't you think?"

"TV?"

"Teslyn Veronica." The color in Tess's cheeks brightened. "Now let's get off this subject and back to the business at hand."

Ezzie smiled in amusement. "Okay, TJ." He started polishing the bar top with his cloth again. "Are you going to be staying in the cabin or in Bakers Creek?" he asked.

"The cabin—at least until things are running smoothly around here," she replied.

"When did you move back to Oregon?" he asked.

"Just last week."

Ezzie looked around at the men, lowered his voice and moved closer. "I reckon these guys kinda gave you a bad time, 'specially Broderick. But he's really an okay guy. He was woods boss for an outfit in Montana.''

Tess gave him a wry smile. ''Don't worry. I grew up around a bunch like this. They're mostly hot air.''

''I know that, but I was afraid maybe you'd forgotten. You better believe they wouldn't pull any of that stuff if your dad was here,'' Ezzie told her flatly, passing his cloth on either side of Tess's hand. ''How's he doing, anyway?''

''Pretty good, considering it's only been three weeks,'' Tess replied. She lifted her bottle, allowing Ezzie to swipe the cloth beneath it. ''An inconvenience like a heart attack's not apt to get Gib down for long.'' A warm feeling crept over her as she said her father's name. The first time she'd called him Gib was when she was nine, after her mother died. During her mother's long illness Tess and her father had grown close, and after the funeral she remembered looking up at him and saying, ''It's just you and me now. What are we going to do, Gib?''

''Go on with our lives,'' he'd assured her. Then he'd added, ''Just remember, we'll always have each other.'' After that she called him Gib, as if he was a friend, until the night, eight years ago, he'd found her with Zak. Then everything had changed. After that came turmoil and bitterness, and she hadn't felt like calling him anything. Neither Dad nor Gib had seemed right....

The cloth in Ezzie's hand stopped. His eyes grew wide. ''Is Gib plannin' on comin' back to work soon?''

Tess raised a brow. "I'm sure he is. His doctor had a devil of a time keeping him quiet in the hospital with him calling out here every day to run things. I knew if I didn't take over, he'd probably be out here in his hospital gown directing operations."

Ezzie laughed. "Gib never was one to sit back when there was work to be done," he said. "What about you? How long are you here for?"

Something about the tone of the old man's voice made Tess hesitate before answering. She looked into his curious eyes and wondered how much Ezzie knew about what had happened between her and Gib, or if, in fact, he even knew about their estrangement. She took a slow sip of beer, then replied, "As long as he needs me."

Ezzie rubbed his chin. "You're a good sport. I know Gib's glad you're back and taking over for him. But then, you always did like it here around the equipment and all. I reckon you can still outdrive any of these men on the Cat—or any of the other equipment for that matter."

Tess shoved a renegade curl behind her ear. "Gib made sure I had lots of experience. I practically grew up riding with him on the Cat."

Ezzie grinned, and from within the bristle of whiskers a gold tooth peeped out. "You were about the prettiest darn Cat skinner anyone around these parts ever saw."

Tess laughed. "And probably the most obnoxious."

Ezzie winked. "I won't argue with that," he said, his grin growing wider. Then he leaned forward, as if about to share a deep secret, and looked into Tess's eyes. "Think you'll be able to handle these boys?"

"You'd better believe I will," Tess said. "One way or another, I'll get some work out of them."

Ezzie's eyes brightened with amusement. "I'm sure you will." He raised a brow. "And speakin' of work, I've got to get busy."

"And I've got to fetch my boots from the cabin."

Ezzie moved away, swirling the cloth along the counter, and Tess left the cookshack and headed for her Jeep. As she walked past the old splitting stump, she paused. Her eyes focused on the network of ax marks on the top of the stump, and an uneasiness swept over her. It was here that she'd first seen Zak, the year the timber carnival was held at Timber West. It was ten years ago, when she was fourteen and Zak was twenty-two, but she still remembered how his lean body glistened beneath the summer sun as he swung his ax, practicing for the wood-splitting contest.

She'd stood watching, impressed by the play of smooth muscles in his arms. Then she'd noticed that he didn't hold the ax the way Gib had taught her to hold it. When Zak paused to wipe the sweat from his brow, she'd walked up to him and shaken his arm, saying, "Hey, mister, you're not holding that ax right."

Zak looked at her with amusement. "My name's not Mister, it's Zak—Zakhra Bertsolari de Neuville."

Tess eyed him dubiously. Unable to pronounce the long Basque names, she'd said, "You're either putting me on or those are very weird names."

Zak laughed, then shoved his beret back on his head, allowing the bright sun to spill across his damp forehead and into his steel-gray eyes. "They're not weird names if you're Basque," he'd said.

Tess thought of when Gib had taken her to the Basque community of Navarre, thirty miles away, on the other side of the mountain. It had been like a different world. They'd seen old women in long dresses and men wearing berets. And in the hills near Navarre they'd seen shepherds in baggy pants herding strange-looking sheep with curved horns, patrician noses and curly wool that hung like blankets. Taking note of Zak's baggy blue pants and tall black boots, she'd asked, "Are you from Navarre?"

"I am," he'd answered, resting the ax on his shoulder.

She shaded her eyes. "What are you doing around here?"

Zak looked toward the forest separating his cabin from the logging camp. "I've got a cabin through those woods," he replied, pointing, "and I'm working at the wildlife park down the road. Who are you?"

"TJ O'Reilly."

"Well, TJ O'Reilly, I suppose you can swing an ax and split dead center," he said, holding the ax out to her.

"Sure," Tess replied, adjusting her hat so her thick mane of hair would stay tucked inside. She grabbed the ax. "Go ahead. Set up a log."

Zak smiled, then placed a log on end and stepped back.

Tess focused on the X chalked across the end of the log and chewed her lip for a moment. Then she swung the ax high overhead and sent it cracking into the log, splitting it into two sections. Zak picked up one of the pieces and studied it. "Hmm. Not bad."

Tess looked up with narrowed incensed eyes. "What do you mean, not bad? It's right on the line." She pointed to the chalk line visible along the edge of the split.

"Oh, so it is," Zak kidded. Then he gave her a smile that lit up his entire face and added, "Learn to hold that ax correctly and maybe someday you'll be able to pick up some speed." He took the ax from her hands and held it as before. "Now you'd best run along and join your friends," he said, motioning to a group of young boys who stood watching them a short distance away.

At the time Tess was not yet fifteen. Now, after all these years, she still remembered the way Zak had looked at her later that day, after she'd won the pole-climbing contest.

She'd scurried down the pole and waited with the other contestants—all of them about her age, but all of them boys. When she looked at her dad, he gave her a thumbs-up and a wide grin, and she held her breath as the announcer boomed over the loudspeaker, "Well, folks, we have a repeat winner. TJ O'Reilly has done it again." The crowd cheered. Tess raked her hat from her head and tossed it into the air.

Her father rushed over, swooped her into his arms and spun her around. "I knew you could do it, baby," he said. "Now it's my turn. I'm heading for the crossbuck contest." He settled her back on the ground, retrieved her hat and plopped it on her head.

"Go get 'em," she called after him as he walked away. She glanced past the retreating figure of her father and saw Zak watching.

He approached her, a broad grin on his face. "Learn to swing an ax the way you climbed that pole," he said, "and I'll bow out of the contest. That was good climbing."

Tess was vividly aware of Zak's lean face and square jaw, the dark hair springing from under his beret, his soulful gray eyes as they looked at her. She felt as if all her strength had been sapped from her body, and for the first time in her life she couldn't think of anything clever, or otherwise, to reply. So she stood gaping at him, wishing she'd won anything but the pole-climbing contest—like the other girls, who took prizes in quilting or baking. Suddenly she wished she looked more like a woman. Although she was blossoming, she knew that the flannel shirt tucked inside her jeans and held in place by wide red suspenders hid every vestige of her changing figure.

Zak reached out, grasped the bill of her hat and lifted it from her head. "What's your real name, TJ?" he asked, his quiet voice sending a chill through her young body.

"Teslyn . . . Tess," she replied softly.

"That's a pretty name, Tess. You should use it." He slipped the hat into her hands, smiled and walked away, leaving her staring after him. Zak never called her TJ again. To him she was always Tess.

For the rest of the summer she'd looked for Zak every time she left the camp, but he appeared to have moved from the cabin next door. She didn't see him again until the next summer, when Zak's father bought the property next door. He contracted with Timber West to log the land, and Gib hired Zak to help. That was the summer Tess turned sixteen—the same summer her relationship with Zak bloomed and he vowed to love her always—then left....

At the sound of her father's truck pulling into the clearing, Tess raised her eyes from the grid of ax marks on the old splitting stump. Gib O'Reilly parked beside a bulldozer resting on heavy timbers near the machine shop. Tess drew an agitated breath and marched in long strides to where the tall lanky man was climbing from his truck.

Gib waved and smiled at Tess. "I'd hoped to catch you before you went inside to face the men," he said, "but I see I'm too late."

"Dammit, Gib," Tess replied, "you know you're not supposed to be here."

Gib straightened. "Doc Evans said I could do things in moderation."

"Yes, and you know exactly what he meant by that," Tess said. "He specifically told you to stay away from Timber West until after your next checkup."

Gib's eyes moved restlessly around the compound, then shifted back to meet Tess's unwavering gaze. "I wanted to make sure Herring's doing his job."

Tess glared at her father. "Making sure Herring does his job is my responsibility now." She noted the lines of stubbornness etched around his mouth and sighed. "I have enough to worry about today without you adding to it by coming out here—"

"Another reason I came," Gib broke in, squaring his thin shoulders. "I figured the boys aren't as apt to give you a hard time if I'm around."

"If they give me a hard time, I'll handle it," Tess said. Her dark eyes flared. "I'm not exactly new to this, you know." She thought of the long hours she'd worked helping David with their construction business in Portland. Even after their four-year marriage ended in divorce, when she became Tess O'Reilly again, she'd joined Pacific Coast Construction in Seattle, continuing to work as a general contractor.

"You haven't worked with these men," Gib insisted. "They're not used to having a woman boss."

"We both knew that when you agreed to let me take over this job," Tess replied.

Gib eyed her with concern. "You might find you've bitten off more than you can chew with Jed Swenson."

"I'm not easily intimidated by male chauvinism," Tess said. "And from what you've told me, that's exactly what I'll be facing with Swenson." She studied the shadows beneath her father's eyes and the angles of his sullen face and realized how much older he looked since his heart attack. The discovery made her feel anxious. "Please, Gib, go back home and let me handle things here on my own."

Gib's thin lips pressed together in determination. "I need to stop by Carl Yaeger's first—make sure he knows I don't have one foot in the grave yet. Ezzie said he'd been by asking questions about the equipment, and I know damn well he'll be pushing to buy us out again. He's interested in that tract of land owned by Pacific Development, too."

The insistent flutter Tess had felt in her stomach all day settled momentarily as her annoyance with her father grew. "This is exactly what Dr. Evans was talking about," she said in a tight voice. "You come out here and suddenly you've got to see Carl Yaeger, and heaven knows what else, when all you're really supposed to be concerned with is your heart." She sighed. "Please, Gib, just go home. I'll stop by tomorrow and fill you in on everything."

Gib's eyes moved impatiently over the bulldozer, then settled on her. "Damn, you're a stubborn woman," he said. "Come hell or high water you're determined to do things on your own, whether it's running this place—or running away from home." He turned and walked toward his truck.

"Gib?" Tess called after him, feeling the knot in her stomach tighten again with his last statement, knowing their old grievance was still there.

He glanced back and waited.

"Wish me well."

Gib studied her for a moment, then smiled. "Just don't be too hard on my men."

Tess warmed under her father's rare smile, but as she watched his truck roll out of sight, the apprehension that had plagued her over the past few weeks returned. His heart attack had jolted her. Now she felt a desperate need to restore the relationship they'd once had, before it was too late. Leaving her job in Seattle and returning to Bakers Creek to take over his logging operation was a start. He'd seemed pleased, and at last, after eight years, they were speaking civilly.

She climbed into her Jeep and headed down the logging road toward the main highway, where her cabin lay nestled among giant cedars and firs. Five minutes later she pulled to a halt in front of the small rustic building, reached for her bags and hopped out.

She stepped onto the porch, turned the key in the old iron lock and pushed the door, which creaked open on rusty strap-iron hinges. The aroma of smoke-impregnated stones filled the air inside the cabin. Her eyes rested on the stone fireplace. Images of cozy evenings spent in front of crackling fires took her back in time. She saw Gib standing there, tall and strong, his graying hair flecked with wood chips. But then the image gave way to another—Gib with hunched shoulders, tired eyes, pallid skin. She closed her eyes, but the vision wouldn't fade. So much still needed to be said, and there might be so little time.

She sighed, set her bags down and surveyed the familiar surroundings—the old oak cupboard stalwart against the far wall, the drop-leaf table Aunt Ruth had insisted they take to the cabin because it was too dilapidated for their house in Bakers Creek.

She looked back at the cupboard. Curious, she crossed the room and opened the pair of long doors. The chess set she'd given Gib was still there. They'd played chess most evenings while staying at the cabin, and by the time she was fourteen, Tess could play a pretty fair game, occasionally even beating her father. Those had been some of their most precious moments together. She lifted the box out of the cupboard and set up the board in its old place on the round oak coffee table, just in case Gib stopped by....

Her practical conscience interrupted her reflections. It was almost one o'clock and she still had to oversee moving the equipment and talk to the tire jobber in Bakers Creek before the shop closed. She pulled on her work boots, settled her hard hat on her head and stepped onto the porch, pulling the door closed behind her. Through the trees, the de Neuville cabin lay only a few hundred yards away. Shrugging off that disquieting thought, she climbed into the Jeep.

As she drove back to the logging camp, her eyes were fixed on the winding dirt road, but her mind was focused on Zak. At what point had she realized he wouldn't be back? Was it during her last bitter argument with Gib, the night she'd run away and married David? That had been after two years of waiting for Zak to return, a time when she could no longer bear the constant tension of confrontations with Gib because of him. David Barton had offered her another option—marriage, a new life somewhere else. But even that had failed. Although they'd worked well together in their construction business, their personal life had been trying, and after four years, Tess realized the marriage would never work, because she simply didn't love David.

Perhaps she'd never really gotten over Zak. After eight years, she still wondered where he was, and felt a vague hollowness.

CHAPTER TWO

WHILE ZAK DE NEUVILLE listened to his father's tirade, he studied Pio, his six-year-old son. The boy's
youthful face helped to take the edge off Jean-Pierre
de Neuville's angry words. A neighbor had just called
to inform them that Gib O'Reilly had cut four trees on
their land near Bakers Creek.

"...and furthermore I'll see O'Reilly rot in hell.
This time he's gone too far," Jean-Pierre said, his gray
eyes flaring with anger. Running restless fingers
through his shock of white hair, he paced between his
desk and the window. "He'll pay dearly for those
trees, every last one of them." He bellowed down the
hall to his wife. "Gratianne! Call Bill! I'm taking
O'Reilly to court!"

Gratianne de Neuville appeared from the hall, her
clear blue eyes moving between Zak and her husband. "What's the point, Jean-Pierre?" she asked in
a calm voice. "The trees are gone, so what's to be
gained—besides more white hair and high blood pressure?" She remained standing in the doorway, chin
raised, her high cheekbones thrown into relief by the
cool morning sun.

"My blood pressure's likely to be even higher if I do
nothing." Jean-Pierre emphasized his words by

pounding his fist on his desk. "Those damned O'Reillys have been thorns in my side ever since we bought that piece of land and they logged it at scalpers' prices."

Zak was annoyed by his father's indirect reference to Tess. The land-clearing contract they'd given Timber West eight years before had been considered more than fair at the time. His father had even drunk a toast to the deal. It was when Gib O'Reilly had discovered Tess with him at the cabin that things had changed. Zak remembered vividly the ugly scene the next night, when O'Reilly had come to Jean-Pierre with threats. And after that, the feud was on: warnings that de Neuville sheep would be shot if they strayed onto Timber West land; arguments about log trucks causing erosion and washouts on de Neuville land; accusations that Timber West workers had damaged de Neuville fences...

And now, with the trees, the feud continued. Had anyone but the O'Reillys cut the trees, Jean-Pierre's attitude would have been different, more tolerant; he'd simply negotiate in a calm businesslike manner.

"You forget, Father, that you bought that land out from under O'Reilly," Zak reminded him. "Maybe he has a legitimate gripe." He knew at once he'd said the wrong thing, but it was too late to retract the words.

Jean-Pierre's eyes narrowed. "He came out pretty damn good with the logging contract I gave him on that land."

Zak looked at his father's angry face. One of the few times he'd ever heard him use profanity was when

Gib O'Reilly was the topic. "It's only four trees," Zak said. "Hardly worth paying an attorney."

"There's a principle involved," Jean-Pierre insisted, his tone reflecting his determination to stand behind his conviction. "Gib O'Reilly will be sorry he cut those trees." He gave a snort of exasperation and left the room.

Gratianne shrugged. "You've seen it at the festival, son. Two old rams go head to head, butting until one finally drops." She passed off her husband's tirade with a nonchalant wave of her hand, adding, "He'll get over it, but he has to chew on it awhile."

Zak looked at his mother's handsome sun-bronzed face and quiet smile, and he relaxed his grip on the armrest. The reminder of the feud induced the same reaction it always had. He felt like cursing the two of them, the father he loved, for the intolerance accompanying his pride, and Gib O'Reilly, for his own ornery stubbornness. "He'll chew on it until Vince walks in and stirs things up," he added.

Gratianne sighed. "Maybe you'd better stop by the store on your way back to work and warn your brother not to cross your father tonight. I'm sure he's in no mood for an argument with Vince. You know how those two are."

"Don't I ever." Too often Zak had heard the arguments. Vince refused to accept their father's resolve to cling to the old ways. With the issue of the trees pending, this was not the time for such a debate. He looked down at Pio, who was pushing a toy truck across the rug, his small hand guiding the little vehicle along the narrow patterned border. "If you run quick and change out of your school clothes," he said, "we can go for a hike before I leave."

Pio snatched up his truck and stood. "Can we go to the river again?" he asked, his wide gray eyes sparking with anticipation.

Zak rumpled Pio's thick black hair. "We sure can. And maybe Grandmama will have some cookies when we return." He winked at his mother.

Pio raced out of the kitchen and five minutes later returned wearing play clothes. Zak followed him outside, then watched him scurry ahead, realizing how much he enjoyed being with his son. But having sole care of the boy still seemed unreal. Since Mirande had taken Pio back to France four years before, he'd seen his son only on infrequent visits. And always the parting was painful. Sometimes he felt it was better not to see Pio at all than to go through the trauma of separation each time. Then three months ago the tragic news came. Mirande had been killed by an automobile while riding her bicycle, and Zak became a full-time father.

The months after Pio's arrival in America had been difficult for both of them—Pio trying to adjust to the loss of his mother while struggling with life in a new country, a new school and a new language; and Zak trying to deal with the frustrations and complexities of single parenthood while assuming his new job at the wildlife park. But now Zak felt the bumpiest part of the road was behind them. Pio was a constant in his life, and he couldn't imagine being without him. They were already making plans for next month, when Pio would be out of school for summer vacation and could live with Zak in the cabin in Bakers Creek.

Although Zak tried to be everything to Pio—father, friend, guardian—he recognized that he couldn't do it all, that if Pio's life were to be whole, he needed a mother. And Zak had to admit he rather liked the idea of remarrying, although he saw no prospects on the horizon.

As the trail descended toward the river, Pio paused and looked longingly toward a high platform at the top of a giant oak tree. He started climbing up the weathered planks of a tree ladder.

"No, Pio!" Zak yelled, quickening his pace. "The boards are rotten."

"Please, can't I go, Papa? Just a little way up?" Pio looked at Zak with pleading eyes.

Zak realized he let Pio get his way far more than he should—he disliked restricting the boy unless absolutely necessary. But this was one of those times. "No," he insisted. "It's too dangerous up there. And I want you to promise me you won't come here alone or climb that ladder while you're staying here with Grandmama and Grandpapa."

Pio didn't respond.

"Pio? Did you hear me?"

Slowly Pio lowered his foot to the ground and looked at Zak, disappointed. "Yes, Papa."

Zak peered up at the old platform perched high above the forest floor and made a mental note to remove both the platform and the ladder some weekend when he was home visiting.

They continued down to the river, Pio stopping along the way to collect pinecones, feathers, rocks and other forest gems to store in his cap. For a little while Zak helped him build a pebble dam across a tiny trickle of crystal water bubbling out of the ground.

All too soon it was time for Zak to leave, and they started back. After telling his parents goodbye, Zak crouched down to hug Pio. "Work hard in school, son, listen to Grandmama and Grandpapa, and remember that I love you."

Pio wrapped his arms around Zak's neck and clung to him. "I don't want you to go, Papa."

Zak looked into Pio's somber eyes. "I don't want to go either, son, but I've got some injured animals at the wildlife park. I'll be back next weekend," he assured him. When Pio only hung his head, Zak added, "Maybe Lilly will have her kittens this week."

Pio's face brightened. "Can I have one if she does?"

"You sure can," Zak promised.

Pio broke from Zak's arms and raced toward the kitchen. "Grandmama, Papa says I can have one of Lilly's kittens...."

With Pio's happy face in the forefront of his mind, Zak climbed into his truck and left. Fifteen minutes later, he entered Navarre, pulled around the courthouse square and parked. Glancing toward the arcade, he watched a group of young people dressed in faded jeans and outlandish T-shirts saunter inside. Next to the arcade was the video store where Vince worked.

Zak entered the store and looked around for his brother, recognizing him from behind by his dark shoulder-length hair. A young woman with long dingy-blond hair and wearing tight jeans and a leather jacket leaned against the counter, talking to him. "Vince?" Zak called out.

Vince looked up from sorting videotapes and smiled when he saw Zak. "You leaving?" he asked.

"I have to get back to the park," Zak replied, catching a flicker of light from the gold stud in Vince's earlobe.

Vince moved from behind the counter and stood beside the young woman, his eyes shifting to her momentarily before settling on Zak. "So, how did you leave things at home?"

"That's why I'm here," Zak replied.

"Let me guess," Vince said. "Mother sent you to remind me not to cross Father tonight—"

"Try it for once, okay?" Zak suggested. "If for no other reason than for Mother's sake. Besides, Father's pretty upset right now. It seems O'Reilly is at it again." He explained about the trees.

Vince pursed the corner of his mouth. "Look," he said. "I never start anything. If Father's in a huff about some trees I can't help that."

"You can avoid antagonizing him," Zak said. "Tonight's not the time to bring up subjects like putting dual carburetors on your car or going to Portland to look for a job." His eyes shifted with curiosity to the young woman, who seemed to be edging closer to Vince.

Vince wrapped an arm around her shoulders, drawing her to him. "Dede Palmer—my brother, Zak."

Zak acknowledged the young woman, whom he knew Jean-Pierre de Neuville would find totally unacceptable.

Vince's arm tightened around her. "I tell you what, big brother. To ease your mind, I promise not to rile Father tonight. I'll be the perfect son—obedient, submissive, compliant."

Although Vince's tone was light, Zak caught the underlying sarcasm. "Under the circumstances, I think you've made a wise decision."

"Right on," Vince said. "Besides, I'll be bringing Dede over."

Zak fixed dark pensive eyes on Vince. "Tonight?"

"It's as good a night as any," Vince replied. He looked toward the door when a customer entered.

Zak felt uncomfortable at the idea of Vince's bringing his girlfriend to the house, but he knew from past experience there was nothing he could say to dissuade his younger brother, although he was certain there would be repercussions. He nodded to Dede, then reached out and clapped Vince on the shoulder. "Just take it easy. I'll be back next weekend."

"Yeah, see you then."

Zak left the store and climbed into his truck. Pulling away, he passed the pub and a group of men wearing berets and baggy blue pants, then headed toward Bakers Creek. As he left Navarre, he felt saddened. Ten years ago there had been no garish arcade or video store, and Basque had been the principal language. But now, times were changing. Although the elders tried to hold on to the old ways, the new generation, like Vince, shunned the Basque traditions. Zak wanted Pio to move ahead with the times, but he also wanted him to retain his birth language and to have pride in his heritage.

An hour later, Zak pulled into the compound at Spencer Wildlife Park and stopped in front of a long concrete-block building housing offices for park administration, storerooms for veterinary supplies and cages for sick and injured animals. He found his new job satisfying and his work with endangered species rewarding.

When he stepped into the building, his assistant poked his head from behind a partition between cubicles and said, "I hope you can put off the nest flight for a week or so. I just got word that the plane's in for an engine overhaul."

"Can't we pin the mechanic down and get the plane back sooner?" Zak asked. "If we put the flight off too long, the young birds will have fledged—and an empty eagle's nest won't do us much good."

"The plane's in Portland."

"Hmm," Zak responded absently, wondering where they might get a plane. "I'll call the airpark in Bakers Creek tomorrow and see if they have something for hire." He knew timing was critical. If they didn't locate nests before the young birds fledged, he'd have to wait until next spring to complete the project. He'd hoped to have the eaglets moved to Santa Catalina island by now.

He stepped to his desk and collected his messages. A coyote pup had been brought in with an injured leg, and a golden eagle with a broken wing. He also learned that the concrete for the cheetah pens wouldn't be poured until Wednesday—another delay. With the first cats due to arrive from Africa sometime in July, they had less than three months to complete the project. After attending to the injured animals, Zak gathered his topographic maps, climbed in his car and left for his cabin.

On the way, a dark blue Jeep passed him going in the opposite direction. His fingers curled around the wheel. His eyes darted to the rearview mirror and rested there for a moment as he watched the Jeep receding, a puzzled frown creasing his brow. The thick dark hair had caught his attention first, but the face he'd only glimpsed for an instant hovered in his mind. It could easily have been that of Tess O'Reilly.

His eyes moved to the rearview mirror again. As he watched the Jeep disappear over the crest of the hill, he felt the same nameless longing that always accompanied thoughts of Tess. He shifted restlessly in the seat and thought about Pio, wondering what it would have been like to have had a son with Tess. What kind of mother would she have been? Or possibly... *was?*

As he passed the turnoff to Timber West and saw the cabin where Tess once spent her summers, he noted the split wood stacked on the porch. Gib O'Reilly? The muscles in his jaws tensed. Was he back? Ever since Zak's return to Bakers Creek six weeks before, the O'Reilly cabin had looked unoccupied, which puzzled him. Timber West was logging, and O'Reilly always stayed in the cabin to oversee the operation.

At the thought of O'Reilly, an ominous feeling settled over him. There would be a confrontation about the trees, and Zak didn't look forward to that. He hadn't talked to the man since the night eight years ago when O'Reilly had found him with Tess. With a heavy sigh, Zak wheeled the truck into his own drive, jumped out and headed down the long trail leading to his cabin.

Four hours later, Zak rolled up the topographic maps scattered on the table in his cabin and slipped them into a tube. The afternoon had been unproductive. His mind hadn't been on eagle nests or the Grizzly Mountain Wilderness Area. His thoughts kept turning to Timber West and Gib O'Reilly. Zak knew he wouldn't be able to concentrate until he'd checked out the trees O'Reilly had cut on their land.

Rolling out the survey map, he studied the area where the trees were purported to have been cut—it was near a small hollow above the ravine that crossed through the two tracts of land. He knew the area well. Perhaps the names he'd carved in the old oak tree were still legible. . . .

He could still see Tess the way she'd looked when she led him to the spot eight years ago. "Gib will never find us here," she'd said when she showed him the cavernlike hollow where a spring bubbled out of the ground—the place they'd named the Grotto.

Zak had swept her into his arms and lowered her onto the mossy forest floor. She snuggled against him, and after they made love, she looked at him, her dark eyes sparking. "Zak," she whispered, "let's carve our initials in this tree." She reached out to touch the oak tree hovering protectively over them.

Zak playfully nibbled at her breast, mumbling, "I'll leave my mark here first." Then he rolled away and slipped the knife from the trousers he'd left lying on the ground. While he carved the tree, Tess laughed a cheerful rollicking laugh at the sight of him so intent on his task while standing naked. Afterward, standing beside him, cradled in the curve of his arm, she smiled in delight when she read, "Adam loves Eve." From that time, whenever they met secretly in the Grotto, Tess always called him Adam, and she was Eve....

Zak took one last look at the survey map, then tugged on his boots, grabbed the machete and headed toward the northeast boundary—and the Grotto.

Twenty minutes later he chopped his way through heavy undergrowth. The path that had been well worn eight years before was now obscured by tangles of hawthorn and wood sorrel, twists of ivy and ropes of oak vine. With each slash of his machete, he made his way toward the edge of the woods where the four downed trees should lie.

As he stripped small limbs from an encroaching maple tree, the sharp voice of a woman rose above the whacking of his blade. "Hey! What the hell do you think you're doing!" she called out.

Zak looked up, the machete freezing in his hands when he saw the dark-haired woman marching toward him in long angry strides.

TESS HAD NO IDEA who the devil was slashing through their woods, but he'd better have a damn good explanation. "You're on Timber West land," she yelled, raising her hand to shade her eyes from the low afternoon sun.

The man stopped chopping and stood with the machete clutched in his raised hand. "My God!" he said. "Tess?"

The familiar voice brought Tess to a halt. She cupped both hands over her forehead to shade her eyes, then stared at the tall dark-haired man standing at the edge of the forest. "Zak?" she said uncertainly.

Zak lowered the machete and started across the clearing. "How long have you been here?"

All the clever things Tess had imagined herself saying to him if they ever met again escaped her. The only thing she was aware of was the tall broad-shouldered figure quickly closing the gap between them. "Here?" she repeated, taking in the details of a face that had almost faded from memory—the wide forehead and strong nose, the firm chin with the deep cleft she'd once teased with the tip of her tongue. Her pulse quickened. She looked into smoke-gray eyes and blinked several times. "I just came to see who was in the woods." Her eyes moved to the broad mustache Zak had grown, the unexpected brushing of silver at his temples, then returned to meet his gaze.

Zak scanned the yellow hard hat perched on Tess's head, the snug-fitting flannel shirt and faded jeans hugging her trim figure, her scuffed boots. He'd never known a woman who looked as good as Tess did in work clothes. With an effort, he collected his thoughts. "I meant, how long have you been at Timber West?" he asked.

"Oh, about a week. That is, about a week in Bakers Creek. One day here," Tess replied, the words seeming to stumble over each other. She cleared her throat. "I'm looking after Timber West until my father's back on his feet. You knew he had a heart attack, didn't you?" She pulled off the hard hat and shook her head, allowing her hair to spring free.

Zak noticed the deep rich highlights of Tess's hair— hair he'd once buried his face in, run his fingers through... "No. I'm sorry to hear that," he said, aware that his tone was unconvincing. He felt uncomfortable with his lack of sympathy for Gib O'Reilly, but the old anger still smoldered inside.

Tess studied Zak. Beneath his guarded exterior, she sensed the hostility toward her father that had been there eight years before. Restlessly she fingered the hard hat, her palms feeling cold and damp against its smooth surface. She looked at the machete in Zak's hand. "What are you doing with that?" she asked, noting the strength of the fingers curved around the handle.

Zak glanced back at the woods. "I came to check on the trees your father, uh, accidentally cut on our land."

Tess looked toward the forest where Gib had ordered some trees to be thinned. Her eyes rested on the four tree trunks, now limbed and dragged into the clearing. "Gib didn't cut any trees on your land. He's thinning the trees along the property line."

Zak shifted uneasily. "But those trees weren't on Timber West land," he said. "According to the survey my father just had done—I have the map at the cabin—this strip doesn't belong to Timber West."

"Then the map's wrong," Tess insisted. "Gib knows where his land runs."

"The map's not wrong," Zak countered. "The county did the survey."

"Gib doesn't cut timber off someone else's land," Tess replied.

"Well, he did this time," Zak said. "Has he even bothered to look at the map?"

Tess's voice betrayed her annoyance. "He doesn't need to. If you'll remember, he owned this land long before your father did."

"I realize that," Zak replied, "but he obviously doesn't know where the property line is." He drew a long breath. "Look, if we're going to be neighbors again, let's not get into the old feud. Come by the cabin and I'll show you the survey and you can square your father away before he cuts any more trees. My father's angry enough about losing four. He's threatening to get a lawyer."

Tess closed her eyes for a moment, then looked at Zak. "Gib doesn't need this right now. He's supposed to be staying quiet. If your father makes an issue of the trees, regardless of whose property they're on, Gib will be on his doorstep, you know that."

Zak sighed. "Then you'd better see that he doesn't cut any more trees. According to the map, the line goes right through the...hollow by the spring."

Tess noted that Zak carefully avoided the word *grotto*. "I suppose you've been back there already?"

she said. Then she wondered why she'd asked a question about something as intimate as the Grotto.

Zak curled his fingers around the handle of the machete. Just thinking about the Grotto brought memories of Tess's smooth flesh beneath his palms. "I found a survey stake about forty feet your side of—" he hesitated "—the old oak tree there."

Say it, dammit, Tess wanted to scream. *Admit it's our tree—our Adam-and-Eve tree.* Her heart pounded and blood rushed to her face. She backed away. "Look, I have to get back to camp," she said, hearing the shakiness in her voice. "Please, just don't let your father do anything for a while," she pleaded, turning to go.

Zak reached out, taking her arm and drawing her around. "Why don't you come by my place this evening and we'll look at the property line on the survey, and maybe we can figure out something before our fathers end up at each other's throats again . . . keep a couple of stubborn old goats from locking horns."

"I won't be finished until late," Tess said, glancing in the direction of the log camp.

Zak gave her arm a firm squeeze and released it. "Then I'll see you at my cabin when you get there. Okay?"

Tess's lips darted into a smile. "I guess . . . if it'll help keep Gib at home where he belongs." She turned and walked quickly toward the camp, her legs weak, her stomach tight and her chest hollow. She welcomed the diversion of dealing with the bunch of obstinate men she would find there.

CHAPTER THREE

IT WAS EARLY EVENING by the time Tess and the men had finished moving equipment and setting it up so that they could cut pole timber on Monday. When she dismissed the crew, she felt relieved. It had been difficult concentrating on the job after she'd seen Zak. She wondered when he had returned to the area, and she felt uncomfortable knowing he was so close. She couldn't shake the feeling that going to his cabin tonight was a serious mistake. If she was to rebuild her relationship with her father, Zak could not be a part of her life. Yet the subject of the property line had to be addressed.

Feeling weary and emotionally drained, she closed the camp for the weekend and returned to her cabin. Instead of her usual shower, she climbed into a tub of hot bubbly water. Leaning her head against the smooth porcelain, she inhaled the fragrance of jasmine. She'd never used perfumes or bath oils when she was sixteen; Zak often commented on her fresh forest scent and seemed to dislike perfume of any kind. But now she found the caress of bath oils and the smell of flowers refreshing.

After drying herself, she slipped into a robe, then dusted her cheeks with a soft rose blush, accented her eyes with a bit of mascara and touched her lips with light pink gloss. Then she sorted through her clothes, wondering what to wear. She was a different Tess O'Reilly than the one Zak had left behind. She was older and definitely wiser.

Holding up a pale blue blouse with a high neck and softly billowing sleeves, she smoothed the fabric against her chest and peered into the mirror. Eight years ago she'd been content to wear jeans and work shirts—Zak liked her dressed that way. But David had encouraged her to emphasize her femininity. And during the four years they were married, she realized she enjoyed feeling pretty. Without further consideration, she slipped into the blouse and fashioned the long neck ties into a loose bow draping down the front.

She also opted for slacks instead of jeans. Selecting a pair of light wool slacks in muted shades of tan and blue, she stepped into them and pulled them over her hips, then slipped into a pair of casual shoes. She swept up her hair into a knot on top of her head and clipped it in place with a large wooden barrette. Finally she draped a tan sweater around her shoulders, grabbed a flashlight and set off on foot along the path that led to Zak's cabin.

As she followed the beam of light dancing in front of her, she considered what she and Zak might talk about after such a long time. She knew she wouldn't ask what happened, why he'd never come back after Gib had found them together. She had her pride, and nothing would be gained by hashing over the past when they had no future.

Finding her way to Zak's place in the dark reminded her of the times she'd sneaked out of her cabin years before, after Gib had forbidden her to see him. At first she and Zak had spent quiet evenings sharing thoughts and feelings. But the bond between them quickly grew, and soon they were talking about their dreams. When their dreams merged and a future together seemed to lie before them, she became obsessed with seeing him, and loving him, and being a part of him....

The memory faded abruptly when she realized that she'd arrived at Zak's driveway. She crossed the gravel and followed the narrow trail to his cabin, then stepped onto the porch. Raising a tentative hand, she knocked lightly.

Zak opened the door and stared, unprepared for the Tess O'Reilly who faced him. He'd never seen her looking lovelier. His eyes moved to the curve of her throat where it emerged above the soft folds of her bow, and he noticed the gentle swell of her breasts beneath the silky fabric of her blouse.

Tess gave him a quick nervous smile. "Well, am I invited in or not?"

Zak blinked. "I'm sorry," he apologized. "I didn't mean to stare. It just seems strange to see you here after all these years." He moved aside, inhaling the vague hint of blossoms as she passed. She'd never smelled so enticing before.

Tess stepped into the room and stared at Zak, feeling an indefinable yearning. She fidgeted with a button on her sweater, wondering what to say next. It had seemed so easy for them to talk eight years ago, but now... What was there to say to a man who had once promised to love her forever, then left and shattered her dreams?

Zak lifted a bottle of wine from a wooden rack. "Would you like a glass of our latest—Florencia?" he asked. He looked back at her steadily and waited.

Tess felt her eyelid twitch nervously and wondered if Zak had noticed—but his gaze was inscrutable. She managed another small smile. "Sure," she replied, sitting on the edge of the sofa.

Zak handed her a wineglass, his fingers brushing hers, then filled it from a bottle with the distinctive black-and-gold de Neuville label. "My father's very proud of this run—it won a gold medal at the national competition."

Tess took a slow sip. The bouquet filled her nostrils as she let the wine moisten her dry mouth. "It's delicious," she said, realizing she'd never tasted any of the de Neuville wines. "Why is it called Florencia?"

"That's Basque for 'high-mountain flower,'" Zak replied. "It's made from flower petals—an old process that's been passed down through Father's family."

"Are you working at the winery now?" Tess asked, assuming he was. It was part of the life they'd planned. She'd never seen the winery, but she used to dream of one day working with Zak to develop prime wines, help design the labels and proudly market their product. Her grandfather had made wine on a small scale, and she remembered how much she'd enjoyed the damp musky aroma of fruit fermenting in his cellar.

Zak arched a brow. "No," he replied. "I'm working at Spencer Wildlife Park. I help at the winery when I can, but my work at the park takes priority."

"Oh," she said. In a way, she wasn't surprised. She knew Zak had always been fascinated by animals. She remembered him saying how much he'd enjoyed his summers working at the park when he was younger. But now she felt oddly disappointed that he wasn't working at the winery. "Have you been in Bakers Creek long?" she asked lightly, attempting to quell her inner turmoil.

Zak smiled. "About six weeks—ever since I was appointed head of the endangered-species program."

Tess cocked her head. "Endangered species? When did you get involved with that?"

"When I finished college about two years ago."

Tess's brows drew together. "College?" Eight years ago, he'd had no interest in college. He'd worked at the winery, as well as the wildlife camp, ever since graduating from high school—until the summer his father bought the property adjoining Timber West. He and his father seemed to be at odds over everything that summer, and Zak had admitted that signing on with Timber West to clear his father's land was an easy escape. Perhaps college had also been an escape.

Zak smiled at the curious look on her face. "You act surprised."

"Curious," Tess replied, "but not surprised." Zak had always been full of surprises, though. She thought of the day he'd given her a little gold ring and made vows to her that she'd only dreamed of in her fantasies. . . .

She looked up, disturbed by her line of thought. "What are you doing now?" she asked. "At the park, that is."

"We're trying to reinstate the bald eagle on Catalina island," Zak replied. "We'll be taking chicks from nests around here and sending them to California. But first we have to fly over established nests to see if they're occupied." He paused, studied her for a few moments, then tentatively added, "Do you still fly?"

"Fly?" Tess said, surprised that the subject had arisen—again. Only last week Gib had offered her the use of his plane whenever she wanted. But later Aunt Ruth had taken her aside and made her promise that if she went flying, she wouldn't tell Gib; he might want to go along, but as yet his health was too precarious.

Tess knew Gib's offer had been more than a gesture. It was a peace offering. They'd had some wonderful times together flying in their little Cessna. Gib had let her take the controls when she was eleven, and after that she vowed she'd someday have a plane. When she met David at the airpark, it seemed that her dreams had come true. David owned a plane. Flying was the one interest they'd shared....

"Tess?"

Tess realized Zak was waiting for a reply. "Uh, yes, I still fly. David and I had a little Cessna like Gib's."

"David? Your husband?" Zak asked in a cautious voice. He found the thought distasteful. Tess wore no ring, but he'd been contemplating her marital state all evening, wondering how to ask.

"Ex-husband," Tess replied. She sipped the last of her wine. "We were divorced about two years ago."

"I'm sorry," Zak commented. He started to tell her about Pio, but then reconsidered, reluctant to talk about his marriage to Mirande, or even discuss the past at all. There was time. He found himself staring at Tess again; in fact, he was unable to take his eyes off her. She looked so beautiful with the golden glow of the lamp highlighting the slender column of her neck and the upsweep of her hair. He'd never seen her wear her hair like that. She looked older, more sophisticated. He wondered if she had any children. Somehow, even though they'd once talked of having children together, he'd never really been able to picture her with a child in her arms. Chain saws and split logs had always seemed more natural—until now. To his surprise, the thought of her bearing another man's child bothered him. "Any children?" he finally asked.

"No," she said slowly. "David and I had a construction business and it was too demanding of our time. And whenever we did have some spare time, we spent it flying."

"Then you did finally get your pilot's license," Zak ventured, remembering Tess's resolve at sixteen to get her license and one day own a plane.

"Yes," she replied. "David encouraged me to get it right after we were married. Before that, Gib and I—" she swallowed hard "—hadn't flown much." She looked down at her hands. Nor had they laughed, or spent time together, or talked unless necessary. After Zak left, there had been little communication between her and her father. Only hostility and anger.

"Have you flown recently?" Zak asked.

"Just my certification flight," Tess told him. "But I sort of planned to go up on Sunday—my last chance before being inundated with logging." With the problems of the job—Swenson not showing up and the men reluctant to cooperate—she knew that after this weekend she'd need to stay close to camp.

"Sunday?" For a moment Zak said nothing, wondering if he dared ask her to take him up. He did need to fly over the nests, but he found that he also wanted to spend time with her and get to know her again. He gave her a tentative smile. "Would you consider taking a passenger?" he asked. "The park plane's in for an engine overhaul and I need a lift over the mountains to check some nests before the chicks fledge, and time's running out."

Tess studied Zak while considering his request. He seemed so eager. But to take him up in Gib's plane was out of the question. "Where, exactly, did you want to go?" she asked, curious.

Zak gave her a broad optimistic smile. "Over some nests around here, then to the ranger station at Pine Mountain Wilderness," he replied. "Do you know the park ranger there, Ralph Tolsted?"

"No," Tess said. "But I know where the Pine Mountain station is. Gib and I flew over it a few times, even landed there once. He wasn't too thrilled with the landing strip, though—says it's the shortest one he's ever used. Why do you want to go there?" she asked, trying to unravel her motives for continuing this interrogation when she knew she wouldn't take him up.

"There's a nest there I want to check. And I've got to talk to Tolsted about others in the area," Zak replied. "It shouldn't take more than about two hours. I'd really appreciate a lift." He grinned, and sparks danced in his eyes. "Think of it as a way to help our national bird."

Tess's gaze was riveted on his smile and the charming way his mouth curved up at the corners. Then she looked into his eyes. "I suppose it would be all right," she found herself saying, "if it's only a couple of hours."

Zak's grin broadened. "Good!" he said. "And I'll owe you a gourmet dinner when we get back." The thought of sharing a quiet cozy meal alone with Tess seemed beyond reality. He'd believed that they would never be together again. But now, against all odds, there was a chance, and he vowed that, if they ever recaptured what they'd once shared, Gib O'Reilly wouldn't stand between them again.

How much time did they have? A week? A month? How long would Tess be at Timber West, and where would she go after O'Reilly was running things again? The thought of Tess's leaving disturbed him. "What about you? Do you plan to stay on at Timber West after your father's back? He is coming back, isn't he?" That thought also disturbed him.

Tess found herself staring at Zak's thick black mustache. At sixteen, she'd hated mustaches; she'd talked Zak out of growing one, in fact. But now, it made him look distinguished, virile...

"Yes, Gib is coming back," she replied, reflecting on his first question. "And no, I don't plan to keep logging. Actually, I'm thinking about going to college—University of Oregon in Eugene—and taking business." It was the first time she'd mentioned her plans to anyone except Aunt Ruth and Gib. Somehow, saying it seemed to make it so, and it felt good. She'd toyed with the idea for months, and when she'd suggested it to Aunt Ruth and Gib, they'd been surprised and supportive, but she felt they hadn't really taken her seriously.

"Business?"

Tess grinned at the curious look on Zak's face. "I already have a good foundation in it from running the construction business, but now I want a job where I can have soft hands and polished fingernails."

Zak smiled at the thought of Tess with polished nails. She had strong capable hands with long graceful fingers, hands that used to drive him wild. But she'd certainly never worried about breaking a nail or ruining her manicure the way so many other women did. He had to admit, though, that work-roughened hands didn't seem to fit the woman poised on the sofa across from him. The thought of her soft feminine hands caressing him intimately appealed to him and, he realized with alarm, aroused him—a reaction he just didn't need right now. "I guess we've avoided it long enough," he said, moving to the kitchen table. "Come take a look at the survey."

Tess stepped to the table and peered down at the map, speculating about Gib's reaction to Zak's return, not to mention the issue of the trees. "I sure hope you're wrong about this," she said, "because if you're not, Gib's going to be the devil to live with."

Zak moved behind her, his chest lightly brushing her shoulder as he reached around her and pointed.

"Here's your cabin," he said, his warm breath feathering the loose hair on top of her head, "and this is the road between your cabin and the camp." His finger traced the road on the map. "This is where one corner stake is located—" he pointed to a spot near the south end of the property "—and this is the other." His finger moved along an invisible line and stopped precisely on the Grotto.

Tess's heart quickened. Standing in the curve of Zak's arm, looking at the spot that had once been their secret retreat, seemed so intimate, and it brought back forbidden memories—Adam and Eve in the forest primeval. "But the Grotto has always been on Timber West land," she said, the words bursting from her lips. Heat rushed up her face.

Zak started to respond, but he, too, found himself thinking of other things. He lifted his finger from the map, hoping to dispel thoughts of toes curling against cool moss, liquid brown eyes watching him, soft warm breasts pressed against his chest. "According to the survey," he said, his voice faltering, "Timber West land stops ten feet this side of the logging road. The trees your father cut are clear over here." He straightened. "Why don't you take this map and show him where the property line runs?"

Tess studied the survey map and saw that Zak was right. Timber West did not own the land from which the trees had been taken. But the fact was, she didn't care whose property the trees were on. She didn't want to get Gib upset over four trees. "I'll pay for the trees and see that no more are cut," she assured Zak. "But please, just make sure your father doesn't do anything right now."

Zak drew a long breath. "It's not that simple," he said. "My father's talking about stretching a fence along the line—he wants to move the sheep up to the high meadows for the summer—and this has to be resolved."

Tess felt a heaviness in her chest. "Can't you stall the fence work—just for a while?"

Zak saw the concern on Tess's face. "I'll see what I can do," he said. "Don't worry about paying for the trees. We can haul them back over here and call it square. And I'll tell my father that your father inadvertently logged on our land and that no more trees will be cut. With luck, he'll be satisfied with that for now." He reached out and squeezed Tess's hand. "I hope this won't change our plans for Sunday—I mean about going up in the plane."

Tess gazed at Zak's anxious face. For the moment everything seemed to fade except the light shining in his eyes, the warmth of his hand on hers. She needed the strength to say, *Yes, things are changed, you can't go with me,* but instead she found herself replying, "No, nothing has changed. I'll pick you up at noon."

"Noon it is then," Zak said.

Tess slipped her hand from his and moved to the door. "I've got to get back," she said quickly, knowing if she didn't leave, she might reach out . . . feel the hardness of Zak's chest . . . lose herself in the circle of his arms . . . know the fire of his kisses once more. And that would be disastrous.

Zak pulled the door open, then paused, his hand resting on the doorknob. "It's good to see you again," he said in a low quiet voice. "And, I'll see you . . . tomorrow."

"Yes," Tess agreed, "tomorrow." She held his gaze for a moment, then clicked on the flashlight and stepped into the darkness, her heart pounding, her pulse racing.

As she made her way back to her cabin, she tried to unravel her motives for agreeing to take Zak up in the plane while considering the potential consequences. Gib had not given her the use of his plane so that she could take Zak flying. He'd be livid if he knew. So she somehow had to keep it from him—at least for now. In spite of her hasty decision, she didn't want anything to come between Gib and her just when they were beginning to rebuild their relationship.

When Zak had proposed that she take him up, it was as if she was helpless to say no. He still had the same effect on her as he had eight years ago. But they were different people now. She'd changed; he'd changed. They didn't even really know each other anymore. After tomorrow she would surrender to no more of Zak's requests. She refused to set herself up for more heartache.

It wasn't until she reached her cabin that she realized she'd forgotten to ask if he was married. The thought of Zak with another woman disturbed her in a way she didn't care to analyze.

CHAPTER FOUR

TESS TOSSED RESTLESSLY during the night, trying to push thoughts of Zak from her mind. She couldn't forget the way he'd looked at her, with a sort of restless longing she couldn't explain. He was the one who had left; he'd severed the ties. Yet she felt as though he wanted her even now. The thought both troubled and excited her. She realized she wanted Zak to want her. She just didn't understand why.

She dragged herself out of bed and dressed. Gib and Aunt Ruth expected her for breakfast, but she wasn't sure she wanted to face Gib, knowing she had promised to take Zak up in his plane.

She considered canceling the flight, but didn't. She had to admit she *wanted* to be with Zak, wanted to find out where he'd been the past eight years, what he'd been doing... if he was married. He'd given no indication that he had a wife, which puzzled her. Zak was a very desirable man. He'd have no trouble finding a wife if he wanted one. Perhaps tomorrow she'd get the answers. With a weary sigh, she climbed into her Jeep and headed for Bakers Creek.

Twenty minutes later she pulled up in front of Gib's house—the white frame cottage where she'd grown up. She glanced across the street and waved to Mr. Wadley, who was working in his yard just as he'd done every Saturday since Tess could remember.

Mr. Wadley snapped a rhododendron blossom from a bush and looked up. "Tell Gib I'll be over this afternoon to checkmate him," he yelled.

Tess grinned. "Considering you just did that, maybe you'd better take a dive. You know now Gib feels about losing."

Mr. Wadley chuckled. "No deal. That old barnacle needs the wind taken out of his sails once in a while. Besides, it'll keep his heart pumping."

Tess waved him off, then hopped onto the porch in two leaps. When she stepped into the living room, she detected the unmistakable aroma of cinnamon and warm yeast. Aunt Ruth stood on a low stool, a feather duster in her hand, reaching for cobwebs that evaded the tips of the feathers.

"Let me do that," Tess said, moving to where the short round woman stretched toward the ceiling.

Aunt Ruth's brown eyes brightened with her smile. "Hi, sweetie," she said, stepping off the stool. She ran her hand across her peppery hair, smoothing it back into the tight bun at her nape. "You can dust for me later. Right now, go into the kitchen and assure your dad that you got through your first day at the camp all right. He's been in a stew all morning waiting to hear from you."

Tess took the duster, hopped onto the stool and swept it across the ceiling, snaring the cobwebs. "There," she said. She jumped down. "Did anything arrive from the university?"

"No," Aunt Ruth replied. "What were you expecting?"

Tess shrugged. "I sent for a catalog."

"You're really serious about this college thing, aren't you?" Aunt Ruth asked, her head tilted to one side.

"Dead serious," Tess replied. "I've just about had my fill of working a bunch of obstinate men, and I'm tired of wearing pants and looking like one of the crew all the time."

Aunt Ruth raised her eyes heavenward and smiled. "Praise the Lord," she said. "I never thought I'd see the day."

Tess looked toward the kitchen where she saw her father reading the morning paper. "How's Gib been doing—other than worrying himself into a frazzle about Timber West?"

Aunt Ruth pursed her lips. "He's as cantankerous as an old dog. I only put up with him because I know that underneath that crusty exterior he's soft as a kitten."

Tess laughed. "You're right," she said, passing the duster along the dark surface of the upright piano. "He just doesn't want the rest of the world to know. Did you give him hell for going out to the camp yesterday morning?"

Aunt Ruth scurried toward the kitchen. "You better believe I did," she said. "I turn my back for a couple of hours and he's gone. Well, he's not getting away today."

Tess trailed the duster along the surface of the buffet as she followed Aunt Ruth through the dining room. "How did he take it?"

Aunt Ruth glanced back at her and smiled. "He grumbled something about domineering women, and I reminded him that it was a matter of survival of the fittest." She tapped Gib's shoulder on the way to the stove. "Tess is here." She put the coffeepot on to heat, slipped an oven mitt on her hand and lifted a tray of fresh cinnamon rolls from the oven.

Tess kissed Gib lightly on the forehead. "Well, I survived my first day at Timber West," she said, pulling out a chair and sitting across from her father. Aunt Ruth set a pitcher of orange juice and three glasses on the table, then filled the glasses.

Gib lowered his newspaper. "I suspected you would," he said. His blue eyes darkened. "Did you have any problem with Jed Swenson?"

Tess eyed the platter of cinnamon rolls. "No." she replied, reaching for a roll. "He never showed up. Am I supposed to put up with behavior like that, or can I fire him?" She sank her teeth into the sweet warm bread.

A worried frown creased Gib's brow. "Don't be too quick to fire him," he said. "He's a good worker—knows logging and equipment. But he can be kind of stubborn at times."

Aunt Ruth winked at Tess. "Well, if that's not the pot calling the kettle black, I don't know what is." She lowered her compact frame into the chair and reached for a cinnamon roll.

Tess smiled at her aunt, then looked across at Gib again. Her face sobered. "Swenson wasn't at the meeting in the cookshack after lunch, or at my office later—as I requested. He's openly defying me. Do *you* put up with that?"

Gib took a sip of juice. "I haven't been around him that much. I hired him a few weeks before my heart attack, and I was lucky to get him. Before you fire Swenson or anyone else you'd better have someone in mind who'll step in. Word's out that Carl Yaeger may have just bought the north slope tract—the section between Timber West and the ridge—and if he did, he'll be hiring. If you get rid of Swenson you might find yourself without a woods boss, and no one else to take his place."

"Ezzie claims that Curt Broderick was a woods boss in Montana."

"He was, but he doesn't have the experience Swenson has."

"Well, Swenson's not any use to me right now," Tess said. "If he doesn't show up soon, I'll have to let him go."

She touched the tip of her tongue to her fingers, licking the warm icing from them, then glanced at her father. "If Yaeger bought the north slope, what do you think he'll do about our road to the ridge? Let us keep going through like we always have?"

"I hope so," Gib replied. "If he doesn't we're in trouble. There's no other access to the pole timber unless de Neuville lets us go through his land—and we already know the answer to that."

Tess said nothing. After a moment she ventured, "Have you ever had our property surveyed?"

Gib picked up the newspaper again. "No," he said, scanning the headlines. "There's no need for a survey. I know where the line runs."

"How do you know exactly where it runs if you've never had it surveyed?" Tess asked. "You could end up accidentally cutting timber off the de Neuville land, or maybe off Carl Yaeger's. It just seems like a good idea to make sure—when you're up and around that is."

Gib eyed Tess with mild annoyance. "I'm not going to pay some half-wit from the county office to come with his fancy equipment and try to tell me what I already know."

"Then I'll do it for you," Tess insisted. "We'll get someone out there and find out *exactly* where the line is, so we won't have to worry."

"I'm not worried."

Tess raised her chin. "Well, maybe I am. I'm running the operation now and I think we should have it surveyed."

Gib plopped his folded newspaper on the table. "If I thought it was necessary—which it isn't—we still couldn't have it done because Timber West can't spare the money. We'll be lucky if we make it through another season."

Tess gazed at him over the rim of her cup. "You're just feeling pessimistic because Aunt Ruth won't let you go out there and finish yourself off."

Gib's bushy brows drew together above concerned eyes. "I'm being realistic," he replied. "All the mills shutting down just about finished us off. And with taxes and loan payments due, we can't even afford a machine breakdown, or that'll be it for Timber West."

Tess studied the lines of worry etched in her father's face. "I can't believe it's as bleak as that," she said.

"Then take a look at the books," Gib replied. "Meanwhile, no breakdowns, no raises—and no surveys." He shoved his chair back and left the room.

For a few moments no one spoke. Gib's abrupt exit signaled that the subject was closed, and Tess knew better than to pursue the matter. The confrontation, as always, left her feeling drained.

The blip and bubble of the coffeepot recalled her attention. Aunt Ruth retrieved two cups from the cabinet and poured the coffee. "How was the cabin?" she asked, sitting down again. "I'd hoped to get it cleaned up before you moved in."

Tess stared at the steam rising from the hot coffee while inhaling its rich aroma. "Gib left it in pretty good shape. A little scrubbing and it was livable."

Aunt Ruth sighed. "I don't know why he's holding on to the place," she said. "Everything needs painting or fixing. He'll work himself to death out there."

"He'll die quicker if he sells out," Tess replied. "It would be like admitting to himself that he's old and washed up, and he's not ready for that yet. And when he does decide to sell, I know he'll hold out until he gets what he thinks the business is worth."

"You're probably right about that," Aunt Ruth agreed. "But it'll be years before the timber industry recovers from the slump. And running the camp's not a life for you."

"I don't plan to do it forever," Tess said. "But I do want to help get the business out of the red and get Gib through this period."

Aunt Ruth shifted uneasily in her chair. "I don't like the idea of your staying out there all alone," she said, "with no one else around."

Tess gave Aunt Ruth a confident smile. "The men are just up at the bunkhouse," she replied, lifting the coffee cup to her lips and blowing lightly.

"Well, you don't know that much about those men," Aunt Ruth fretted. "A pretty woman all alone out there can be a real temptation to some. I just wish there were a few close, more permanent neighbors around."

Tess's hand jerked, sending coffee sloshing over the rim. She quickly set the cup down and blotted the coffee from the table with her napkin. Then she gave a short nervous laugh. "Help's as near as the telephone."

"But the telephone's up in the office," Aunt Ruth said, her voice wavering in concern. "It won't be much good if you need help at the cabin. With all the dense woods around, someone could be hiding out."

Tess looked at Aunt Ruth. "Zak is next door."

For a moment Aunt Ruth said nothing. Then her forehead puckered. "Zak de Neuville?" she said uncertainly, her fingers curling around her napkin.

"Yes. That's who brought up the subject of the survey and why I asked to have it done. Gib told one of the men to thin the trees along the west boundary—the strip of land between the dirt road and the de Neuville property—and those trees are *not* on Timber West land. They're on the de Neuvilles' place. Four trees have already been cut."

Aunt Ruth eyed Tess over the rim of her cup. "I'm sure Gib knows what he's doing. Certainly he knows where the property line runs."

"That's the problem," she said. "He *thinks* he knows, but he's wrong. Zak showed me a survey map." She reached for the pot of coffee with a shaky hand and refilled her cup. "Zak said his father's threatening to sue Gib for cutting the trees."

Aunt Ruth looked directly at Tess. "Have you been seeing Zak?" she said in a guarded voice.

"No," Tess replied, then added, "well, that is, yesterday I saw him briefly, when he showed me the survey map, but I'm not . . . seeing him."

Aunt Ruth drew an extended breath. "Does Gib know he's back?"

"No."

"Then I see no reason to say anything about the property line or mention that Zak de Neuville is around. It'll just get him riled again. And you'd better see that no one cuts any more trees, regardless of what your father says—at least until after his checkup next week."

Tess toyed with the idea of telling Aunt Ruth about taking Zak up in the plane, then discarded it. Aunt Ruth had enough on her mind without brooding about Gib's reaction to that.

THE NEXT DAY, Tess pulled into Zak's drive and was surprised to find an old Chevy—various parts of the car in different stages of restoration—parked beside Zak's truck. The car's rear end was jacked high with oversize tires, and inside, a pair of plastic-foam dice hung from the rearview mirror.

With mounting curiosity, Tess headed up the trail to the cabin. Zak opened the door before she had a chance to knock. "Come on in and sit down," he said. "Vince was just leaving. You remember my brother, don't you?"

Tess looked into the dark blue eyes of a young man in a black leather jacket, faded jeans and dirty tennis shoes. Where the jacket gaped open, she could see the grotesquely contorted face of a rock star painted on a rumpled T-shirt. "Yes," she replied, trying to assimilate the change from a bright-eyed youth of thirteen to this angry young man of twenty-one. "It's nice to see you again, Vince."

Vince's eyes moved over Tess with obvious approval. "Likewise," he replied.

In the doorway to the bedroom, a young boy rolled a truck across the floor. When he turned curious gray eyes to Tess, her lips parted with a swift intake of breath. It was as if she were peering into Zak's eyes. The boy scrambled over to the sofa to stand beside Zak, and he studied Tess from within the circle of Zak's arm. His young face was topped by a shock of wavy black hair and his chin had a small cleft. Looking at the boy, Tess waited for Zak to continue.

Zak drew the boy against him. "And this is Pio," he said, "my son."

Tess said nothing. All thoughts and feelings were momentarily turned off. At first she stared blankly at the boy, then she focused on his features. There was no doubt. This boy was indeed Zak's son. And the boy's mother, Zak's wife? Where was she? Tess gave Pio a nervous smile. "Hi," she said.

The boy didn't smile back. "Hi," he replied in a clipped tone. He looked up at Zak, and asked to be excused. When Zak nodded, Pio picked up his truck and scurried outside.

Tess sank into the cushions of an overstuffed chair and looked out the window at the boy pushing his truck along the dirt road. He appeared to be about six or seven. Zak must have married shortly after he left. How could he have been so faithless? Eight years ago they'd said their vows and planned to marry when she turned eighteen. There had been no one else in his life then, she was sure of it. Had his feelings for her been so shallow that when Gib intervened he simply walked away and married someone else?

"Father's damn traditions are straight out of another world," Vince said, his heated words punctuating the pounding of Tess's heart. It seemed he was continuing a conversation that had started before her arrival. "And I'll tell you another thing—I won't marry a Basque girl just because he's decided I should."

Zak looked at Tess. "Excuse us for a minute," he said, taking Vince's arm and leading him toward the porch. "I'll be right back." They stepped outside and Zak pulled the door closed behind him.

"He's a proud man," Zak said, "and the old traditions have been right for him. It's only natural that he wants the same for you."

"That's fine for you to say," Vince rasped, "you're *etcheko primu*—" he spat out the words "—firstborn. The ranch and winery will be yours—if you marry a Basque woman and fit into father's mold, of course."

Zak sighed. "You know you always have a place there."

"I'd die of boredom in Navarre."

The silence that followed was finally broken by Zak. "You don't have to turn your back on all the values you were taught in order to be your own person."

"And I don't have to hang around here and listen to this either. I thought at least *you'd* understand, but I see you're no different from him. You'll do exactly as Father says. You'll marry a Basque woman, settle into his niche at the ranch and live his life for him. I hope you enjoy it."

Zak didn't respond. He knew that was exactly what was expected of him. When he finally spoke, there was resolve in his voice. "We're caught between two worlds, not fitting into either, but there is a happy medium between the old ways and the new. We just have to find it—and then convince Father."

Vince laughed shortly. "Ever try moving a mountain?"

Zak laughed, too. "You won't have to move a mountain. Meanwhile, try not to irritate him—"

"Which means, tell him what he wants to hear. I can't do that."

"Try," Zak said. "And thanks for bringing Pio along."

Vince said affectionately, "There was no way I could get out of it. He had to tell you about the kittens."

Zak crouched and smiled at Pio. "I'll be anxious to hear what you name your new pal," he said.

Pio's face grew bright. "When can I bring him here?" he asked in an animated voice.

"Not for a while—at least six weeks," Zak replied. "Meanwhile, to help the time go by, I'll come for you next weekend and we'll go find some eagles, maybe do a nest climb. How would you like that?"

Pio grinned. "I'd like that, Papa." He hugged his father, then scampered along the trail toward Vince's car.

Zak smiled at his son's eager pace. "I suspect he's anxious to get back to his kitten," he said to Vince. "Now, no hot-rodding between here and Navarre," he warned.

Vince gave Zak a sheepish grin. "Don't worry. One more ticket and I lose my license. I fall in line with the old ladies now."

Zak watched Vince amble down the path, then he turned and walked back inside. "I'm sorry about Vince," he said. "He's trying to do his own thing, and he and my father can't seem to agree on exactly what that is." He realized he was avoiding mentioning Pio. He'd planned to tell Tess about him today, and next week have them meet properly. He could only imagine how surprised she must be. Gathering some maps from the kitchen table, he said, "I guess I should have told you about my son. I didn't expect Vince to come by with him—I intended to tell you about him today."

Tess pressed her lips into a smile, trying to hide the turmoil inside because of what she'd overheard. "I guess we have some catching up to do."

As they walked down the path toward the driveway, Tess asked, "How old is your son?" She felt oddly cheated that Zak had a child who was born of another woman.

"Six," Zak replied.

"And your wife?" she said in a tight voice. "Where is she?" Although she'd asked the question, she wasn't sure she wanted to hear the answer. The thought of Zak's having a wife bothered her more than she would have imagined.

Zak's face sobered. "Pio's mother died about four months ago."

Tess looked up in surprise. Zak, a single parent and a widower of only four months? "I'm sorry," she said. "It must be very difficult for you."

"It is for Pio," Zak replied. "My wife and I separated quite a while ago."

"Basque?" Tess asked.

Zak looked at her with a puzzled frown.

"Your wife—was she Basque?" Tess asked again, waiting for Zak to confirm what she already suspected. According to Jean-Pierre de Neuville, Basque married Basque. She'd been aware of that eight years ago, when she and Zak had talked of marriage, but somehow, at sixteen, the world didn't seem so cut and dried. Life was always ready for change. With Zak's father that was not the case. Life was very simple. Basque married Basque.

Zak lifted a brow. "Yes, she was Basque," he said, swinging up into her Jeep.

Tess climbed into the driver's seat. So he did leave her to marry a Basque woman. And his next wife, the mother he'd choose for Pio, would she also be Basque? Of course! It appeared that Jean-Pierre set the rules and Zak followed. "Your parents must have been pleased," she said in a tight voice, then wondered what made her say such a thing in reference to Zak's dead wife. Turning to Zak, she said, "I'm sorry, I shouldn't have said that."

Zak saw that Tess was gripping the wheel more tightly than necessary. He wanted to tell her, almost felt obligated to tell her, about his disappearance and his marriage. Things certainly hadn't been as they appeared. But the time wasn't right. They needed to get to know each other again, and he needed to regain her trust before he dared tell her the truth.

He gave her a tentative smile. "I had no idea how complex it was to be a single parent—shuffling job and family, being there when Pio's sick, worrying about what he should or shouldn't eat." He sighed and gazed out the side window. Nothing in life had prepared him to take on the single-handed raising of a son. At times it seemed an almost overwhelming responsibility. "There's no doubt," he said in a weary voice, "a young child needs a mother."

Tess was acutely aware of the heaviness in Zak's tone. Gib must have faced the same dilemma. When he took over the role of both parents after her mother died, nothing seemed to go right. The meals were terrible, the house was a mess, and neither she nor Gib really cared. And she seemed to have no direction or guidance. Fortunately Aunt Ruth moved in and took over, and their everyday lives seemed to fall back into place again. She glanced at Zak. "Had you thought about living with your parents, letting them help?"

"I've thought about it some," Zak replied. "As it is now, Pio stays there during the week so he can go to school in Navarre, and I go home on weekends. But next month, when school's out, he'll be moving into the cabin with me for the summer. We need to make our own adjustment."

Ten minutes later they arrived at the airpark. After filing a flight plan, Tess gave the plane its preflight check and she and Zak climbed on board. She taxied to the end of the runway, checked the flaps and took off. They headed toward Timber West and the ridge where Zak hoped to spot the first nest.

Sitting in the small cabin with her shoulder pressed against Zak's conjured up images from the past. She felt a sudden pang, remembering how she used to rest her hand on his thigh... snuggle against his shoulder... reach out and touch his face...

"When we locate the nest, dip the wings so I can get a good look inside," Zak said, intruding on her reverie.

Tess shifted her thoughts to the panorama below. Within minutes, they skimmed over Carl Yaeger's land. She spotted her cabin and the logging camp. Beyond, she saw the clearing where Zak's cabin stood.

"Where should we start looking for the nest?" she asked.

Zak scanned the forest below. "Somewhere on the ridge, in the old-growth timber up there," he said. "Probably in an old snag."

Tess turned the plane in a wide arc toward the ridge and flew low over the treetops. "There's a pretty big stand of old-growth just above where we're getting ready to log," she replied. "And there's some on Carl Yaeger's tract, the piece of land Gib wanted to buy a few years ago. He could have paid for it fast with those old trees."

Zak's eyes darkened. "That's our biggest problem with the eagle population—the harvesting of old-growth trees," he said. "If it isn't stopped, there won't be any trees strong enough to support nests."

Tess felt mildly annoyed. "We always leave lots of good-size second growth," she told him tersely.

"Are the trees big enough to support a two-ton nest?" Zak asked.

"Aren't you exaggerating a bit?"

"Some older nests are eight feet across and six feet deep. They can easily weigh two tons," Zak replied, feeling uneasy about the possibility of spotting nests near Timber West's logging operation.

For a few minutes they rode in silence. Then Zak sat up straight. "Over there." He pointed to a massive nest of coarse limbs atop a huge Douglas fir. Tess maneuvered the plane near the nest and dipped the wings.

"Twins!" Zak exclaimed. "Great. When they're two chicks in a nest, then we can take one of them.

Looks like the tree is fairly accessible, too. I'll climb
that one if it's not dead. Can you circle one more time
over the old-growth before we head out? I want to
look for perch nests.''

"Sure," Tess replied. "What's a perch nest?"

"Sort of a second home. It's an unoccupied nest
that the eagles use as a perch for spotting prey. They
roost there at night, too."

They circled over the old-growth forest once more
while Zak logged his findings, then they headed east.
"We should be over Odelle and Crescent lakes in
about fifteen minutes," Tess said. "Then it's only
about another ten minutes to Pine Lake from there.
How many nests do you want to check?"

"Three more," Zak replied. "Most of them should
be within two hundred yards or so of the lakes—eagles
feed mainly on fish. They should be easy to spot."

As they headed east toward the rugged Cascade
Mountains, slowly gaining altitude, the corners of
Tess's mouth tipped up with excitement. It was wonderful to be flying again. The short flight she'd had the
week before wasn't the same as having the freedom to
soar above the mountains as they were doing now. Her
thumbs stroked the wheel. "My biggest regret about
the divorce was that David got the plane," she said.

Zak fingered the map rolled in his lap. "How old
were you when you married?" he asked, wondering
exactly how long Tess had waited after he'd left.

"Eighteen."

Zak's eyes moved over the rugged terrain below.
"Was he from Bakers Creek?" He kept his voice casual, but his fingers drummed against the rolled map.

"Seattle," Tess replied. "He'd been flying into Bakers Creek every week to work on a big house he was building, and we met at the airpark."

"Oh." A muscle twitched in Zak's jaw. "Where is he now?" he asked, scanning the forest below.

"I don't know," Tess told him bluntly. "He declared bankruptcy shortly after we divorced—the building slump. Then he moved east. I went to work for his competitor and I haven't heard from him since."

The plane bucked its way along the valley and headed northeast toward the mountains. Capricious winds dropped them suddenly downward, then sent them soaring upward.

Tess glanced at Zak. "What about you? Where have you been for the past eight years?" Obviously not pining away for her, she realized.

Zak rolled the topographic map out and over the small steering wheel in front of him. "France, Washington, Oregon," he replied. "I've sort of moved around."

"France?"

"The western Pyrenees—my father sent me to learn about Basque wines," he said, studying the map. He looked into the distance. "According to the map, Crescent Lake's just ahead."

Tess's fingers curled around the wheel. "When?"

"When what?" He continued studying the map.

"When did you go to France?"

Zak's gaze moved over the swirls of contour lines on the map, but his mind recalled Gib O'Reilly's enraged face the night he'd burst into the cabin and found them together. "About eight years ago," he replied, "when I left Oregon." He blinked several times and the map came into focus again.

Tess's thumbs moved in short agitated strokes on the wheel. Zak still hadn't offered an explanation, or even a casual comment about why he'd left so quickly. It certainly hadn't been just to learn about Basque wines. Nor had he told her anything about the woman he'd married so soon afterward. Uncomfortable with that thought, she drew her attention back to the panorama below, where silvery streams braided through dense mountain forests and across velvet-carpeted meadows. As the landscape rolled out beneath them, she squinted, then sat up straight. "There it is. Crescent Lake. And over there, Odelle."

"Good," said Zak. "Circle low if you can."

Tess turned the plane in a wide arc, allowing Zak to search the dense timberland below. As they followed the lakeshore, he cried, "There, on top of that old snag. It looks like it's occupied. And look over there—" he pointed to another old tree "—a pair of young ones."

Tess banked the plane in a sweeping turn, descending toward the treetops. Leveling off, she flew over the area and saw the two large birds with solid brown plumage. "They look pretty big," she remarked. "When do they get their white feathers?"

"When they're five," Zak told her. His head snapped around as they passed over the second nest. "Damn, another single. And we can only take chicks from nests with twins."

Tess didn't reply. Her attention had turned to the small grayish specks flipping against the windscreen. She eased the controls back. The plane leveled off before slowly rising as they headed for the ranger station at Pine Lake. For a while they cruised smoothly, Zak intent on watching the thick virgin forest closing in on the valley below.

Tess scanned the view for other reasons. "That's oil on the windscreen," she stated. "We have to land."

Zak looked up and saw the specks of oil. "Land? Where? There's nothing but dense forest down there."

"The ranger station should be just over that ridge," Tess said. "Start looking for the lake. There's a grass airstrip beside it." She focused again on the specks of oil, which had now merged and were forming grayish streaks up the windscreen. "We've got to get down—fast!"

Zak's eyes riveted on the streaks of oil. The engine began to sputter. "Jesus," he said. "The engine's about to cut out!"

"We can glide in—if we can find the airstrip," Tess said. "Just keep looking for the lake. It can't be more than five minutes from here—I hope." But she really couldn't remember exactly how long it took to fly from Crescent Lake to the ranger station. When she'd flown with Gib so many years before, it had seemed just minutes away. But then she'd enjoyed flying so much that every stretch seemed too short.

Squinting through the murky windscreen, she scanned the terrain in the distance, and as she did she spotted a silvery patch amid the green of the forest.

"There it is!" she exclaimed. "Pine Lake—but I don't see the landing strip yet."

Zak leaned forward, his eyes focused on the opening in the woods where the lake lay. "Just to the west—next to the water."

Tess peered through the oil-splattered windscreen and saw the cleared area. "That's it. Damn, it's short."

Zak's gaze moved over the thick stand of evergreens boxing the runway. "Can you handle it all right?" he asked.

"I don't know," Tess replied. "I've never landed on such a short field. I hope the wind's right—we can't chance going around to approach from the other direction. We'll have to dip in over those tall trees at this end." She banked the plane in a sweeping turn to align with the runway, throttled back, lowered the flaps and continued to nose the plane down.

As they dropped toward the runway, Tess saw a wind sock perched atop a tree and realized, with mounting fear, that they were approaching with the wind. "The last thing we need," she mumbled. "The wind's wrong. We're going to come in too fast." She knew that would further shorten her landing space. She scanned the field for obstructions and studied the trees at each end of the narrow grassy strip. "I don't think we can make it," she said as the engine sputtered, cut out and sputtered again.

"We sure as hell better do something fast," Zak said. "We're about to lose power."

Tess advanced the throttle slightly. "This is going to be a hot landing—and it had better work. We won't get a second chance,'' she said, her heart pounding so fast she felt light-headed. She gripped the wheel. ''Okay, now. Here we go. Put your head in your lap for the landing and be ready to jump out and run....''

CHAPTER FIVE

THE CLEARING CAME UP FAST, too fast, and within seconds they skimmed close to the tops of the tall trees. Tess cut the power as the plane plunged toward the airstrip. Peering through a windscreen now almost completely obscured by oil, she maneuvered into the clearing and touched down, feeling a jolt as the main gear made contact with the ground. Holding her breath, she struggled to ease the controls forward until the nose wheel touched down. The plane shuddered and bounced over the uneven ground. Throwing all her weight onto the pedals, she applied the brakes. The plane careened toward the wall of trees at the end of the runway and skidded to a halt at the edge of the clearing—a breath away from the mammoth tree trunks rising before them.

Tess sat still for a moment, staring into the dense growth, wondering what quirk of fate had spared them from plummeting into the impenetrable wall of trees. When the horror on Zak's face finally registered, it precipitated a chain reaction, and she suddenly felt herself go clammy with belated fear.

Zak blinked several times, then looked around to verify that they were really down. When he saw Tess, he realized she was shaking. "We're fine," he assured her, his own shock abating as he pulled her into his arms.

Tess gripped Zak's arm. "I never thought ground could feel so good," she said, her voice cracking, tears of relief brightening her eyes.

"Neither did I," Zak replied, holding her, feeling her heart pounding against him. It seemed so right to have her in his arms again, to feel her cheek against his shoulder and her arms clinging to his. When she moved away, he reached out and brushed a finger beneath each moist eye and asked, "Are you okay?"

Tess laughed a nervous high-strung laugh. "This was my first forced landing."

Zak grinned. "Well, you did one hell of a good job bringing us down."

The door on Tess's side of the plane flew open and a hoarse voice rang out, "Everybody in here all right?"

Tess looked down. "Yes, we're fine," she said, still shaken.

Eyes the color of spring clover peered up from beneath thick dark brows. "You're damn lucky—the whole front of the plane's covered with oil," the man said. "I'm Ralph Tolsted, by the way."

"Tess O'Reilly," Tess said, "and—"

"Zak de Neuville," Zak added, reaching around Tess to shake Ralph's hand.

"Oh!" Ralph exclaimed. "You're from the wildlife park. I didn't expect such a dramatic arrival. That was a nice piece of flying." He stepped aside to let Tess climb out. "I'm sure glad you folks got down okay."

"So am I," Tess said, still gripping the wheel to quiet her shaking hands. "For a minute there, I didn't think we'd make it." Feeling the agitated pounding of her heart, she eased out of the seat, then stepped from the plane on weak legs.

Zak moved to stand beside her and they stared at the plane. Oil bathed the windshield and streamed along the side of the fuselage and under the belly. Tess raised the engine cowling and peered inside, locating the problem immediately. "A broken oil line," she said, "and it looks as if we've lost most of our oil. Gib better have a spare hose. I've got to get back this afternoon." She certainly didn't want to have to explain any of this to her father. She climbed back into the cockpit and searched through the toolbox for a spare hose, but found none.

"We can call the airpark and send for a hose," Ralph suggested. "There's still lots of daylight left— it's only a half-hour flight up here."

Tess looked anxiously at Ralph. "Would you mind calling right away?" she asked. "I really do need to get back today."

Ralph smiled. "No problem. Come on in the house." He ushered them toward the compound of moss-green buildings and the modest house provided by the forest service. He turned to Zak. "I got your letter about the chick-transplant program and I've been watching the aerie over there," he said, pointing to the tangle of sticks atop an ancient fir overlooking the lake. "I looked down at the nest from the ridge, and from what I could tell through the glasses there's only one chick."

Zak glanced back at the nest as they walked. "I was afraid of that."

Ralph guided them up a narrow path leading to the house. "There was quite a bit of other stuff in the nest, too," he added. "Looked like some bottles."

Zak laughed at the surprised look on Tess's face. "Eagles are real pack rats," he told her. "We've found bottles, light bulbs, old shoes—even a framed picture in one." He glanced back. "From the size of that aerie, I'd say it was twenty-five to thirty years old, so there could be just about anything in it."

"Thirty years?" Tess said.

"Probably," Zak replied. "Some nests stay active as long as fifty—added to or repaired each year. That's why it's so important to preserve old-growth timber massive enough to support them."

Ralph led them into the living room and poured them each a mug of coffee. He glanced at Tess. "That's a Cessna 152, isn't it?" he asked.

"Yes," she replied. "We'll need a replacement hose, new fittings and five quarts of oil."

Ralph excused himself and went to call the airpark on the radio. When he returned, he announced, "They're not sure when they'll be able to get a plane out here, but they'll send one as soon as possible."

Zak stood. "Since we have some time, I'd like to climb to the ridge and look into the nest. Is there a trail?"

"Yes," Ralph said. "Come on. I'll show you where it starts."

Tess stared out the window at the clouds that were starting to build over the rugged mountain peaks. "I'd better wait here in case the plane shows up before you get back," she said. "I'm anxious to replace that hose and get out of here before we get socked in."

"Come on. You have plenty of time," Ralph assured her. "It's only about a fifteen-minute hike to the ridge, and it'll be at least an hour before the plane can get here."

Tess reluctantly turned from the window and followed Ralph and Zak to the plane, where Zak grabbed his binoculars and their jackets. Tess fell into place between Zak and Ralph. As they hiked, a damp musty-smelling breeze filled her nostrils.

At the trailhead, Ralph stopped and turned. "Take your time," he said. "When you hear the plane coming you won't be more than a few minutes away." He waved and headed back to the house.

Zak led the way and they began a steady climb up the steep grade, winding between high weedy banks with crumbling dirt walls from which twisted roots reached out, groping at nothing. Higher on the trail, the forest thinned and the path turned to follow the edge of a cliff. Tess looked down at the steep drop-off, feeling both surprised and uneasy at how high they'd climbed in such a short time. At a level spot on the trail, Zak paused and held the binoculars to his eyes, peering down into the nest. "Ralph's right—one chick. I can't tell exactly what else is in the nest, but it looks like a bottle."

He lowered the glasses and turned to find Tess looking at the nest, her silhouette edged in gold as the sun peeked through an opening in the dark clouds. As he stared, the wind whipped her hair into a torrent of dark curls, all but obscuring her delicate face. He felt an overwhelming urge to take her in his arms, to hold her and press his lips to hers. But this was not the impulsive sixteen-year-old girl he'd left behind. Tess was quieter now, more subdued and mature. And he had to admit, he didn't really know this woman she'd become. They'd only just begun to get reacquainted, and he didn't want to upset the fragile balance of her trust.

Tess turned to catch Zak watching her. She held his gaze and contemplated his ruggedly handsome features. His face was animated and flushed from the hike. Feeling uneasy with the way he looked at her, she gave him a nervous smile and glanced down at the binoculars in his hand. "May I see?" she asked.

"Sure," Zak replied, walking over to hand her the glasses.

Tess held up the binoculars and looked into the shallow depression of a nest lined with grass. She turned the focusing ring until a woolly eaglet came into view. "It's gray," she said, expecting to see a chick with mottled brown-and-white feathers.

"That's postnatal down," Zak said. "The chick's younger than the others you've seen—probably no more than a couple of weeks old."

As Tess watched the young bird through the glasses, an adult swooped into view and perched on the edge of the nest, a fish dangling from its hooked beak.

"That's probably the mother," Zak said. "For the first few weeks the father hunts and the mother feeds. Look closely and you'll see her show her chick how to rip the kill into bite-size pieces."

While Tess watched the eagle feed her young, a series of chortling cries, like the loud laugh of a maniac, came from high above, the sound rolling and echoing against the bald granite face of the bluff. Tess looked up to see another eagle gliding overhead.

The mother bird left the nest and flew up to join her mate. Together the majestic pair circled in a wide arc, their snow-white head and tail feathers contrasting with the gray of the sky. Then suddenly they came together and plunged toward the earth, rolling and tumbling faster and faster until it seemed certain they'd crash. At the last moment, in perfect control, they broke apart and pulled out of their free-fall, soaring swiftly and silently away on a current of wind.

"That was incredible," Tess breathed, then turned to find Zak watching her again.

His eyes moved slowly over her face. "When they're courting," he said in a quiet voice, "their aerobatics can be pretty spectacular." His gaze moved over her lips and back to focus on her eyes. "Just then, you saw them lock talons and begin their cartwheel toward the ground in a sort of . . . love ritual."

Tess blinked. "Love?" The word drifted from her lips and hovered between them.

"They mate for life and live with fierce devotion to each other," he said, his voice low, "sometimes staying together as long as twenty-five years." He moved imperceptibly closer, realizing now that he was talking about more than the eagles. "When one dies, the other begins a lonely journey, roaming the skies until it finds a new mate, and leads it back to the familiar nest." He wanted to touch his lips to hers, feel her lips become soft and sweet. And he wanted more, so much more. He wanted time with her—time for them to get to know each other again, to grow to love each other again. He realized with sudden clarity that he desperately wanted her love again. And he wanted to give her his love in return—a love that had never died.

Tess closed her eyes as he bent down and brushed his lips against hers, absorbing the sweetness of a kiss that was almost reverent in its tenderness. As he tilted her chin toward him with his finger, a warmth radiated through her that could not have been stronger had Zak enfolded her in his arms. He slowly drew his lips from hers. "It's been a long time," he whispered.

Unprepared for the bittersweet yearning growing inside, and wary of her own vulnerability, Tess moved away. Feeling the first drops of rain on her face, she pulled the hood of her parka up and said in a wavering voice, "We'd better start back."

"What are you afraid of?" Zak asked.

"Nothing," she replied, tying the hood with shaking hands. "It's about to rain and I think we should get back." Without waiting for his response, she turned and headed quickly down the trail.

By the time they arrived at the house, the sky had turned a rich purple and lightning flashed like neon in the distance. Ralph met them on the porch. "Clouds have moved in at the airpark and the ceiling's too low, so they can't come until tomorrow morning," he told them.

"Oh no, that can't be!" Tess cried. "We have to get back today—now! Isn't there any other way out?"

"Not from here," Ralph said. "But I told them you needed to leave as early as possible tomorrow."

Tess closed her eyes momentarily, then opened them quickly as Gib's face appeared in her mind. Flying off on her own and getting stranded was one thing. Being stranded because she'd taken Zak up was entirely another. The thought of her father's inevitable reaction caused a knot to coil in her stomach. "I've got to call the logging camp," she said, feeling a heaviness settle inside. Her only hope was to get word to Jed Swenson, if she could, and tell him to start the men cutting pole timber early the next morning.

All afternoon Tess, Zak and Ralph tried to contact Timber West, but the stormy weather interfered with the radio transmission, and it was almost eleven at night before Ralph established a reliable phone patch with Ezzie at the camp. Ezzie assured Tess that he'd get her message to Jed Swenson and the logging crew. After signing off, Ralph gave Zak a pillow and blanket, showed Tess to the spare bedroom and retired for the night.

Later, as Tess scurried down the hall from the bath to the bedroom, Zak intercepted her. He closed his hand on her forearm. "I'm sorry about all of this," he whispered, gazing at her solemnly, his eyes luminous in the subdued light.

"So am I," Tess replied, her heart beating so rapidly she felt it might leap from her breast. She braced her palms against his chest, wanting to keep some distance between them, yet fearing that if he kept looking at her the way he was, she wouldn't have the strength to push him away. "I should never have agreed to take you up in my father's plane," she said. "It's as simple as that."

Zak stared at her silently for a long moment, then slid his palms down her shoulders and curved them around her waist. "But you did agree," he replied, drawing her closer, his voice low, strained. "And since I'm to blame, I want to make things right...." He bent his head toward hers.

Her heart pounding at the realization that Zak was going to kiss her again, Tess could only reply, "Don't..." But her words were snatched away when Zak's mouth came down on hers.

Every muscle in her body seemed to go slack. "Mmm." The protest she'd intended slipped out as a moan of pleasure. She curved her arms around Zak's neck, allowing his tongue to tease hers, probe deeper, until her mouth throbbed beneath his kiss.

"You feel so good in my arms," Zak said in a ragged voice. "So right." He cradled her close, the warmth of him against her spreading like wildfire.

Clinging to him, Tess felt an almost ethereal sense of bonding. But the feeling quickly faded, replaced by a state of confusion. A cool sweat broke out on her brow. He'd left her once. He'd leave her again. There was no place in her life for Zak de Neuville now.

"No, Zak," she said, her voice firm and filled with purpose. "This shouldn't happen." She backed out of his arms. "Everything is different now. You have a child to raise and I have things to resolve with my father, and that's the way it will have to be." Turning, she dashed into the bedroom, feeling an almost overwhelming sense of loss as she closed the door.

For one brief frivolous moment, she had nearly believed their lives could come together. But even if Zak did offer her an explanation for his disappearance and she could learn to trust him again, there were still too many obstacles between them.

THE NEXT MORNING Zak helped Tess replace the oil hose, and by the time they arrived in Bakers Creek, it was almost noon. When Tess stepped out of the telephone booth at the airpark, her face reflected her inner turmoil. "Aunt Ruth said Gib stormed out this morning when someone called from camp," she said to Zak.

Zak tried to convince himself that Gib O'Reilly would be so relieved that Tess had landed safely, he wouldn't press the issue of who'd been with her. "We'll square things away when we get there," he replied as they walked toward Tess's Jeep. He didn't look forward to that encounter.

"We?" Tess said, concerned. "I really don't think you should see Gib right now. He's already hot enough under the collar."

"I got you into this," Zak said in a firm voice. "I don't intend to walk away from it." Nor did he intend to be intimidated again by Gib O'Reilly's threats.

Tess pursed her lips. "Just what, exactly, do you plan to say to him?"

Zak noted the worried frown on Tess's face and replied, "I'll just explain the circumstances."

"No. I want to talk to him alone," Tess insisted as they climbed into the Jeep. She slammed the door. "The doctor said he shouldn't even be at the camp.

And I don't want him losing his temper—which is what will happen if you're around."

Zak climbed into the passenger seat. He stared out the window. "I'll have to talk to him eventually," he said. "We still have the property line to discuss."

Tess pulled out of the parking lot onto the highway and headed toward Timber West. Her eyes brightened with tears of frustration. "I wish they'd get off each other's backs," she said.

Zak reached over and took her hand, encircling it with his. "So do I," he said. "But they won't."

For a moment, Tess made no attempt to move her hand. Zak's fingers curled so comfortably around hers, and the pad of his thumb stroking the back of her hand felt so natural, so familiar, that it made her think of how it used to be when they drove somewhere together... and it was as if the eight intervening years had never been. She shifted her gaze to their hands. But the years *had* been. Gib's anger had been. Zak's disappearance had been. She slipped her hand from his. "I hope Swenson showed up like he was supposed to."

Zak rested his hand on the back of her seat and looked away. It was there again—Tess's uncertainty, her distrust. She had a right. If they were to ever rebuild their relationship, he'd have to tell her everything. How long until he'd feel comfortable doing that? A week? A month? He sighed. "Well, you know Swenson got the message. That's about all you could have done."

"I could have been up at the pole-timber area this morning at six, like I was supposed to be," Tess said.

"I wanted so much to do things right, to run the camp the way Gib wanted. And now..." She turned away, saying nothing more.

Fifteen minutes later, as they approached the turn-off to Timber West, Zak looked toward the ridge where several massive gray snags thrust above the stand of second-growth timber. He hoped none were trees that held perch nests. They were too close to the logging operation. Facing Gib O'Reilly about cutting four trees was one thing; stopping his logging operation was another.

Tess pulled into Zak's drive and stopped, but left the engine running. Zak opened the door and jumped down. "I appreciate the plane ride," he said. "But I wish you'd let me explain to your father. I feel responsible for what happened...."

"It's not your fault that the hose broke," Tess insisted. "Now, I'd better get this over with." She backed onto the highway and drove to her cabin. Quickly she changed into work clothes, pulled on her boots and grabbed her hard hat. Jumping back into her Jeep, she drove to the compound, and as she pulled into the clearing, she spotted Gib standing by his truck, which he'd parked near the property line. When she looked beyond him, her heart thumped wildly. She saw the four logs he'd cut the week before, but now four more had been dragged onto the pile, and a noticeable cleft appeared in the once solid forest wall at the edge of the clearing. *"Damn!"* she yelped. She jumped from the Jeep and rushed over to her father. "What are you doing, Gib? This is *not* Timber West land!"

"The hell it's not," Gib said, impatient eyes flicking over her face.

Tess noted the hard lines about his mouth. "You're not even supposed to be here, and you know it."

Gib looked at Sean Herring, who was limbing one of the downed trees. "Somebody's got to run the camp."

Tess glanced around, a heaviness settling in her chest. "Isn't Swenson here?"

Gib's eyes followed Herring's choppy movements. "I'm surprised you'd ask," he said, his tone clipped.

Tess was swept by uneasiness. "Why do you say that?" she asked, her gaze moving restlessly around the compound to where several men stood chatting idly.

"Because you're pretty quick to go flying off with that damn Basque sheepherder and leave the whole operation to run itself!"

"It was a business arrangement," Tess said in a restrained voice.

Gib's eyes narrowed. "I wasn't aware you operated a flying service."

Tess felt the blood pounding in her temples. "Zak asked me to fly him over some eagle nests," she replied, her heart hammering rapidly.

"So you fly because he says fly, then ditch the plane and take off with that—"

"I *didn't* ditch the plane," Tess insisted. "It's back at the airpark now." She saw the stubborn lines about her father's mouth and the defiance in his eyes.

"Why the devil did he come back here, anyway?"

"He lives here, remember?"

"Or maybe he just likes the young girls around here better. I take it he's still prowling around seducing children."

Tess's fingers curled into her palms. "I'm tired of your caustic remarks about Zak," she said, straining to check her temper. "I loved him and he loved me, and he wasn't some kind of pervert."

Gib flailed a hand in the air. "You were too young to know what you wanted, so you let that no-'count sheepherder crawl in your bed by promising to make legal what never should have happened in the first place!"

Tess glared at him. "Just who do you think you are, deciding the course of my life?" At once she regretted flaring up. Gib wasn't ready for this. She'd back off.

Gib closed the gap between them and stood so close Tess could see the veins throbbing in his temple. "A father, that's who. A father who gives a damn!"

"Well, you have a hell of a way of showing it!" Damn, she'd done it again.

Gib drew in a shaky breath, pressed his hands against the fender of the truck and closed his eyes.

Tess reached for his arm. "Gib? You okay?"

He turned to her and continued in a low voice, "A lot of years have separated us," he said, "and if I could, I'd give my soul to have those years back. But if it came down to letting the daughter who was my entire life go off with a grown man who had no apparent direction, and I had it within my power to prevent it, I'd do the same thing again, so help me God, Teslyn, I would."

Tess looked up into Gib's tired eyes and felt the pain he must have suffered over the years she'd taken away from him. And into her distraught mind came the realization that he'd done what he had to do—because he loved her. For the first time in years, she put her arms around him and buried her face against his chest. When she looked up, tears moistened the deep furrows beneath his eyes. "Dad?" she said, blinking to clear her eyes. "Can we start over, try to recover what we threw away?"

Gib looked down at her. "How?"

Tess brushed at a vagrant tear making its way down her cheek. "By discussing Zak objectively."

Gib mumbled unintelligibly and began to walk away.

Tess's anger flared again. "That's part of our problem, Dad," she said. "When you're angry, you don't talk. You only grumble and walk away. We need to keep talking about this."

Gib turned to face her. "Well, I can't get excited about Zak being around."

"I'm sorry about that," Tess said. "But he *is* here, and you'll just have to get used to that."

Gib sighed. "I'm not sure I can."

"Can you at least try? For us?"

Gib gave a weary sigh and looked at her. "It's really important to you, isn't it?"

"Yes," Tess replied. "I want us to understand each other, and the only way we can is to stop tippy-toeing around the subject of Zak. We're very quick to argue about him, but we've never once discussed him in a rational way."

"Okay then," Gib said. "Start by answering one question." He looked directly at her. "Do you still love him?"

Tess shrugged. "I don't really know him anymore—it's been eight years. We've both been married and divorced, and Zak has a son. Even if I did still love him, I'm not sure I'm up to taking on a ready-made family."

"But you care enough to want to spend time with him. You did take him up in the plane."

"Only because he asked me to. He's head of the endangered-species program at the wildlife park and he's working with bald eagles," Tess explained. "That's why he asked me to fly him over the nest sites. If the oil hose on the plane hadn't broken, or if there'd been a spare in the toolbox, we would've been back yesterday."

Gib gave her a repentant smile. "I'm sorry about that. The important thing is that you got down safely."

Tess noticed he didn't say you *and Zak* got down safely. But at least Zak's return was out in the open. There was, however, still the issue of the property line. "Now, about those eight trees," she said, motioning toward the stack of logs. "They were cut on Zak's father's land. Our land stops ten feet from this road."

"Like hell it does. Our land runs fifty feet beyond where the trees were cut."

"The survey map shows clearly—"

"Enough about the trees," Gib broke in.

Tess pursed her lips. "Will you at least look at the survey?"

Gib folded his arms. "Don't you have a camp to run?"

Tess studied the firm set of his jaw, the unyielding look in his eyes. They *would* get back to the trees, and Gib *would* look at the map, she determined. She sighed. "Like I said earlier, didn't Swenson show up?"

"He said he had some personal business," Gib replied, looking toward the cookshack. "He only got here just before you arrived."

"Personal business?" Tess queried, her voice impatient. "Look, Dad, I can't run a logging operation with a woods boss who refuses to work for me. I don't know why you even kept him on if this is the way he operates."

"He worked fine for me," Gib said. "I suggest you give him the benefit of the doubt and see what he has to say."

Tess breathed deep through flared nostrils. "I'll give him the benefit of the doubt," she said, restless eyes moving to the cookshack, where the sound of laughter rumbled inside, "then I'll give him his last paycheck. Now, will you please go home. I'll stop by in a few days so we can go over the books and do the monthly report."

"Mmm," Gib responded.

Tess walked with him toward his truck and kissed him lightly on the cheek. "I've got the chessboard set up," she said as he moved to open the door.

Gib smiled. "Is that a challenge?"

"Sure," Tess replied, "if you think you're ready to take me on again."

"I can take you on anytime, kiddo," he said. "There's one thing an old die-hard chess player never does..."

Tess looked at him with curiosity and waited.

Gib winked. "And that's tell his prize student all the plays." He turned and climbed into the truck.

Tess laughed. "I may have a few of my own tucked away," she said, stepping back as he started the engine.

When Gib's truck had turned out of the clearing and disappeared, she yelled to Herring over the buzz of a chain saw, "Spread the word, Herring. Absolutely no more cutting around here—even if my father gives the orders. Is that clear?"

Herring nodded and turned off the saw.

Tess looked toward the cookshack, distracted by guffaws and laughter. It appeared that the boys were taking an extended break on Timber West time. And Jed Swenson? Was he also enjoying a leisurely afternoon in the cookshack? She marched toward the small building, determination in her stride. It was obviously time to assert her authority.

CHAPTER SIX

"COME ON, YOU BUCKS, put your money here. Who'll step down? Swenson or TJ?" bellowed Curt Broderick.

"She's one tough cookie, that TJ," yelled Mac Royer, a solid hulk of a man who closely resembled a smiling bulldog, "but she's no match for Swenson. I don't think it's who'll step down, but how long TJ will last."

A voice blared from across the room as a coin clanked to the floor and spun at Curt's feet. "A quarter says she'll last one more day."

Curt crouched above the coin. "A lousy quarter? Come on, men, ante up. Make it worthwhile. Let's see some green!" A dollar bill floated down. "That the best you can do, Pryor? How 'bout a five?" Pryor switched a five for the one. "That's more like it," said Curt. "Place your bets, men. Winner takes all. I hear a 'one day.' Take this down, Royer."

Hands tossed crumpled bills into the circle.

"I'll give her five days."

"Five days for Dempsey."

"Two days!"

"Two days for Royer. Anyone for a week? One whole week? Come on, you guys—"

A knife blade flashed and buried itself in the wood with a thunk. The men looked into the narrowed eyes of Jed Swenson.

"That's for forty-five seconds," he snorted. He crouched, yanked the knife from the floorboard and stabbed it through a five-dollar bill. Settling back on his heels, he scratched a fingernail against the stubble on his chin and said, "It'll be a cold day in hell when I let a woman tell me how, or when, to do my job, and you boys can tell *that* to *Mizzz* O'Reilly."

"You can tell me yourself," Tess said from the doorway, her eyes focused on the big man. She walked over to where Swenson crouched. The voices died as Swenson rose, hooked his thumbs in his belt and glared at her. Hands on her hips, Tess glared back. "You're the elusive Jed Swenson, I presume."

Swenson scratched his head. "Hey! You're head honcho here. You oughtta know your own woods boss." He grinned over at his men. Subdued snickers rippled, then died.

Tess surveyed the crowd. Gradually their faces sobered. She turned to focus on Swenson, who hitched up his britches and slowly chewed the wad of tobacco in his mouth, his narrowed eyes openly defiant.

Tess crossed her arms. "Mr. Swenson, I'd like to see you in my office," she said, holding his gaze.

Swenson glanced around, yellow teeth exposed by a twisted smile. "There's nothing needs saying in your office that can't be said right here in front of my men."

Tess faced Swenson squarely. "Have it your way," she said. "First, they're not your men. You're not running this camp. You're woods boss—hired to direct cutting at the site and operate the skidder. You'll take your orders from me, and when I tell you to be somewhere, I expect you to follow orders. Is that clear?"

For an instant, Swenson's jaws stopped moving. "Hell, lady, you couldn't be clearer."

"All right, where were you on Friday?"

Swenson shifted his weight and hooked his thumbs in his pockets. "I had to go to my...grandmother's funeral."

Tess drew an impatient breath. "Where were you this morning when you were told to start the men cutting pole timber?"

"I had to—" Swenson gave her a belligerent smile "—get my teeth cleaned."

"Very well then, you can pack your gear. You're through." Tess turned and looked around at the blank faces. "And if anyone else wants to clean their teeth on company time, please don't hesitate to follow Mr. Swenson right out that door."

Swenson folded his arms and glared down at her. His mouth contorted into an ugly grimace. "You're pretty damned high-handed for a woman."

Tess's eyes flashed. "Your paycheck will be at the office this afternoon. Good day, Mr. Swenson."

Swenson's lips spread into a sneer. He scanned the faces of his men, the sneer fading as each, in turn, looked away. With mounting fury, he ground out, "I'll give you about one day to come begging for someone to run your damn camp." He yanked the knife from the floor and charged out of the cook-shack.

Tess stared at the open door. A gut feeling told her she had not seen the last of Jed Swenson. She turned to the men. "Curt?" she said, "I understand you've had some experience as woods boss in Montana."

"Well, yes." Curt squared his thick shoulders.

"Think you can handle the job here?"

Curt's lips twisted in a confident smile. "Sure."

"Good! Now we'll need another skidder driver to replace Swenson. Anyone here have any experience?"

Harv Dempsey stood up and shrugged. "I've done some—it's been a few years, though."

"Good. Meet me at the ridge in thirty minutes and we'll see what you can do."

TWO DAYS LATER Tess realized Harv Dempsey wasn't going to work out. More than once she'd had to call him down for not wearing his safety belt, and she had also noticed the jerky and erratic movement of the skidder when he drove. Things hadn't improved. Now, as she headed toward the cutting area, she was prepared to pull him off the skidder and put him back on limbing.

As she drove up the dirt road, she spotted a large sign nailed to the old gate where Timber West land met the north slope tract. The Jeep plunged to a halt and she read the words boldly painted across the wood surface:

ROYALTY ON ALL LOGS CROSSING
THIS PROPERTY IS $15 PER THOUSAND

> J. de Neuville—Owner
> J. Swenson—Manager

Tess stared at the sign. Jean-Pierre de Neuville, owner? Carl Yaeger was supposed to have bought the tract. And Swenson, manager of de Neuville's land? This was all she needed. Having to cross Jean-Pierre de Neuville's land would not sit well with Gib—nor would the increased log royalty. Timber West never paid more than a dollar per thousand board feet when Pacific Development owned it. Gib would be livid.

Zak had warned her there might be problems because of the trees Gib cut. He was right. The Jeep bolted forward, mud spewing from the spinning tires. Well, she'd pay Jean-Pierre de Neuville's royalty. The timber on the plateau would more than cover it. It was prime pole timber, and utility companies were paying a premium now.

By the time she pulled into the clearing where the men were working, her palms throbbed from gripping the wheel, and her clenched jaws ached. She spotted Curt Broderick coming toward her, a chain saw in his hand. "I guess you saw de Neuville's notice?" he said.

Tess hopped out of the Jeep. "Oh, yes," she replied.

Curt lowered the chain saw to the ground. "Swenson came by earlier. Claims he's workin' the north end of de Neuville's place—near the ridge. It won't surprise me if real trouble starts soon. Swenson doesn't take lightly to being put down, especially by a woman—nothin' personal intended."

"I know, but we'll just have to handle things as they come. Meanwhile, let's move timber," she said.

Curt grabbed the chain saw and pulled the cord, then revved the motor and walked back to where he'd been limbing. Tess leaned against a tree, folded her arms and watched Harv Dempsey pushing logs. He took too many passes to position the big machine, and when she heard him grind the gears, she walked toward him and indicated that she wanted to talk to him. He climbed down, and she realized he wasn't wearing his safety belt again.

"Dempsey, you've been told several times that wearing a safety belt is required in this operation," she said.

"It's too much hassle when I have to keep getting on and off," he replied.

"That may be," Tess said, "but we can't chance the liability. Thanks for trying, and don't feel bad about it, but I'm putting you back on limbing. Your saw's in my Jeep."

Without further comment, Dempsey shrugged and headed for the Jeep. Tess signaled to Curt, and when he walked over to her she said, "I interviewed another driver and he'll be here in the morning. Meanwhile, I'll handle the skidder."

"You?"

Tess smiled. "Don't look so surprised." She headed toward the big machine. It had been years since she'd operated a skidder, and looking at it now, she felt a renewed sense of excitement. It was hinged in the middle with the back wheels turning independently from the front ones, and whenever she drove it, she felt as if she were riding a giant double-jointed bug. She climbed the steps to the enclosed cab, swung up onto the seat and fastened her safety belt. Adjusting her hard hat and smiling, she turned the key and pressed the starter button.

Before the machine moved out, Curt motioned to her. "Hey, TJ!" he yelled over the sound of the engine.

Tess peered down from her lofty perch. "Yes?"

"I forgot to tell you. When Swenson was here earlier, he made some...threats. Want me to sort of keep an eye on him for you?"

Tess looked at Curt with apprehension. "What sort of threats?"

Curt shrugged. "Nothing specific—just said you'd be hearing from him."

"Well, maybe you'd better go back and watch things at the camp for the afternoon," she said. "I'll move the logs to the landing and meet you later."

Trying to shove thoughts of Jed Swenson from her mind, Tess put the skidder in gear, took the wheel and pulled on the throttle. For now, she intended to ride this giant bug.

Three hours later, she mopped the dust from her face and neck with a wet towel. As she prepared to climb into her Jeep, Zak's truck pulled into the clearing. He jumped out and walked over. Touching her cheek with his finger, he wiped a smudge away, then picked a leaf from her hair. "You look like the Tess I remember," he said.

Tess laughed. "I guess it's my lot in life to have dust on my face and leaves in my hair."

Zak studied her flushed face and bright eyes. "It's good to see you again. How did it go with your father the other day?"

"Amazingly well—after the storm had passed," Tess replied. Her face sobered. "Why didn't you say anything about your father buying the Pacific Development tract?"

Zak shrugged. "I thought you already knew."

"I didn't know, and neither did Gib—or about your father raising the royalty on our road. This is not going to go over very well, you know that. Raising the royalty might just be enough to make Timber West fold—which I imagine would make your father happy, because then he could buy this land, too."

"I admit he'd like to buy out Timber West, if only to stop your father from cutting trees on the wrong land," Zak said. "That's one of the problems between those two. They're both so damn bullheaded. Your father's too stubborn to admit he's wrong about the trees—and the property line—so he simply refuses to look at the survey map. Well, he's going to end up in court if he continues cutting—you are aware that five more trees are down, aren't you?"

"Five?" Tess said, looking at Zak with a start, her heartbeat quickening. "I found four the morning we got back from the airpark, but gave specific orders that no more were to be cut on that strip. Who cut the fifth?"

"I don't know," Zak replied. "Swenson found the tree freshly cut, and he started dragging it over onto our land. He and your new woods boss had a scuffle over it—"

"Curt? Swenson and Curt had a fight?"

"Swenson accused your man of cutting the tree, and I guess that didn't sit too well, so they got into a scrap."

"Well, I'm sure Curt Broderick didn't cut the tree," Tess said. "The question is, who did?"

"Swenson insisted it was your man—said he heard the chain saw, and when he got there no one was around but Broderick. And Broderick claims Swenson was the only person in the area. He claims he saw Swenson hooking a cable to his Cat and dragging the tree onto our land right after it was cut."

"That doesn't make sense," Tess said, a perplexed frown on her brow. "Regardless of what Swenson says, Curt didn't do it. Swenson made threats earlier today. He's still in a tiff about losing his job. I think he cut down the tree and tried to blame it on Curt."

"Swenson is pretty hotheaded, from what I hear," Zak admitted. He noted the furrows in Tess's forehead and the anxious lines around her mouth, and he felt ashamed. She didn't need any more worries. She had enough problems trying to work a crew of obstinate loggers while two bullheaded old men breathed down her neck. He combed his fingers through his hair. "I'm sorry I brought more problems," he said.

Tess looked into Zak's apologetic eyes. "I'm sorry, too," she admitted. "It's just . . . I get so frustrated because of Gib's stubbornness." She backed away and slapped at her jeans, sending crusted mud crumbling to the ground. When she looked up, Zak was smiling. "What's so funny?"

Zak scanned her attire. "You still look good in tight jeans," he said, ambling closer. "But I think I like you better the way you looked last week, when you stopped by my cabin." He raised his hand and gently pulled a twig from her hair. "You smelled good, too. Like flowers."

"Jasmine," Tess said, her pulse quickening as she felt Zak's warm breath on her temple. "I didn't know you'd noticed." She realized she was being coy, but she wanted to hear more.

"You better believe I did," Zak said. "I noticed other things, too..."

"Like what?"

"Like the curve of your neck—" he trailed his finger along her nape. "I've never seen you wear your hair up before. I liked that, too."

"I wear it that way quite often," Tess said, enjoying the little tingles radiating from where Zak's finger lightly moved toward her throat.

His finger stopped at the hollow between her collar bones and lingered there, then moved along her neck again. "I also like you in blue," he said, stepping even closer.

"Blue?" Tess asked, struggling to retain the gist of the conversation.

Zak slipped his hand behind her neck and pulled her to him. "You've matured into a desirable woman— one I'd like very much to kiss right now..." His voice drifted off and his lips moved toward hers.

Tess pressed against his chest. "Someone might see us," she said, knowing that wasn't the real reason for her resistance. Zak still hadn't offered any explanation for his disappearance eight years ago. He had been the most important person in her life then, and she'd thought she was the most important person in *his* life, too. But he'd simply... walked away....

Zak felt Tess stiffen, and he understood. He rested his hands on her shoulders. "I'd like to spend some time together. Talking."

Tess looked into his anxious eyes. She wanted that, too. She needed to know what had happened. Suddenly she smiled. "I think I'd like that," she replied at last, feeling the strong beat of Zak's heart against her palm.

With her smile, Zak felt as if the wall between them was toppling. "Good," he replied. "And I want to forget about trees and property lines. For once I just want to concentrate on us."

Tess nodded, happy at the prospect. "Meanwhile, I'd better talk to Broderick and Swenson about this tree thing. Are you going to your cabin right now?"

Zak looked at her curiously. "Yes. Why?"

"I'd feel better if you were with me when I talk to Jed Swenson," she said. She'd dealt with Swenson before, but she wasn't sure she wanted to face him alone in the woods. Although she wasn't easily intimidated, she wasn't a fool, either.

Zak smiled. "I'd feel better if I was along, too. I'll wait for you at my cabin and we can go from there."

"Give me a few minutes," Tess said, climbing into her Jeep. "I'll stop by camp first and talk to Curt."

Zak nodded and waved.

Tess found Curt in the machine shed working on the bulldozer. He told her he'd found Jed Swenson hauling the tree, and when he started asking questions, Swenson jumped him. Tess felt uneasy with Curt's attitude. It sounded almost as if a feud was building between the two men. As she walked back to her Jeep, she wondered if Gib had had this many problems running Timber West or whether she was somehow jinxed.

She met Zak at his cabin. They walked up the road, following the clink and rumble of Jed Swenson's Cat, and found the big man grading the road. When he saw them approach, he cut the throttle and waited for them to walk up to him.

Tess looked up, realizing Swenson's higher vantage point put her at a distinct disadvantage. "Mr. Swenson," she said, "would you please step down. I'd like to talk to you about the tree that was cut in the clearing by the road earlier."

Swenson shifted a plug of tobacco from one side of his mouth to the other and climbed down. His eyes moved from Tess to Zak, then back to Tess. "What about the tree?"

Tess raised her chin. "That's what I want you to tell me," she said, determined to listen to Swenson's side of the story in spite of what she already believed. "From what I understand, you claim Curt Broderick cut the tree."

Swenson held her gaze. "That's because he did," he replied, his eyes fixed on hers. "He was standing by the tree when it fell."

"Where, exactly, were you when you saw him?" Zak asked.

"I was cutting over near the hollow," Swenson replied, pointing.

Zak's eyes narrowed. "And you just happened to be walking near the clearing and saw Curt Broderick?"

Swenson spat tobacco juice on the ground. "I heard the tree fall and when I got there I found Broderick standing over it."

"What did you do after that?" Tess asked, trying to remain calm, even though she knew the man was lying.

Swenson's eyes darted to hers. "I told him to get the hell away from the tree. That it belonged to de Neuville."

"And?"

"And he told me to mind my own business."

"So you jumped him."

"Hell, no. He jumped me."

Tess felt the accelerated beat of her heart. "Was anyone else around, anyone who saw you and Broderick?"

"Hell, how should I know. Broderick had me pinned to the ground."

Zak stared at him dubiously. "You don't look like someone who could be easily pinned, Swenson. Are you sure you have the story right?"

"Are you sayin' I'm lyin'?"

"I'm not saying anything. I'm just trying to find out what happened."

"I told you what happened. You can believe anything you damned well please. I have work to do." He swung up onto the Cat, shoved it in gear and lowered the blade. When the bulldozer started moving forward, Tess felt Zak's hand on her arm, drawing her out of the way. "I don't think we're going to get anything more from him," he said, watching the bulldozer disappear over a rise. "That's the same story I got."

Tess folded her arms. "Well, I refuse to pay for that tree until we get to the bottom of this," she said, her voice growing shrill.

"Take it easy," Zak said, sliding his arm around her shoulders. "I'll see if I can get more out of him later—something that will prove him wrong. Meanwhile, I've opened one of the old trails through the woods. Let's go back that way."

Tess shrugged. "Sure. Why not?"

Zak took Tess's hand and she didn't pull away. As they walked through a forest of deep green cedars and tall hemlock, Zak contemplated an outing he hoped to arrange with Tess and Pio. He wanted them to get to know each other. Although Pio's response to Tess had been a disappointment, he felt sure the boy would warm up to her when he got to know Tess better. He also realized that it was becoming increasingly important to him that Pio's attitude toward Tess became positive.

He squeezed Tess's hand. "Do you still like the smell of creosote?" he asked, remembering the time she'd wrapped her arms around a telephone pole and sniffed it, telling him how much she liked the aroma.

Tess laughed. "Heavens, no! Creosote reminds me of coating fence posts, which reminds me of having black fingers and digging fence-post holes. Whatever made you think of that?''

Zak shrugged. "I guess, being with you in the woods again. We spent so much time together here.... I think of lots of things you said when I'm out on the trails.''

"I guess we did spend quite a bit of time here," Tess admitted. "I can't imagine why you'd remember anything I said about that, though. I was very young then, and very silly.''

"You were delightful. A free spirit. You reminded me of a wood nymph.''

Tess remembered the times she had literally been a wood nymph, and the vision brought a rush of heat to her cheeks. It had seemed so natural to lie naked with Zak on a bed of cool moss in the Grotto. She'd had no inhibitions with him. Their intimate times together had been as natural as walking or talking or sharing a picnic in the woods. She had adored touching him, caressing him, doing intimate little things that drove him wild. She'd been so in love then....

Zak felt Tess's hand tighten around his and he looked down. She seemed far away. "Hey," he said, giving her hand a little shake. "Where are you right now?''

Tess looked up with a start and blinked several times.

Zak smiled. "Do you realize you're blushing? I've never seen you blush before." Even that seemed to make her more feminine—and more beautiful. "Could we get together on Saturday?" he asked, eager to set a date now that Tess had consented to spend some time with him. "I'll be climbing a nest tree on the ridge, and Pio will be with me. The three of us could make a day of it."

Zak's suggestion made Tess's heart beat faster, but even though she wanted to be with him and get to know his son, she knew she couldn't spare the time. "I'd really like to," she replied, "but I need to go over the account books while Gib's away—he and Aunt Ruth are going to Portland for his checkup, then visiting their sister for a week or so. I've got to figure out how to pay for all the equipment repairs, and the trees."

"Look, if you need a loan, I can—"

"We don't need a loan," Tess broke in. "At least, not another one. We already have one big loan payment due in about two months. What I need is the chance to look over the books without Gib breathing down my neck, so I can do some figuring and decide what to do."

At the edge of the woods, before they stepped into the clearing where Zak's cabin stood, Zak paused and looked at her. "Have you approached him about selling?"

"Sure," Tess said, "but he won't even talk about it."

"Well, if he ever brings it up, let me know. I'm sure my father's last offer still holds. He mentions it from time to time."

"I know Gib's not thinking about it right now," Tess told him.

"Does going over the books take all day?" Zak asked.

"Not really," Tess replied. "Maybe a few hours in the morning."

"Then come with Pio and me."

As she looked into Zak's hopeful eyes and saw the corners of his mouth twitch with a tentative smile, she realized how important this outing was to him. A day with Zak and Pio might be fun. She shrugged. "I suppose I could spare a few hours."

"Good!" Zak took her other hand in his and pulled her toward him. "Will you be done with your book-keeping before noon?"

"I'll try." Tess realized that if Zak wanted to kiss her now, she'd let him. She had no idea where the relationship was going or if anything could come of it, but with the way he was looking at her now, she was powerless to resist him.

"We'll be by tomorrow about noon—with a picnic basket," Zak said, curling his fingers around hers. "We'll go to the park to pick up my climbing gear and I'll show you the breeding pens we're setting up."

"That sounds nice...." Tess's voice drifted off as Zak moved toward her and gently claimed her lips. She slid her hands up his back and curled her fingers into his hair, drawing him closer, reveling in the feel of his eager mouth, the taste of his seeking tongue. In his arms, she felt complete—yet there was still so much she needed to know about him, about the past. But she didn't want to analyze that right now. She didn't want to break the spell.

CHAPTER SEVEN

ZAK LOOKED ASKANCE at Pio, who sat staring out the side window of the truck, his face sullen. "Hey, sport," he said, reaching over to pat Pio's leg, "I thought you wanted to go on this tree climb with me. Grandmama told me you've been talking about it all week."

Pio shrugged but said nothing.

"I know you've never seen a young eagle," Zak continued. "You'll be surprised how big they are—they're actually bigger than their parents when they leave the nest, then they lose weight when they start to fly."

Pio pursed his lips and continued to stare out the window.

Zak tried to reconstruct the morning. When he'd arrived in Navarre, Pio had rushed out to meet the truck as usual, and he'd seemed especially excited. He'd grabbed Zak's hand and dragged him into the laundry room to see Lilly's kittens, chattering all the while, telling Zak the names he'd chosen. Then they tried to determine which of the kittens were boys and which were girls, deciding that Tuffy, the little orange kitten Pio had selected, was a male.

After a quiet breakfast, Pio did his chores and they left to pick up Tess. But once they were in the truck, Pio grew increasingly broody.

"Okay, son, out with it," Zak said. "You've been moping since we left Navarre. Did something happen? Did you get in trouble?"

"No." Pio folded his arms.

"Did Grandmama fuss at you for something? Maybe for not doing your chores."

Pio turned to Zak. "Does *she* have to go with us?"

"You mean Tess?" Zak asked, surprised.

Pio's eyes darkened but he said nothing. He just continued glaring at Zak, his lips compressed.

"Why would you not want Tess to come with us?" Zak was baffled. This wasn't like Pio. Normally he was a friendly likable little guy. "She's lots of fun, and she wants to get to know you better," he added.

"I don't like her."

"You don't even know her."

"I still don't like her." Pio turned to the window again and sat silently staring out.

Zak's brows drew together. It must have been something his grandfather said, something about the O'Reillys. And Pio had picked up on it. "Did Grandpapa say something about Tess, maybe something unkind?"

"No," said Pio, annoyed.

"Well, I'm sorry you feel the way you do," Zak said, at a loss what to say. "But we *are* spending the afternoon together and I'll expect you to be polite, even if you don't like Tess." This wasn't going at all as he'd expected. Tess had done nothing—unless it was the way she'd looked at Pio the first time she saw him. There was no question that she had been shocked. Pio could have taken the surprised look on her face for dislike.

In Bakers Creek they stopped to pick up a bucket of fried chicken and a carton each of coleslaw and potato salad. And at the grocery store Zak bought soft drinks, potato chips and fresh-baked peanut-butter cookies. It wasn't a very healthful selection of food, he realized, but at least it was everything Pio liked. When they got back into the truck, he gave Pio a cookie. Pio took it with indifference and nibbled on it as they continued toward Tess's cabin.

Tess met them at the truck, a platter of fresh sliced vegetables and a container of cream-cheese dip balanced in her hands. "You didn't tell me what to bring, so this is my contribution." She climbed into the truck and smiled at Pio. "Hi," she said, settling in the seat beside him.

"Hi," Pio replied in a cool tone, his face sober.

Tess peered over Pio's head and saw the look of disgust on Zak's face. Obviously something had happened between Zak and Pio, and she was in the middle of a minor feud. Well, she refused to let a father-son scrap ruin her day. She looked at Zak and said brightly, "This is a wonderful idea. And if we're lucky, those clouds up there will stay white and fluffy."

Zak gave her a tentative smile. "If we're lucky."

Tess rested the platter of vegetables on her lap. "Do you like fresh vegetables?" she asked Pio.

Pio stared at the neat rows of cucumber wedges, carrot and celery slices, and flowerets of broccoli and cauliflower. A look of distaste settled on his face. Tess was disappointed. She'd loved fresh vegetables when she was young and had hoped Pio would, too.

Pio turned to Zak and said something to him in Basque that Tess did not understand, but guessed was about the vegetables. Zak nodded his head and Pio folded his arms and glared at the platter. Zak sighed. "Okay," he said, exasperated, wheeling the truck into a turn in the road.

Pio looked relieved as he scooted away from Tess and closer to his father.

"What was that all about?" Tess asked.

Zak glanced at her, his face troubled. "He wanted to know if he had to eat the vegetables, and I said he did . . . then I said he didn't. I'm afraid he's not much of a vegetarian."

"I'm sorry," Tess said to Pio. "I guess I should have brought cookies or cake or something like that instead."

When Pio didn't respond, Zak gave her an apologetic smile. "No, that's fine. I love fresh vegetables, and Pio loves fried chicken—we brought a big bucketful." He glanced at Pio, who leaned heavily against him, obviously keeping his distance from Tess.

Zak patted Pio's leg, but Pio refused to smile. "He didn't really want to come today," he told her, trying to explain Pio's poor behavior. "He has a new kitten at home and he didn't want to leave it. But I convinced him we'd have fun and that his kitten would be waiting for him when he got back to Navarre."

Tess glanced down at Pio. "A kitten? How exciting!"

Pio looked up at Zak with disgust.

Zak felt increasingly irritated with his son. Pio had never been so rude or disagreeable before, and he wasn't quite sure how to handle the situation. For now, he felt like taking Pio back to Navarre, although that would be giving him his way. This six-year-old boy was quickly trying his patience.

Thirteen miles down the road, Zak pulled into Spencer Wildlife Park, nodding to the guard as they passed through the entrance. "I want to show you the cheetah pens first," he said to Tess, wheeling the truck through an open area where water buffalo grazed.

Feeling the boy's hostility, Tess glanced across Pio at Zak. She'd smiled at Pio several times, but he refused to smile back, and she had no idea what the problem was.

The truck passed through the remote-controlled gates into an area where a pride of lions stretched lazily on rocks. Driving through more gates, Zak pulled up to a complex of concrete pens that were still under construction. He hopped out of the truck and Pio followed.

Tess climbed down and joined them, and Pio immediately moved around to stand on the other side of Zak. Tess tried to analyze the boy's obvious resentment. She suspected Pio viewed her as a threat to his relationship with his father. Trying to overcome her hurt and disappointment that Zak's son disliked her, she turned to Zak. "I didn't know there would be so many pens," she said, staring at a vast matrix of concrete walls.

"We'll be housing twenty cheetahs to start with," Zak said, contemplating the pens. "The first are scheduled to arrive from Africa this summer."

Tess studied the maze of walls. "It seems like they'd be better off roaming free in Africa."

"Unfortunately they're not," Zak replied. "They're dying out because of a genetic problem, and on top of that they're considered predators, so farmers shoot them to protect their livestock. Instead, we're trying to persuade the farmers to trap the animals live for shipment to wildlife parks."

"Will they ever go free again?" Tess asked.

"Probably not," Zak replied. "There may be as few as two thousand cheetahs left in Africa—seven hundred were killed in one year alone. Given the current rate of habitat shrinkage and their poor reproductive rate, the cheetah may only survive in captive-breeding programs like ours by the middle of the next century."

Tess glanced around at the network of roads and fences. The place had grown almost beyond recognition since the last time she'd been there, the summer before her mother died. Leaning on the rail, she folded her hands. "My mother and I used to come here when I was about Pio's age," she said. "I sometimes try to imagine how my life would have been if she hadn't died. I know raising me was hard on Gib. He wasn't so cantankerous when Mom was alive."

"Do you feel as if you're the reason for that?"

Tess shrugged. "I don't know. Maybe. You said it's really hard to be a single parent."

Zak moved to stand beside her and took her hand. "It is hard—but it's also rewarding," he said, looking at Pio, who was balancing himself along the length of a low concrete wall. "In spite of the somewhat less-than-desirable behavior you're seeing today, Pio's a real joy to me."

Tess saw the warmth in Zak's eyes as he watched his son step along the low wall, arms extended like a tightrope walker. It bothered her to think of Zak and another woman having a child together...living as a family...loving as a couple. She also wondered what went wrong with their marriage. He hadn't told her anything about it.

Zak noticed her pensive expression and squeezed her hand. "You're either puzzled or bothered about something, aren't you?" he said.

"Is it that obvious?"

He smiled. "I said we needed time together to ask questions—and get answers. Go ahead."

Tess glanced down at their clasped hands. "You said you and your wife separated. Why didn't you ever divorce?"

Zak hesitated, not certain how much he wanted to tell her right now, with Pio almost within earshot. They needed time alone, but for now, Tess also needed some answers. "We just never got around to it, I suppose," he replied. "Mirande was from France and she couldn't adjust to being away from her family."

Tess looked at Zak with a start. She'd assumed his wife had been from Navarre—someone he'd known from his childhood—a woman of his parents' choosing. "Then you met her when you went to study wine-making?"

"Yes," Zak replied. "It was sort of a rebound relationship for both of us."

"You planned to stay in France, then?"

"No, it was understood that we'd eventually live in America, since I was expected to take over the winery—and we did move here after Pio was born. The first year, when we lived in Navarre, everything was fine. Then, I started college and we moved to Washington. That's when Mirande really got homesick for France. She wanted to go back to see her folks that winter—they hadn't seen Pio in over a year. I knew I'd be busy in school, so I agreed."

Tess tried to recall that period of her life and realized she'd probably just married David. It had been a time of turmoil for her—trying to decide whether to say yes to David's proposal, wanting to get away from Gib. She shook off those unsettling memories and returned her attention to Zak. "How long was she gone?"

"She never came back." Zak dropped Tess's hand and rested his elbows on the railing. He leaned forward, hands together. "She kept extending her visit, and eventually she told me she didn't want to leave France. So that summer I went over there, hoping to talk her into coming back with me, but she refused. The hardest part was leaving Pio. Mirande wouldn't let me take him to America for any length of time when he was so young."

Tess looked at him, bewildered. "But you're his father. You could have just taken him—at least gotten temporary custody."

"I couldn't do that to Pio—or Mirande. They were very close—" he turned to look at Tess "—and I think a young child needs a mother. Anyway, Mirande agreed to let me see Pio whenever I wanted, as long as he stayed in France."

"How often did you go back to see him?"

"A couple of times a year, and each time it was harder to leave him. But I knew Mirande was a devoted mother and that she was good with Pio, so that helped. For the last two years, she finally let him spend his summers here."

Tess felt troubled by what Zak had just told her. Deep down, she'd hoped to hear him say that he and his wife had separated because he'd never really loved her or that he'd discovered his work was more important than his marriage. But he hadn't said either of those things. "You still didn't say why you never got a divorce."

"We discussed it the last time I visited—about two years ago," Zak replied. "There seemed little point in trying to hold together a marriage divided by the Atlantic Ocean. Then, the time ran out."

Tess wondered if Zak had continued to love his wife all those years, hoping things would work out. Or if he still loved her, even though she was gone. Barring all other obstacles, maybe he wasn't yet ready for a relationship. "How did she die?" she finally asked.

"She was hit by a car while riding her bicycle," Zak replied. "Died instantly."

"That must have been a shock."

"We'd grown apart over the years. We only talked about Pio in our letters. But yes, it was a shock. She was still the mother of my son. I guess it hit me hard because of what I knew it would do to Pio. You can relate to that better than I can, though."

"Yes, I suppose I can," Tess replied, remembering the pain she'd felt when her mother had died. She still didn't like talking about that period in her life.

Zak saw the doleful look on Tess's face and moved close, resting his arm across her shoulders. He watched Pio hurl a dirt clod into the air. "How long does it take to get over it?" he asked.

Tess shrugged and considered her reply. "I don't think you ever really do," she said at last. "You just learn to accept it. But you never stop wondering how it might have been to have a whole family."

Zak closed his hand on her shoulder, squeezing gently. "You said that you and your husband never had time for children. Did you ever want them?"

"Oh, sure," Tess answered. "I wanted them a lot— most of our friends had young families, and I envied them. But David insisted we wait until the time was right. When we had money saved, or when the business was stable, or when we had a house. But for David, the time was never quite right, so eventually I just stopped thinking about it."

Zak enjoyed the warm feel of Tess leaning against him, and he wanted to know more about her life now—her likes and dislikes, her hopes for the future. "So what does a retired construction boss do in her spare time—when she's not off flying airplanes?"

Tess smiled. "Would you believe I like to cook—not everyday ordinary cooking, but gourmet meals?"

Zak laughed. "I have to admit I find that a bit surprising. Seems to me I remember you having a definite aversion to anything domestic."

"I'm still not wild about spending the day cleaning house," she admitted, "but after the wedding David's mother gave me a gourmet cookbook—I guess she didn't want her little boy to starve—and I tried out some of the recipes. Everyone made such a fuss, I kept cooking. I can make a great bouillabaisse, and you should taste my chicken marengo."

Zak tried to visualize Tess standing in the kitchen preparing a fancy meal. It certainly presented a far different picture from what he would have imagined eight years ago. He smiled at the image of her wearing a dainty apron and shuffling through the pages of a cookbook. "I'd like a sample," he said.

"Of which?" Tess asked. "The bouillabaisse or the chicken marengo?"

"Neither," Zak replied. "Of you." He bent over and teased her mouth with the tip of his tongue, then pressed his lips to hers, holding them there—until he felt an impatient tug on his arm. He looked down to see Pio staring up at them, his disapproving eyes traveling from Zak to Tess and back again. "Can we go see the eagles—now?" he asked in Basque.

Zak sighed, hearing the impatience in his son's voice. "Yes," he said.

Pio glared at Tess, turned quickly and headed toward the truck.

Tess watched the boy scamper away. "I assume that had something to do with me," she speculated, "since he said it in Basque."

"No," Zak replied. "He wants to see the eagles." He took Tess's arm and walked with her toward the truck. "We often speak to Pio in Basque at home—we think it's helping make his adjustment easier—and sometimes he forgets when he's away."

Tess considered Zak's words. She'd had Gib to hang on to after her own mother's death. If she'd been forced to give up her home, her country and everything familiar, and learn a new language, as well, she wasn't sure she could have coped. Pio had a right to be angry and confused. His message was very clear, though. He had no intention of sharing his father with anyone.

They climbed into the truck and followed a road through a wide fenced meadow where a flock of emu gazed curiously from their round-bellied long-legged huddle. Zak pulled up in front of the main office and they stepped into the concrete-block building.

Zak released Pio's hand and the boy went scurrying down a hall. "He wants to see if any new birds have arrived," he said. "A lot of injured ones are brought here." He guided Tess toward the hall. "We have two golden eagles, a bald eagle and quite a few owls—including a great gray that just came in," he said, leading her past the row of large cages that housed the injured birds.

After loading the truck with tree-climbing gear, Zak fetched Pio and the three of them left for the nest tree on the high ridge behind Timber West.

Thirty-five minutes later the truck followed the switchbacks of an old logging road winding up the steep slope. Zak stopped where a small stream meandered through a lush mountain meadow. "We can have our picnic now, then hike from here," he said. He hopped out, moving aside to let Pio climb down. "I trimmed back a trail, so it shouldn't take more than fifteen or twenty minutes to get to the tree."

Tess waited with the food as Zak spread a blanket on the ground. A moment later they gathered around the bucket of chicken while Tess scooped potato salad and coleslaw onto paper plates. She and Zak shared the vegetables while Pio sat on one corner of the blanket, his back to Tess, and picked at his food. Zak tried to encourage him to eat, but after twenty minutes he gave up. "I guess we'd better get going," he said, "before I end up climbing the nest tree in the rain."

Tess looked up. Dampness filled the air, and low, thick clouds scudded above the green canopy of trees. "Wouldn't it be better to wait for another day?" she asked anxiously. "It can get pretty windy at the top of a tree when it's raining." She remembered times when she'd climbed trees to limb them before felling them and how the wind whipped around her while she was strapped to the tree a hundred feet above the forest floor.

"I've already waited longer than I want," Zak replied. "If I don't start taking the young now, they'll leave the nest and we'll have to wait for next spring's chicks."

Gathering the gear, they hiked through a glade of huge firs rising from a thick green undergrowth of lush ferns, spongy mosses, low bushes and delicate woodland flowers. Fifteen minutes later, when they approached the nest tree, the parent birds began circling and swooping, their sharp cries echoing through the forest.

Zak removed coils of rope and other gear from his backpack and prepared for the climb. Pulling an arrow from his quiver, he threaded it with fishing line.

"What are you doing?" Tess asked.

"Making a lifeline to attach to myself while I'm climbing," Zak replied. "I'll shoot the line over the limb of that other tree and... Just wait, you'll see in a minute." He leaned back, drew the arrow and shot. It curved over a limb high above and descended on the other side. With careful teasing, the arrow made its way to the ground. Zak tied the fishing line to one of the ropes and pulled the rope up and over the limb, securing it to a tree. Repeating the procedure with his climbing rope, he draped it over a high limb of the nest tree. When he looked around, he saw Pio preparing to climb a nearby tree. "Pio!" he yelled. "No climbing—and no wandering off. Stay near Tess."

Pio jumped down and stood a short distance from Tess.

Zak turned to Tess. "Would you keep an eye on him for me?"

Tess glanced at Pio. "Sure," she said. "Come on, Pio." She smiled and reached for Pio's hand. He backed away, eyes darkening. She didn't insist, but instead, watched him from a distance. "Is there anything else you want me to do?" she asked Zak.

Zak strapped on the backpack that would hold the eaglet. "You can take up the slack in my lifeline as I climb so I won't have so far to drop—if I fall," he said.

With stirrups attached to the climbing rope and spikes fastened to his boots, Zak began his ascent. Partway up he paused. "Go ahead and pull on the lifeline and wrap it around that heavy limb," he called to Tess, pointing to a massive branch.

Tess grabbed the rope and tugged until it was taut, then secured it. She watched as Zak gradually made his way up the tree, aided by the rope and climbing stirrups. She could hear his breathing becoming labored and heavy.

"Keep pulling up the slack," he called down.

Tess tightened the rope again, then glanced around at Pio. He stood staring up, intent on watching his father.

Zak approached the huge limb from which the climbing rope hung, balanced himself on a branch and unhooked his safety line. Tess had never been afraid of heights, but seeing Zak ninety feet above the forest floor with no safety line made her knees feel weak. It wasn't until he had pulled himself onto the limb and rehooked the safety line that she realized she'd been holding her breath.

One hundred and fifty feet above the ground, with one foot resting on the stub of a small broken branch and the other spiked into the dry crumbling bark of the huge dying fir, Zak gazed across the forest of second-growth timber and made a mental note of the location of several old snags.

The parent eagles continued to circle above the nest, their shrieks shattering the solemnity of the forest. Zak knew he'd reached the most critical stage in the climb—when he'd have to lean back, clinging to the nest, and reach up over the rim to capture the chick. He stepped onto a smaller limb, pausing to regain his balance, and peered over the edge of the nest at the twin chicks. They crouched there, looking at him with alarm, their brownish-black plumage rippling from a gust of wind.

The adult birds swooped down to defend their nest, passing close to Zak's head. Pulling himself higher, Zak reached across the tangle of interwoven limbs and gently encircled one of the eaglets with his hand. The young bird gripped the nest tightly with its talons, refusing to relinquish its home. Zak tugged, but the talons held. He tugged again, and at last the young bird slackened its grip.

With the chick tucked under his arm, Zak lowered himself to a limb below the nest and carefully placed the bird in the soft canvas backpack. He climbed down to where he could lower the pack into Tess's waiting hands, then grabbed the climbing rope and rappeled down. When he reached the ground, he glanced around, then looked at Tess in alarm. "Where's Pio?"

Tess looked toward the spot where Pio had been standing. The boy was gone. "He was here just a minute ago," she said.

Zak quickly transferred the eaglet into a nesting crate. "Pio!" he yelled in a worried voice.

"He was just here," Tess said. "He can't be far."

Zak rested his hands on his hips, his eyes scanning the dense forest. "I hope you're right. It would be easy to lose him around here. Pio!" He waited but heard no response. *"Pio!"* he repeated, this time with alarm. He ran a short distance and called again.

Tess skirted the area surrounding the tree. She should never have let him out of her sight, but he'd seemed so intent on watching Zak she assumed he'd stay close. And Zak had distinctly told him not to wander off. She heard Zak calling, his voice farther away—and more urgent.

She hurried back to the nest tree and tried to reconstruct what had happened. They'd been standing together, both looking up while Zak retrieved the eaglet. She contemplated the mound of climbing gear, scanned the area, then looked back at the gear. Something was missing. A rope—a shorter one with a metal safety clip on the end.

Following what looked to be a crude narrow trail, she found a spot where the brush was matted down. She scanned the area and saw something move. Her eyes locked on a dangling rope dancing its way up a tree a short distance away. "Pio!" she yelled through the forest. "Zak, he's here!"

Zak pressed his way through the brush, moving toward the sound of Tess's voice. Seeing Tess looking up a tree, he rushed over and called to his son. "Pio! Come down."

The rope dropped to the ground, and when Pio climbed down, Zak took his arm. "I told you not to climb the tree and I expect you to listen to me when I tell you something, do you understand?" He disliked scolding Pio just when they were beginning to get their lives together.

Pio held his father's gaze and nodded but said nothing.

"Now stay close because we have to get back right away." Zak released Pio's arm and the boy scampered a short distance away to walk along the mossy surface of a downed tree.

When Zak did nothing more, Tess looked at him with apprehension. "Aren't you going to punish him?" she asked.

Zak shrugged. "I just scolded him. That's enough."

Tess had little experience with children, and it wasn't her place to make suggestions to Zak about how he should handle his son. But she knew something about losing a mother at a very young age, and she had the feeling that Pio was testing his father, that he wanted to be given bounds. "A little while ago you told him not to climb, to stay close by," she reminded Zak.

"He's just lost his mother. He's upset."

They started back along the trail, Zak laden with climbing gear and Tess carrying the caged eaglet. Pio was ahead. Tess was still bothered by Zak's permissive handling of Pio.

"When I lost my mother," she said, her eyes on the trail, "I was angry. It seemed like she didn't have the right to just . . . leave like that. Everyone told me how sorry they were, and when I misbehaved they did nothing—yet I wanted to be stopped. I didn't like the way I was behaving, but I thought no one cared enough to do anything about it. So one day I got on my bike and rode it in the street—which I'd been forbidden to do. When Gib saw me, he spanked me and took my bike away for a month. And you know what?" She turned to Zak. "That was the first time I felt that anyone really cared, and I stopped being angry."

"Pio knows I care."

"You didn't care enough to discipline him when he wandered away and climbed the tree. Next time he might wander farther away to prove his point, and you might not find him."

"Most of the time he listens—"

"That's because he wants your approval. But I think he also wants to know that you care enough to put restrictions on him, to keep him from doing things that could harm him."

Zak thought about what Tess said. She knew better than he what Pio was going through right now, and he couldn't argue her point. He sighed. "I suppose you're right. We're still trying to figure each other out."

"Meanwhile," Tess said, "I know he doesn't think much of me. I suspect he's not ready for another mother, so until that time, he'll view anyone you're with as a threat."

"How come you know so much about kids?" Zak asked, smiling, wishing his hands weren't too full to hold hers while they walked.

"I was a half-orphan once, like Pio," Tess replied. "It's not that easy to forget. But eventually you learn to live with it and be open to . . . change."

"How long does it take?" Zak asked.

"That depends. When Aunt Ruth moved in and started telling me what to do, I resented it for a month or so, then I adjusted, and everything was fine."

For a few moments, Zak was quiet. Then he looked at her and ventured, "What if she'd been Gib's new wife?"

Tess held his gaze. "I would have hated her."

"For how long?" Zak asked.

Tess shrugged. "I don't know. I never had the chance to find out."

As they drove back down the ridge, Zak was particularly quiet, and Tess suspected it had something to do with Pio's misbehavior. It wasn't until they reached the bottom of the ridge and started toward her cabin that she learned differently. He looked over the top of Pio's head. "When I was up in the tree, I spotted what looked like one of the abandoned nests I wanted to locate."

Tess smiled. "That's good."

"Maybe, maybe not."

Tess studied the firm lines about his mouth. "Why do you say that?"

"Because it looks like it's pretty close to where you're logging now."

"What difference does that make?"

"If the tree's within three hundred feet of where you're operating, you'll have to stop logging."

Tess looked at him in consternation. "You can't really be serious," she said. "We've logged that area for years and the eagles are still there."

"That doesn't mean they'll stay," Zak replied. "It's their habitat, and nesting time is the most critical."

"But it's an empty nest."

"It's a perch."

Tess glanced in the side mirror at the pole-timber area behind them. "Well, I can't stop logging because of an empty eagle's nest," she said, visualizing Gib's angry face when he learned who ordered the logging stopped. "There are several other old-growth trees in the area that can be used for perches."

Zak sighed. He really didn't want to get into this right now, just as their relationship was beginning to grow. Perhaps the logging wasn't in the primary zone, after all. He noted Tess's anxious frown. "Well, for now let's not worry about it," he said. "I'm sure everything will work out."

He stopped to let Tess off before returning to the wildlife park. When they arrived at her cabin, Pio stayed in the truck while Zak walked Tess to the door. He leaned over to kiss her.

Tess braced her hands against his chest. "No, Zak," she said. "This has gone far enough. Until you give me some kind of explanation about what happened eight years ago—why you simply walked out of my life—you can't expect just to pick up where we left off."

"You're right. I do owe you an explanation, which I intend to give you, but it's not a simple matter." He glanced back at Pio. "And this is not the right time."

"When?" she asked him.

Zak thought a moment. "I'll be kind of tied up for the rest of the weekend getting the chick settled..." He paused, then added, "Will you be here tomorrow afternoon?"

Tess wanted more than anything to spend time alone with Zak, to learn the answer to the one question constantly nagging her—why he went to France and left her without any explanation. At least he seemed open to talking about it. "Yes, I'll be here," she replied.

Tess waited for him to suggest they spend the whole afternoon together, just the two of them, talking; but instead, he said, "My parents are coming to pick up Pio, and my father wants to talk to you about the trees—and the property line. Maybe we can talk afterward."

Tess looked up at him, feeling disappointed, then she grew alarmed. She'd never met Jean-Pierre de Neuville—he rarely visited his property—and she felt uncomfortable with the thought of meeting him now. "Is this some sort of warning?" she asked.

"In a way," Zak replied. "I'm sorry you'll have to deal with him. I convinced him to take it up with you, since I know you're worried about your father."

"I am concerned about Gib," Tess replied. "He may be as stubborn as a Missouri mule, but he's my father and I love him."

"I know," Zak said. "I also know I don't want us to find ourselves in the middle of this feud." He trailed his finger along her arm. "Your father's stubborn as hell, my father's rigid as hell, and who knows how it will turn out. But we don't need to be involved."

"That's easy for you to say. But I'm sitting on a piece of land they both claim, and while they're fighting it out, I'm trying to run a logging camp. I *am* in the middle."

Zak's hands settled on her waist. "Just don't let my father intimidate you," he said, his eyes moving over her face.

Tess blinked several times. "You'll be coming, too, won't you?" she asked in an uncertain voice.

"I'll try," Zak replied. "But I may be late, since I have to meet the vet at the park—he has to examine the chick."

Tess's brow furrowed as she watched the truck pull onto the highway and drive away. Although she wasn't easily intimidated, the thought of facing Zak's father alone made her anxious. From what she'd heard, Jean-Pierre de Neuville was as stubborn and unyielding as Gib. Tomorrow's meeting, she suspected, would confirm that.

Turning into the cabin, she decided to block out thoughts of Jean-Pierre de Neuville and concentrate on her day with Zak. Each time she was with him, she felt they were growing closer, the love of their youth renewed and matured. Although she didn't have the answers she wanted about his disappearance, she let herself believe he had a logical explanation, which he'd soon share with her. But whatever his reason, she couldn't help thinking that even if their lives finally merged, Gib, Pio and Jean-Pierre de Neuville might always stand in the way of any happiness she might regain with Zak.

CHAPTER EIGHT

TESS OPENED THE DOOR of her cabin and looked into eyes that shone like honed steel. "Miss O'Reilly," the man said. "I'm Jean-Pierre de Neuville."

Tess stared unblinking. Zak's father was perhaps the handsomest older man she'd ever seen. His thick white mustache and shock of white hair set off his lean sun-bronzed face, and softened the lines etched about his mouth. "Mr. de Neuville," she said, nodding. "I was expecting you." Her eyes brushed lightly over his suede coat and Western-cut slacks, then shifted to the woman standing beside him.

Jean-Pierre reached out, taking the woman's arm. "This is Mrs. de Neuville," he said in a crisp businesslike voice.

Tess turned to Zak's mother. "Mrs. de Neuville," she acknowledged, peering into clear blue eyes that matched the shirt beneath her gray leather jacket. "Please come in."

Gratianne de Neuville smiled as she stepped inside. Tess took in the handsome high-cheeked face accentuated by gray hair swept back into a knot and held in place with a silver clasp.

Jean-Pierre looked at Tess. "If the cutting of timber on my property isn't stopped immediately," he said, "and compensation made for the trees that are already down, I will take legal action."

Tess swallowed hard. The man certainly got right to the point. "Please . . . won't you both sit down?" She indicated the sofa and the overstuffed chair.

Gratianne seated herself on the sofa. Jean-Pierre remained standing until he caught Gratianne's eye, then he slowly lowered his large frame into the chair. His eyes rested momentarily on the chess set sitting on the coffee table, then he looked questioningly at Tess.

Tess gave him a quick nervous smile. "My father and I play," she explained, as she sat beside Gratianne.

Jean-Pierre's eyes flashed with impatience. "According to my manager," he said, "nine trees have been taken from land your father believes is his. I assure you, Miss O'Reilly, the land in question does not belong to Timber West. The survey I have just had completed shows that the property line runs forty feet east of where your father thinks it is. I want to remind you that the penalty for wrongfully cutting trees on someone else's property is four times their value, and if he doesn't stop cutting immediately—"

"Mr. de Neuville," Tess interjected with an air of courteous attention, "I'm sorry about the trees and I'm trying very hard to clear up the misunderstanding about the property line with my father. I assure you I'll do my best to see that no more trees are cut."

"My son indicates he was given that assurance once before," Jean-Pierre replied, "and yet after that five more trees were cut."

Tess hesitated. "My father did order four trees to be cut before I had a chance to talk to him about it, but there's a question about who cut that last tree," she said. "I believe the man working for you—Jed Swenson—cut the tree and is trying to blame it on one of my men."

Jean-Pierre rose to his feet. "You're accusing my manager of cutting my own trees?" he said incredulously, his voice a blend of irony and challenge. "That's just about what I expected from an O'Reilly—"

"Jean-Pierre!" Gratianne broke in.

Jean-Pierre looked down at his wife. "I'm sorry," he said, looking from Gratianne to Tess. He lowered himself into the chair once again. Gratianne caught Tess's eye and gave her a brief apologetic smile.

Tess looked back at Zak's father. No wonder he and Gib had an ongoing feud. They were each as immovable as a mountain. She shifted uneasily. "I know you're upset about the trees, and I don't blame you," she said. "All I can do is assure you that I'll do everything I can to see that no more trees are cut. If you'll give me an estimate of what you think the trees are worth, I'll see that you're reimbursed—at least for the first eight. The ninth tree is still in question."

"Jed Swenson did not cut the tree," Jean-Pierre insisted.

"Perhaps not, but neither did Curt Broderick," Tess replied with equal certainty. "I guess the question is, then, who did?"

Jean-Pierre stood. "If you don't mind, I'd like to drive up the road and take a look at the trees."

"Please do," Tess said. "I'll go with you."

"That's not necessary," Jean-Pierre told her, his voice firm. "Gratianne?"

Gratianne gave her husband a smile edged with defiance. "If Tess doesn't mind, I'll stay here."

"That would be fine," Tess said.

Jean-Pierre looked from his wife to Tess, then turned and left. Moments later Tess saw his dark blue Suburban move past the window.

Gratianne looked at Tess. "You'll have to forgive Jean-Pierre," she said. "When he feels he's right about something, he'll defend it to the bitter end— much like Zak."

With a nervous hand, Tess smoothed the crocheted doily draped over the wide armrest of the sofa. She had no idea how much Zak's mother knew about her past relationship with Zak, and she felt uneasy discussing him. "I'm afraid my father's the same," she said. "I guess the problem is they both think they're right, and neither will back down."

"That's Jean-Pierre for you," Gratianne replied, smiling with affection as she repeated her husband's name. "I learned long ago to let him spout off when he thinks he's right—even when I know he's wrong— then quietly put him in his place when he really gets out of line. I guess it works, because we've been married for thirty-six years and the sparks are still there."

Tess visualized Jean-Pierre de Neuville's handsome face and forceful bearing, then considered Gratianne's gracious yet spirited demeanor and knew sparks could indeed be there. Would it be the same way with her and Zak thirty years from now? She straightened, surprised by the direction of her thoughts. She moved to somewhat safer ground. "Zak told me Pio lost his mother recently," she said. "I was very sorry to hear about that."

Gratianne's face grew concerned. "It's been quite an adjustment—for all of us," she replied. "We're pleased with Zak, though. He and Pio have become close in a very short time. As soon as school's out for the summer, Pio will be staying with him, and I think they're both looking forward to that."

Tess tucked a restless finger into the lace of the doily. "I'm glad they get along," she said.

"Of course, Zak can't take the place of a mother," Gratianne added, "but we hope he'll find a nice Basque woman in Navarre and settle down soon. That would make his father very happy."

Tess knotted the doily around her finger. She glanced down at her hand and quickly smoothed the lace, then said, "May I offer you some coffee?"

"No, thank you," Gratianne replied. "Zak should be here with Pio soon and we'll be leaving then—at least I hope it will be soon. Sometimes he gets so involved at the park he forgets the time. He takes his work with endangered species very seriously. I'm sure if he could, he'd try to save the whole world from extinction."

Tess laughed lightly. "He does seem quite dedicated," she said.

"At least he feels he's doing his part," said Gratianne, "but he gets very frustrated with the callous and indifferent attitudes of so many people toward wildlife."

Tess looked away, uneasy with Gratianne's last statement, particularly since Zak had expressed such strong feelings about the logging practices of timber companies. She glanced at the window and saw Zak peering through the glass, a grin spreading across his face. She moved quickly to open the door. "Hi," she said, relieved that he had finally arrived.

Zak nudged Pio through the door and stood holding his hand. "I still have to go back," he replied. "The vet called and said he'd be late." He settled into the overstuffed chair. Pio perched on the armrest.

Tess turned her thoughts to the quiet boy. "How about some milk and cookies, Pio—chocolate ones with double icing?"

Pio looked at Tess and shrugged.

But Tess caught the spark in his eyes and knew she'd finally scored a point. She placed several cookies on a dish and poured a glass of milk, then carried them to the coffee table between the chair and sofa. "There you go," she said. "There are lots more if that doesn't fill you." She realized trading cookies for friendship wasn't the best approach, but she could see her gesture had served its purpose. Pio looked happier, his eyes brighter.

Zak glanced beyond Tess to his mother and asked, "Where's Father?"

"He went to check the trees," Gratianne replied.

Zak's face sobered. "How did it go?" he asked, his eyes shifting to Tess.

Before Tess could respond, Gratianne replied, "I think Tess handled him very well. It seems she's had experience along those lines."

Pleased by his mother's apparent approval of Tess, Zak looked at Tess with a provocative smile. "I hope someone will let me know if I ever get to be an obstinate, bullheaded old man."

Tess held his gaze, wondering if Zak was considering a future with her. The thought triggered a dormant longing, and she quickly looked away.

"Son," Gratianne said with an eloquent wave of her hand, "you're already obstinate and bullheaded."

Zak laughed and reached out to pull Pio across his lap, tickling his tummy. Pio curled around Zak's hand and giggled. "They're all against us, Pio. Remember that," he said, tumbling Pio onto the floor. The boy scrambled up, crawling back onto Zak's lap for more.

Tess watched the interplay between father and son, feeling envious of their closeness. She remembered times when she and Gib had scrapped playfully, even after her mother's death. They'd had a unique sort of camaraderie once, and she wondered if it could ever be regained. At least things were moving in the right direction.

As she watched Zak and Pio's antics, she heard Jean-Pierre's Suburban pull up in front. She opened the door and stepped back for him to enter, but he remained outside.

"The trees are larger than I thought—mature second-growth timber," Jean-Pierre stated, his eyes dark. "We're looking at six to eight hundred dollars a tree. I'll have Jed Swenson measure them and come up with an estimate."

"Swenson?" Tess said. "I hardly think we'd get a fair estimate if Jed Swenson measures the trees."

Zak rose from his chair and walked over to stand beside Tess. "I'll measure the trees," he said.

Jean-Pierre's eyes shifted from Tess to Zak. "I'd prefer that you not get involved in this."

"Don't you think I'm capable of measuring trees, Father?" Zak challenged.

Jean-Pierre met his son's intent gaze. "Very well. I'll expect to have the figures right away." He turned to Tess. "I'll also need your father's assurance, in writing, that he acknowledges the property line as shown on the survey. If he doesn't agree to this, and if there's any more cutting, the matter will have to be settled in court. I'm afraid in that case my attorney would insist that we collect the penalty for wrongfully cutting trees—a substantial amount. Now, if that's all, Miss O'Reilly—"

"That's not all, Mr. de Neuville." Tess squared her shoulders. "We need to talk about the royalty. It's very high. We've never paid more than a dollar per thousand board feet."

"That's an unrealistic figure," said Jean-Pierre, "in view of the fact that the road needs to be graded, shaped and rocked. I've already contracted Jed Swenson to do the work, as well as maintain the road for me. The royalty I'm charging will barely meet those expenses."

Tess looked at Jean-Pierre's uncompromising face. "But we've always maintained the road."

"I prefer to have control of the roadwork," Jean-Pierre said bluntly. "That way I'm assured that the road will be properly maintained."

"The road has been adequately maintained for over five years, Mr. de Neuville. Pacific Development had no complaints. I don't see how the roadwork you propose is justified."

"I'm afraid there's quite a bit of erosion at the south end, and it actually washed away in several spots during heavy rains—"

"Yes, but it was always regraded when that happened—"

"It should never have happened," Jean-Pierre stated, "and it won't happen again when the road is properly drained, graded and rocked. I must also insist that all gates be closed when the sheep are turned into the high meadow, and that there be no hauling during extremely wet weather."

"But if the road is rocked—"

"The road is not designed for heavy log trucks when the ground is saturated. I'm not being unreasonable, and I think you know that." He looked beyond Tess to his wife. "Gratianne, we should be getting back."

Gratianne stood and extended her hand to Pio.

Pio turned to Zak. "You'll come next weekend, Papa?"

"You bet I will," Zak replied. He pulled Pio into his arms and gave him a big hug. "Meanwhile, you take good care of Lilly and her kittens, okay?"

Pio smiled. "I will." He took Gratianne's hand.

Zak stood. "Thanks for coming for Pio," he said to his father.

"We're glad to do it," Jean-Pierre replied. "The house seems pretty quiet without him now." He took Gratianne's arm, nodded to Tess and left.

Tess remained in the doorway until Zak's parents had pulled onto the highway, then she turned to Zak. Her lips curved in a smile. "You're right," she said, "He *is* as stubborn as my father."

Zak looked down at her with an amused grin and rested his hands on her waist. "I'm not going to comment on that," he said. He bent over, intending only to brush her lips lightly, but instead he found himself pulling her against him, bringing his mouth down hard on hers. It felt so good to hold her...to move his hands up her back...to curl his fingers in her hair...

Tess allowed herself the luxury of being in Zak's arms—just this once, she told herself. She languidly savored the sweetness of his tongue teasing hers and enjoyed the feel of his hands holding her close, caressing her. In his embrace, she experienced the old familiarity of his body, and she cherished it.

After a long blissful moment, Zak reluctantly pulled away and glanced at his watch. "I've got to get back to the park now," he said, moving toward the door, "but I want to spend some time alone with you— maybe an evening this week?"

"I'd like that," Tess replied, "but it will have to be toward the weekend. I have a pretty busy logging schedule coming up."

"Then let's make it Friday," Zak said. "Dinner at my place. I still owe you a gourmet meal for the plane ride."

Tess smiled. "Friday then..."

TESS SPENT the next four days logging and yarding, and by late Thursday afternoon logs rose high on the dock. She returned to her cabin that evening, took a quick bath and fell into bed, exhausted. The trucks were expected to arrive early the next morning, and she was thankful she wasn't needed on the ridge for loading. She slept soundly until a vigorous knocking on her front door interrupted her dreams. "TJ! Open up. It's Herring."

Tess groaned and glanced at the bedside clock. Six a.m. Pulling a robe around her, she shuffled to the door and swung it open. She squinted up at Herring. "What's wrong?"

"Big problems!" he replied. "There was a rock slide on the ridge road last night and the Cat's out of commission. The log trucks are boxed in on de Neuville's land and Swenson's charging a parking fee."

Tess blinked. "Wait a minute," she said. "I'll be right out." She threw on some clothes and rushed out of the cabin. "How bad's the slide?" she asked, binding her thick tresses with a leather thong.

"Pretty bad," Herring replied. "The road's buried."

"What's the problem with the Cat?"

"Broken steering hose—lost all the hydraulic fluid."

"Well, that won't take long to fix," Tess said, "but we'll need a new hose. Follow me to camp."

In the machine shed, she searched through boxes, certain she'd seen a hose earlier in the week, but she couldn't find it. "I've got to get to the ridge," she said. "You go to Bakers Creek and get a new hose and put it on our account, then get back as quick as you can."

Ten minutes later Tess crossed the de Neuville land and pulled up behind a line of log trucks parked in the road. She edged the Jeep along the steep embankment to get around the trucks and continued up the road through the Timber West gate. When she arrived at the slide, she was baffled. The heavy night rains they'd been having could have caused rocks to slide, but not in this area where the hills were stable.

Hearing the whine of a motor, she glanced up and saw Zak's truck approaching. He pulled up beside her Jeep and jumped out. "I just heard about the rock slide," he said. "For whatever it's worth, there'll be no parking fee. I talked to Swenson. That was his own idea."

"Thanks," Tess said. "I'll still have to settle up with the drivers for their lost time, though." She stared at the rocks. "It just doesn't make sense. There's plenty of vegetation to hold the rocks in place along the hill here."

Zak scanned the pile of rocks blocking the road, his eyes following the path of the slide up the steep hillside. "I'll hike up there and look around," he said. "See if I can find out what caused it."

"Okay," Tess said with a sigh. "I'll see if I can get things moving down here."

Forty minutes later, Herring arrived with the hose and they started work on the Cat. Before long the bulldozer began moving rock, and Tess joined Zak on the slope. They fanned out, walking among the loose rocks, kicking some over and tossing others aside. When the road was almost cleared, Zak spied something caught in some rocks. He reached down and retrieved a six-inch length of orange cord. "Dynamite!" he yelled to Tess over the rumble of the Cat. "This is a piece of fuse!"

Tess climbed over the rubble to where he stood. "So that's what helped the pile of rocks along." She lifted the cord from his palm and held it to her nostrils. "It's freshly burned." For a moment she stared at the fuse, then she said, "It seems a bit coincidental that the steering hose on the Cat broke just before the land-slide—and it all happened right about the time the trucks were due to haul."

Zak looked down to where the men were working. "Has anything else out of the ordinary happened?" he asked.

"Well, maybe," Tess replied. "Bull lines have been breaking right and left—even when we're skidding logs on flat grade. We're lucky no one's been hurt."

Before Zak could respond, Curt yelled to Tess from the Cat, "About ten more minutes, then send the trucks through!"

Tess waved her okay and turned to Zak. "I've got to go."

"I hope tonight's still on," Zak said. "By then you'll be glad to come home to a nice hot meal."

"Home?" Tess blinked. The word sounded so...permanent.

"My place. Okay?"

She looked at the line of trucks and the big Cat scraping the road. "I suppose you're right. I won't feel much like fixing my own dinner tonight."

By late afternoon the landing was cleared of logs, and Tess was exhausted. The day had been long and tiring, both physically and emotionally. Soon she'd have to alert Gib to some tough issues that could no longer be ignored. Timber West's recent quarterly tax payment had drained their reserves, and now with the expenses of clearing the landslide, the increased royalty and the extra pay to the truck drivers, the logging company's operating capital would be almost depleted—and they still had a large loan payment to meet.

When she arrived at her cabin that evening, she headed for the bathroom to soak away her worries in a tub of warm fragrant water. Forty-five minutes later, dressed in tan slacks and a lightweight rust-colored sweater with a scooped neck, she headed down the trail toward Zak's cabin. Stepping to the door, she rapped lightly.

Zak greeted her with a smile, his eyes scanning her trim figure and moving over the ebony hair that fell gently to her shoulders. "You look like you survived the day rather well," he said.

"Just barely," she replied, her gaze shifting to the navy wool shirt hugging his muscular chest, then drifting down to his faded jeans.

Zak reached for her hand and curled his fingers around hers. "Are you hungry?"

"Starved." Tess continued to hold Zak's hand as he led her toward the dining area. She looked at a table graced with place mats and china, silverware and wine goblets. A bouquet of aster, marsh marigold and mountain sorrel added a touch of color and the fragrance of spring. "You've gone to a lot of trouble," she said, surprised and pleased.

"I promised you a gourmet meal," Zak replied, filling the goblets with wine from a decanter.

Tess watched the clear glass turn to a rich crimson. "Is this from your winery?" she asked.

Zak gave her a wry grin. "No, it's a California burgundy. But don't tell my father." He handed her a glass. "Rare, medium or well done?"

Tess stared at him.

"Your steak?"

"Oh, medium," she replied.

"Just relax and dinner will be ready shortly."

Tess settled into the comfortable sofa. "I'm not used to being waited on," she said, sipping the wine.

"Good, then I'll spoil you."

Zak rattled around in the kitchen and ten minutes later the aroma of steaks browning on a griddle teased Tess's appetite. Sitting quietly in the cabin brought back so many fond memories—clandestine meals...lovemaking in front of the fireplace...their first meeting at the Timber Carnival...

Zak looked over at her, catching her faraway look. "What are you thinking?"

Tess raised her eyes to meet his. "About the Timber Carnival," she replied.

Balancing a platter of steaks, Zak stepped over to the table. "What about the carnival?"

Tess moved to the table and sat, draping her napkin over her lap. "Do you remember the first time we met?"

Zak speared a bacon-wrapped fillet and placed it on her plate beside a foil-wrapped baked potato. "Mmm-hmm," he said, smiling at the image of Tess as a scrawny fourteen-year-old. He was still smiling as he lifted the second fillet to his own plate.

Tess took a slow sip of her wine. "I was just wondering what you thought of me then."

Zak sat at the table and cut a wedge of steak. "Well, I was impressed by your agility—the way you scampered up that pole," he said, his eyes holding hers as he brought the meat to his lips.

Tess dabbed her mouth with her napkin. "I meant the very first time we met, before the pole climb."

Zak cocked a brow. "You mean when you grabbed my arm while I was practicing for the wood-chopping contest?"

"I didn't grab your arm. I only suggested you hold your ax differently," she said, sticking her fork into the baked potato to allow the melting butter to ooze down inside. "But besides that, what did you think?"

"Well, let me see," Zak teased, toying with her question. The corners of his mouth flicked in a quick smile. "You looked up at me and I thought you had the biggest most beautiful eyes I'd ever seen—on a boy."

Tess stared at him. "You thought I was a boy?"

"You disguised your femininity very well then," he said. "I was never so surprised as when you swooped off your hat after the pole climb and all that lovely hair dropped to your shoulders." His eyes moved lightly over the dark hair framing her face, his fingers restless to twine through the silky tresses.

Tess looked at Zak and smiled. "What did you think when we met the next year?"

Zak rested his knife and fork across his plate and leaned forward, a provocative gleam in his eyes. "I was very surprised, to say the least. Only a year later you were a beautiful desirable woman." He smiled. "And when I caught sight of you in that snug blouse and tight jeans, I almost missed the chopping block completely."

Tess laughed. "You still won by a wide margin. I was really impressed."

"I had lots of adrenaline flowing that day, just wondering if you were going to pop a button on your blouse."

Tess's lips curved into a smile. "Nothing fit right that year."

"That's a matter of opinion. I thought everything fit just perfectly. You did strange things to me then," he said, his voice lower, huskier. He looked across at her, catching the flare in her dark eyes, the rich flush in her cheeks. "Just like you're doing right now."

For the next few minutes they ate quietly. When they'd finished their dinner Tess touched her lips with her napkin and rested it on her plate. Zak pushed his chair back and moved around behind her. She stood slowly, took his hand and followed him over to the fireplace. He pulled her down to sit beside him on the rug and she curled into the curve of his arm. "You feel good against me," he said.

Tess stared at the low flames dancing on the hearth, determined that things would go no further until Zak offered an explanation about his disappearance. When he put his finger under her chin to turn her lips to his, she resisted.

"What's the matter?" he asked.

"I told you. There are too many unanswered questions," she replied. "I realize Gib didn't exactly escort you graciously from the cabin, but why did you go to France? You could have stayed nearby, given Gib time to get used to the idea of us together. In spite of what you think, my father is a reasonable man."

Zak raised a skeptical brow. "Is he?" The picture of a wrathful Gib O'Reilly on the night he'd found them together, and later, when he'd confronted Zak's own father, flashed across his mind.

Tess heard the cynical tone of Zak's words and felt the hard pounding in her chest. She looked into his eyes, and in their steel-gray depths she saw undisguised anger that she knew was focused on her father. "Why are you still so angry with Gib? Is it male pride?"

Zak's eyes darkened. "Male pride had nothing to do with my leaving."

She heard resentment in his words. "It didn't? Then what did?" she asked, her voice wavering.

The muscles in Zak's jaws flexed. The only way he and Tess could get their lives together again would be if she got her answers—and he owed her an explanation. But he knew she wouldn't like what she heard. He took a long slow breath and sighed. "The day after your father found us, he came to Navarre and told me to have no further contact with you. He reminded me, and my father, of the implications of our age difference—and the penalties."

Tess looked at him incredulously. "You don't really think Gib would have done anything—prosecuted—do you?"

Zak looked into her dubious eyes. "You were only sixteen. I was twenty-four. I'm absolutely certain he would have."

"Then why didn't you at least get word to me? You know I would have waited, that I would have found some way to come to you."

"I tried, but I learned pretty quick that your father had packed you up and sent you back to Bakers Creek," Zak said, his eyes darkening with the memory. "So I went there, but you were nowhere around. And when I started asking questions about where you were, the police picked me up and slapped me with a restraining order."

Tess noted the hardness about Zak's mouth. "Gib sent me to my grandfather's farm," she said. "I left and took a bus to your cabin, but you were gone. The cabin was boarded up." Swept by sudden anxiety, she felt her throat constrict, remembering her helplessness at finding Zak gone.

Zak held her, pressing her body to his and resting his cheek against the top of her head. "Your father made it clear that I was to go away without your knowing where I'd gone, or why. He wanted me out of your life permanently." He trailed a finger along her chin and raised her face until their eyes met. "So my father sent me to France to learn about Basque wines. He also wanted you out of my life because you weren't Basque."

"Damn them both," Tess said, feeling her old anger resurface. "All that time I waited—and Gib knew you weren't coming back." Her eyes burned and she blinked back tears of frustration and anger. After a long moment of silence, she ventured, "Why did you marry so soon after? I thought we had something special."

"We did," Zak replied, "but with your father's threat and my father's resolve to keep us apart, I saw no future for us. Several months after I arrived in France I met Mirande. Her fiancé had just left her for another woman and she was upset, and I guess we just sort of gravitated to each other—you know, misery loves company."

"Did you love her?"

Zak shrugged. "I suppose so, in a way. We had a lot in common and enjoyed each other's company. Once we'd married, I never really gave it much thought." He gave Tess a little squeeze. "What about you?" he said. "When did you get married—and why did you get divorced?"

Tess snuggled closer. "After you left, I wanted to get away—from Gib, from Bakers Creek, from the past. I waited for two years, then I met David at the airpark. He was a very ambitious man and took lots of chances in business, always trying to push the company beyond its capabilities. Eventually he lost it all. We had a lot of heated arguments about it, but I guess the real reason was that I never found what I wanted...."

Zak looked down. "Nor did I—because I never stopped loving you." He leaned over and kissed her long and hard, tasting the fragrant aroma of wine on her breath, the hint of steak on her tongue. Nibbling his way to her ear, he flicked the tip of his tongue inside and whispered, "You fit so perfectly in my arms."

"You fit nicely, too," Tess replied, sliding her hands around his neck. Zak stroked her back, then moved one hand beneath her sweater and up to cup her breast. She gasped as his thumb began to circle one tight nipple through the lacy fabric of her bra. She tipped her face up, blending her lips with his once again as Zak cradled her head in one hand and lowered her down onto the rug.

Zak nudged the sweater upward and Tess lifted her arms, allowing him to slip it over her head. His finger traced a meandering path across her breast, then circled gently. He unclasped her bra and slipped the straps from her shoulders. The scant garment fell to the floor. As his warm hands fondled her breasts, short breaths caught in her throat. "Zak—" Her words were stifled as Zak's mouth came down hungrily on hers.

After some moments, Zak pulled away and began to unfasten her slacks. He tugged them from her hips, then slipped her panties off, trailing burning lips along her breasts and across her firm tummy. The glow from the flames danced over her body; ocher tongues frolicked along her slender legs and caressed the fullness of her breasts as tiny sparks of light flickered in her eyes.

Tess watched the play of muscles rippling across Zak's sinewy body as he stood, tossed his shirt aside and slipped off his jeans and shorts. Then she lowered her gaze. He looked much as he had years before in the Grotto, only now a thicker mat of dark hair curled on his chest and trailed down his taut stomach. But below that trail of dark hair, he was as she'd remembered—large and hard and ready for her. He lowered himself to the rug once more, and she moved into his outstretched arms, his musky male scent filling her nostrils.

Zak looked deeply into her eyes, one finger moving slowly along her cheek and down her chin, his thumb tracing the outline of her lips, as if memorizing every intimate detail of her features. He thrust his fingers into her hair, pulling her head back, and crushed her mouth with his.

Tess felt the heat of Zak's arousal press against her as they lay together, his body probing, seeking hers. When her breath grew shallow, she pulled her lips from his. "It's been so long," she whispered, savoring the feel of his hands as they moved in languid circles along her thighs.

"Too long." Zak bent over and encircled her breast with his hand, touching her nipple with his tongue and teasing it to a ripe peak. Gentle gasps escaped her lips, and she felt an ache deep and low inside. She molded her body to his, her palms gliding over his firm buttocks and pulling him against her. Only with Zak had she felt this aching desire, a longing so deep she'd never stopped wanting to become one with him, body and soul. She reached down and took him in her hand. As she began to caress him, Zak drew a sharp breath. "God, you've got a velvet touch," he said.

"And you've got a velvet... Ahhh," she sighed, closing her eyes as his fingers began to explore her most intimate realms. At the same time he began to kiss her mouth gently again, then harder, deeper, until her mouth seemed to throb and her body demanded fulfillment.

Tess's faint moans excited Zak in a way he'd almost forgotten. He sat up slowly, then lifted her in his arms and carried her to the bedroom. Gently he lowered her to the bed. Her muscles tensed and low hums droned in her throat as his tongue tantalized her, flicking over the tip of one swollen breast, then the other. He was vividly aware of the pleasure he was giving her, and it aroused him to even greater heights.

"That feels so good," she whispered, tangling her fingers in his hair. She could feel heat radiating from each spot Zak caressed with the moist warmth of his mouth and wherever his hands stroked the long smooth length of her body. Suddenly, fiery waves pulsated in her loins.

Zak felt Tess shiver. He opened his eyes and saw her chest heaving in short quick motions and heard her rapid intakes of breath. When she lowered her gaze to meet his, he saw the smoldering intensity of her eyes, the impassioned desire—and he felt his own aching need. Tears of passion moistened his eyes. He kissed the corners of her mouth, the curve of her chin, the hollow of her throat, hearing her involuntary gasps of pleasure.

He hovered over her, the fiery hardness of his body seeking hers, their lips meeting. Then he lowered his body and felt the urgency in her arms, the slow undulations of her hips. She raised her body to meet his, and in one slow fluid movement, they were joined.

Tess sighed with pure pleasure as she felt Zak's weight on her and his hard fullness inside her. She moved with him, matching his rhythmic thrusts, her palms pressing his firm buttocks. Zak's motions quickened, building in intensity, the darting thrust of his loins meeting the sharp snap of her hips, rising to a crescendo, until sounds burst from their lips and their bodies jerked in uncontrollable spasms.

Glorying in the last ripples of her waning desire, Tess clung to Zak, and they lay entwined in each other's arms. It had never been this intense, this over-powering, with anyone but Zak. She felt spent, but also elated. During her marriage she'd wondered if her passion had died. She'd never had this hunger for David. She smiled with contentment and snuggled deeper into Zak's arms.

As they lay curled together, listening to the rustle of leaves against the window, and the sighing of the wind in the trees, Tess whispered, "Was it this good before?"

Zak kissed her forehead. "It will always be this good," he said. "We belong together. Our bodies belong together."

Tess lay beside him without speaking, enjoying the feel of his hands moving up and down her body. After a while he looked down at her and said, "Do you remember the first time we made love? In the Grotto?"

Tess smiled. "Of course. I was still starry-eyed about the song you wrote and sang to me—and about our wedding. I thought it was the most beautiful wedding any girl could ever wish for. It may have been make-believe, but when you slipped the ring on my finger, I felt very married. It was like a dream, and after we'd said our vows I imagined that this was what heaven was like. I remember the night mist settling around us, the bouquet you made from columbine and wild iris, the little gold ring . . ."

Zak reached for her hand and looked at her bare finger. "Do you remember what was inscribed inside the ring?"

Tess paused for a moment, then slowly enunciated the words. "*Eskualdun fededun*—the Basque is faithful."

Zak stroked her naked finger. "What happened to it?"

Tess looked down at her hand. "I buried it."

"Where?"

"In a bottle inside the hollow of our Adam-and-Eve tree. It seemed appropriate to lay it to rest there."

Zak's brows drew together over questioning eyes. "When did you do that?"

"When I finally decided you weren't coming back— the day before I ran off with David. I went to the Grotto, buried my ring and cried so hard I had trouble convincing myself I was really happy about marrying David."

"How did you feel when you got married?"

"Betrayed. I loved you and hated you. I resented having to repeat the same vows to David, and then was angry for resenting it. I hated Gib for putting me in that position and loved him because I couldn't *not* love him. And I felt like a traitor to Aunt Ruth. She'd always talked about seeing me married in a fancy wedding dress. I think it was the worst day of my life. All I could think of was how could you do this to me? How could Gib do this to me? How could I ever be happy with David?''

She looked up at Zak and kissed his chin. "Even when I was married, you were always somewhere in the back of my mind and soul,'' she said, snuggling in his arms.

"And I thought about you, too, so very much, over the years,'' Zak admitted. "But I never dreamed we'd be together again.''

Tess rested her head against Zak's chest and closed her eyes. Tomorrow she'd worry about who was behind the landslide...Jean-Pierre de Neuville and his trees...and confronting Gib about Zak. But tonight, at last, Zak was hers.

CHAPTER NINE

TESS CLIMBED into her Jeep and headed toward the ridge, her thoughts on Zak. She hadn't seen him since she'd stayed overnight at his place two days before, but she knew he'd spent the weekend in Navarre. Now she was anxious to get the workday behind her, as they'd tentatively planned for him to stay at her place tonight. Their passionate lovemaking had been a fantasy that became reality. Away from him, she felt lonely and realized how empty her life had become. But she also felt anxious and uncertain about what the future held for them.

Zak had a son now—by a Basque woman—and the boy clearly resented her, which, she had to admit, was understandable. Pio obviously wasn't ready to share his father with anyone, but in time perhaps she could help him get over the loss of his mother.

When she was sixteen, all she'd dreamed of was marriage and raising a family with Zak. But after the divorce she had begun to feel a need for something more, and she thought studying business in college was a step in the right direction—she still did. But at least she and Zak were together again. She felt a resurgence of the old anger when she thought of the years

Gib had stolen from them. She'd confront him about that—there were things she had to say.

She crossed the de Neuville land and continued to the pole timber area, where she found Curt on the bulldozer dragging a log to the landing and Sean Herring and Harv Dempsey limbing trees. The skidder sat idle. When Curt saw her he cut the throttle, jumped down and marched toward her. "One of the tires on the skidder's blown," he said.

Tess's stomach lurched. "From what?" she asked as she considered the cost of another new skidder tire. It seemed Timber West was operating in a vicious circle. They needed to keep the equipment running in order to get the pole timber out, and they needed to sell pole timber in order to keep the equipment running.

"It looks like it ran over a spike," Curt said.

Tess examined the skidder tire and found a hole in it the size of a half-dollar. "It looks more like someone put a bullet through it," she replied. "Where's the spike?"

"We couldn't find it," Curt said. "We're just assuming that's what did it."

"Well, I'm not assuming anything," Tess stated. "Meanwhile, we'll have to use the Cat." Her eyes rested on the idle machine. "Where's the new skidder driver?"

"I sent him back to camp."

"Well, with the skidder out, we may have to let him go," Tess said, "at least until we get the thing running again. I can't afford to pay someone just to sit around the cookshack. Meanwhile, I'd better go to

Northwest Tire and see about getting someone out here."

She got back in the Jeep and headed for Bakers Creek. After arranging for someone to look at the skidder tire, she drove to Gib's house. Now that he and Aunt Ruth had returned from Portland, it was time for the confrontation she knew was inevitable. Spotting Aunt Ruth talking to a neighbor a short distance from the house, she tooted the horn and pulled over. Aunt Ruth stepped to the curb and peered through the passenger-side window. "Hi, sweetie."

Tess moved to the passenger seat and kissed her aunt on the cheek. "Hi," she said. "Welcome home. How was Dad's checkup?"

Aunt Ruth smiled. "Fine," she replied. "Now he thinks he can take on the world."

Tess looked up the street at the house and asked, "Did the doctor put any restrictions on him?"

"Only that he isn't to start working yet," Aunt Ruth replied. "His blood pressure's still higher than Dr. Evans would like, but he also said not to mollycoddle him. We should let him spout off a bit."

"Well, he'll get his chance in a few minutes," Tess said. "I have a bone to pick with him."

Aunt Ruth looked at her with apprehension. "Just go easy," she cautioned. "Don't get him too upset."

"What's he doing right now?"

"Working on his truck."

Tess slid back behind the wheel. "Well, I guess I'd better get this over with," she said. "Are you coming home soon?"

Aunt Ruth shook her head. "Not for a few minutes."

Tess drove up the block, parked in front of the house and found her father in the driveway, his head under the hood of his truck. "Gib, I want to talk to you."

"Hand me that five-sixteenths open end," he replied.

Tess looked down, her eyes darting about the array of tools spread out in front of Gib's scuffed black toolbox. She picked up the wrench and placed it in Gib's outstretched hand. Without looking up, he curled his fingers around the wrench and retracted his arm.

"How could you do what you did to Zak and me eight years ago?" Tess demanded, annoyed that Gib wouldn't acknowledge her.

"Here, hold this." He reached out, extending a hand with the wrench. "Now I need the gauge."

Tess lifted the gauge from the pile. "Gib, I asked you a question," she said, handing him the tool. "You sent Zak away. How could you do that to me?"

"You were just a child."

"I was a woman."

Gib handed the gauge back to her. "Now I need the wrench again."

Tess grabbed the wrench and shoved it into his hand. This was typical, what she should have expected, in fact. Gib's method of dealing with an unpleasant confrontation was to ignore it and hope it would go away. Well, this time it wouldn't go away.

She moved opposite Gib and ducked her head under the hood. "Well?"

Her father remained quiet for a few moments, then said, "Hand me the stubby screwdriver."

Tess drew in a frustrated breath, pulled herself out from under the hood and fetched the screwdriver. "Here," she said, slapping it against his palm. "Gib, I'm not going to let this rest. You sent Zak away. You led me to believe he left on his own. How could you?"

Gib's hand closed around the clear amber handle. He turned the screwdriver, then replied, "I did what I thought was right."

Tess looked at her father's lean figure bent over the fender of the truck. Her eyes darkened. "Would you really have prosecuted Zak if he hadn't gone away?"

Gib slowly rose to meet Tess's smoldering eyes. "Yes," he said. "I would have, and he knew it." He frowned and stood quietly, as if considering what to say next. "If you choose a life with him now," he said finally, "it's your choice, but eight years ago you were little more than a child."

"But Zak loved me and I loved him. We planned to be married, but you just wouldn't listen. Why couldn't we talk then? I wanted to tell you about Zak before you found us, but I knew I couldn't talk about him. It was as if he was something dirty."

"In my eyes he was—a grown man taking advantage of a child."

"I was sixteen."

"At sixteen no one's old enough to make a lifetime decision," Gib stated flatly.

"Would I have been any more ready at eighteen—or twenty?" Tess asked. "I knew I loved Zak, that he was everything I wanted. What more did I need to know?"

Gib's eyes met hers. "I'm sorry, Teslyn, believe me I am," he replied. "But I told you before, if I had it all to do over again, I'd do the same thing. Can you possibly understand that and forgive me?"

Tess looked into Gib's eyes while considering what he was saying. Zak mentioned how difficult it was to be a single parent, to make all the decisions alone while trying to do what was right. And right or wrong, Gib had done what he thought was best. She shrugged. "I suppose I'll have to forgive you," she said. "I'd probably have done the same if I'd had a wild thing like me for a daughter."

Gib smiled. "You weren't a wild thing, honey. Headstrong, determined, maybe. But not a wild thing."

Tess smiled back. "Pretty bad, though, huh?"

"Yup." Gib wrapped an arm around her shoulder. "Now, can we bury the hatchet and get on with our lives?"

Tess blinked. "I'd like that."

Gib grabbed a handful of curls and gave her head a jiggle. Tess caught the old glint in his eyes and smiled at her father. For the moment she wanted to turn her back on the logging operation, skidder tires and land feuds, and just be Gib's little girl again.

Gib ducked his head under the hood. "Now, will you give me the gauge again?"

Tess handed it to him. "What's wrong with the truck?"

"Nothing," Gib said, his muffled voice rising over the sound of the idling engine. "I'm adjusting the valves."

"Do you need any help?"

"No, just what you're doing—keeping me company." He handed her the gauge. "Now I need the wrench again."

Tess handed him the tool and smiled, reflecting on the times she'd stood just where she was now, passing tools to Gib while he worked on his truck. She had loved being with him as a child. None of her friends knew how to change an air filter or set the gap on spark plugs, and she'd always felt special because of it. "Do you remember when we flew up to McMinnville for the plowhorse pulling contest?" she asked, recalling how Gib had rewarded her for helping him tune up the truck.

"Uh-huh," Gib replied. "What made you think of that?"

"Well, it should be coming up soon and I thought we could fly up there again—maybe even get some more strawberries." She remembered how after the contest they'd picked a flat of berries from a nearby farm and brought them home to Aunt Ruth. And that evening they'd had strawberry shortcake with fresh whipped cream.

"Sounds pretty good. In fact, I think Ruth's got some berries and fresh cream in the icebox now," he said. Gib stood, wiped his hands again, then shut the hood. "It's done. Let's go get some berries and cream. We'll pick up some more for Ruth when we go to McMinnville."

"Then you want to go?"

"Yes, honey. I'd like that."

When Tess saw Gib's smile, she had second thoughts about bringing up the matter of the increased royalty or Jean-Pierre de Neuville's threat about the trees, but she decided the problems had to be addressed. They didn't need a lawsuit on their hands right now. She took the survey map from the Jeep and followed Gib into the house.

"Why don't you go clean up," she said, "while I whip the cream for the berries?"

Gib squeezed her arm. "Fine by me."

From the refrigerator, Tess retrieved a bowl of large crimson berries and a carton of heavy cream. As she attached the beaters to the electric hand mixer, Gib returned and sat at the table. "Now, fill me in on what's happening at Timber West," he said.

Tess glanced over at Gib, realizing he wasn't aware of the survey map rolled near his hand. While soft creamy peaks of whipped cream were forming, she told him about the rockslide, the skidder tire, and finally about the feud between Curt Broderick and Jed Swenson—mentioning that Swenson was now working for Jean-Pierre de Neuville but omitting the cause of the feud.

She placed a clear glass bowl of berries in front of Gib. He spooned whipped cream on the top while asking, "What are Swenson and Broderick feuding about?"

"It has to do with that strip of property between Timber West and Jean-Pierre de Neuville's place," she replied, sitting across from him.

"What about that strip?"

"Swenson cut a tree there."

"What's Swenson doing cutting a tree on our land?"

"That's my whole point, Dad," Tess said. "Jean-Pierre de Neuville insists that's his land."

"De Neuville doesn't know what the hell he's talking about," Gib said, heaping another mound of cream on top of his berries.

"Go easy on the cream," Tess reminded him. "Cholesterol, remember?" She watched as Gib defiantly spooned out another dollop of cream. "I brought the survey map so you could see what he's talking about. It really does look like that strip of land is his."

"I don't care what de Neuville says, or what's on the map. I know where the line runs—the same place the fence ran for seventy-five years—and I don't much give a damn what some nincompoop from the county office says."

"Regardless of what you believe, if the county office and the judge disagree with you, you'll be paying the penalty for cutting nine trees—which could be more than twenty thousand dollars—and Timber West can't afford it. Now, I want you to please promise me you won't tell Herring or Dempsey or Broderick to cut any more trees."

Gib looked up, his eyes darkening. "No one, not even a judge, is going to tell me I can't cut trees on my own land."

Tess popped another spoonful of berries into her mouth. "Then you'd better be prepared to pay out a lot of money, because Jean-Pierre de Neuville's about to haul you into court."

"Fine. He can just do that. Any other problems?"

Tess sighed. "All kinds of other problems—a broken hydraulic line on the Cat right after the landslide, trucks having to wait for the Cat, deadhead fees to the truckers." She looked across at Gib. "And that's only the beginning. It looks like the rock slide was intentional—caused by dynamite. We found a piece of fuse in the rocks."

"Now wait a minute," Gib said, his eyes fixed on Tess. "You're making it sound like someone's trying to shut us down."

"That's exactly what it looks like," Tess replied. "These 'accidents' have been happening ever since I let Swenson go. I think he's trying to make it impossible for me so I'll quit and you'll hire him back."

"I'd never hire him back," Gib said.

"He probably thinks you would, and making it look like Curt cut the tree might get Curt fired, and him rehired." Tess shrugged. "Who knows what Swenson has on his mind? He might just be getting revenge."

Gib finished the last of his berries. "Don't be too quick to accuse Swenson before you have some facts," he said.

Tess placed the bowls in the sink, then wiped the table. "I should have some facts pretty soon, at least on the skidder tire—whether it was shot or not. Meanwhile, we also have another expense...." She turned and walked to the sink, spraying a rush of water over the cloth.

Gib eyed her suspiciously. "What other expense?"

Tess swallowed hard, keeping her back to him, then turned on both faucets, blasting warm water into the sink. "The log royalty. It's gone up," she said, her eyes fixed on the soap bubbles rising around the dishes.

"Yaeger raised the royalty on us?" Gib replied angrily. "I didn't think he'd do that. But then again, he's kind of riled because I won't sell to him."

Tess plunged her hands into the warm, soapy water. "Not Carl Yaeger," she said, reaching for one of the bowls in the sink. "Jean-Pierre de Neuville. He bought the land between us and the ridge."

"I'd heard something like that," Gib said slowly, "but I figured it was just a rumor. Well, at least he's letting us go through. How much is the royalty?"

Tess's fingers curled tightly around the bowl. "Fifteen dollars per thousand—"

"What!"

The sound of a fist slamming on the table brought Tess whipping around. "Take it easy, Gib," she said, her heart rapping in staccato beats as she held the bowl, soap bubbles dripping to the floor. "He's using the money to fix the road."

"He's spending my money for nothing. That road's only an access road for hauling, not a freeway!"

"It's his land. He can do what he wants."

"He can go to hell!" Gib stood. "And if I want to cut trees on *my* land, I'll cut the damn trees. You can tell that to Jean-Pierre de Neuville the next time you see him." Gib stomped out of the room, leaving Tess staring blankly after him, a puddle of soap bubbles gathering at her feet.

ZAK THREW OFF his clothes and slipped under the covers, then rolled onto his side and kissed Tess lightly on the cheek. "There's a man in your bed," he whispered, sliding his arm around her naked body.

Tess batted her eyelids, then gazed into darkness. When her mind cleared from sleep, she said, "Zak, you're so late. I expected you for dinner."

"I'm sorry," he apologized. "I had no way of letting you know I couldn't make it. Am I forgiven?"

Tess turned into his arms and snuggled against him. "Of course. What happened?"

He wrapped his arms around her and held her close. "We had a lot to do getting ready for the next climb."

Tess peered into the darkness. She'd almost forgotten about Zak's Grizzly Mountain trip. "That's tomorrow, isn't it? What time are you leaving?" she asked.

"As soon as my parents drop Pio off," he replied. "That's another minor problem—I forgot this is the week they fly to Santa Rosa for the vintners' conference."

"Then Pio's going with you on the climb?"

"No. He'll be staying with the woman in Bakers Creek who usually watches him for me."

Tess tipped up her face and their lips met. The slow unhurried kiss left her mouth tingling and her heart pounding. Zak's hands moved up and down her back, his fingers trailing along her sides, following the curve of her breasts as he nibbled on her lips.

Tess nipped at the end of his finger. "I missed you," she whispered.

Zak nuzzled between her breasts and spun a web of kisses from one taut nipple to the other, and as he held her, she smoothed her hand along his back and down to knead his taut buttocks, then trailed her palm along his thigh and up the sensitive skin of his loins. Her fingers began doing tempting little things, and Zak's body hardened to her touch.

He cradled her breast in his hand and his lips encircled her nipple, his warm tongue exploring the puckered tip. She felt her heart thudding against his palm, its rhythm matching the throbbing rhythm in her loins. Her urgency mounted as his fingers followed the curve of her waist and traced her smooth flat tummy, coming to rest on the soft mound of hair. Gently he teased, and when she thought she could bear it no longer, he moved between her parted thighs and she twined her legs around him, raising her hips to allow their bodies to join in the slow familiar union.

Their unhurried movements soon gave way to eager thrusts as their passion rose to a crescendo, at last bursting into a frenzy and carrying them to the pinnacle of oneness. Their hearts pounded in unison as they clung together, the last spasms subsiding. Tess lay her tousled head against Zak's shoulder and he pressed his cheek to the silken tresses. Cradled in his arms, she gave a contented sigh, closed her eyes and drifted into a quiet restful slumber unmarred by thoughts of Timber West.

The next morning, when the sun peeked through puffs of rose-colored clouds, Zak had already gone. Shortly afterward, Tess stepped from her cabin, breathed in the fragrant scent of morning and walked in brisk strides toward the Jeep. When she arrived at the cookshack, her bright mood was broken. There was no aroma of coffee, biscuits or bacon as she'd expected. Instead, she saw the men gathered around a bare table, scowls etched on their faces. "What's going on here?" she asked. "Where's Ezzie?"

Herring looked up. "Don't know. But this is the third time this week he's been late."

Tess cocked her head. "Late from what? He only has to go from the bunkhouse to the cookshack."

"That's the problem," Herring said. "He's not coming from the bunkhouse. He's shackin' up with Becky."

Tess stared at Herring as she tried to conjure up visions of Ezzie courting a woman. "Becky?" she finally asked.

"Becky Tyson," Herring replied, "from the Blue Ox Cafe, where Ezzie's been picking up pies."

Tess looked down at Herring. "But Ezzie always makes his own pies."

"Not anymore."

Tess put her hands on her hips and smiled. "That old coot." Then her smile vanished. "Well, I'd better get some food on the table." She looked around at the men and raised her voice. "Okay, boys, find something to do for fifteen minutes while I fix some breakfast."

The men grumbled their discontent and trudged out of the cookshack while Tess started breakfast for ten hungry loggers. Twenty minutes later the men gathered around the table again. Tess had barely finished grating yesterday's boiled potatoes for hash browns when the platter of the previous night's reheated dinner rolls clattered empty on the counter. The room quaked with drumming fingers and tapping feet. "Pour yourselves some coffee and hang in there," she said.

Royer's response boomed over the drone. "Damned old coot can't even crawl out of the sack long enough to feed us."

Herring's voice blared back. "Come on, Mac. He hasn't got many years of ruttin' left. Let him be."

Tess ignored the comments and launched a pan of hot biscuits down the long table, followed by a platter of sausages and a bowl of gravy. Twenty hands reached out eagerly, and within minutes both platter and pan were empty and Herring was swabbing out the gravy bowl with a biscuit crust.

Tess slapped another four pounds of sausage onto the griddle and checked the oven for the next batch of biscuits. While she dumped the borderline well-browned-to-charred potatoes on a large serving plate, slid the plate along the table and finished turning the sausages, the biscuits burned. By the time she opened the oven door, it was too late. Smoke poured out and rose to the ceiling of the cookshack.

Damn Ezzie! She plopped the platter of sausages and the rest of the burned biscuits on the table. Cooking gourmet meals for two certainly hadn't prepared her for the task of cooking for a group of hungry men—especially on an old wood stove! "Sorry, gentlemen, that's all there is," she said, dusting her hands and removing her apron. "I'll see you at lunch." She slapped her apron on the table and left for Bakers Creek and the Blue Ox Cafe.

An hour later, she gave up her search. No one in town had seen either Ezzie or Becky Tyson, and the cafe was closed for the day. Frustrated, she headed back to Timber West.

As she drove, her mind drifted to Zak. More than anything, she wanted to be with him. During the past week she had spent her days hard at work at Timber West, but her nights had been spent in Zak's arms, sometimes at his cabin, but more often at hers. And now with Zak going away for two days, and Pio soon to move in with him for the summer, she felt as if she were being cheated of the private intimate moments they had only begun to share again.

Without realizing it, she passed the turnoff to Timber West and found herself approaching Zak's drive. She pulled in and scurried up the path, anxious to see him once more before he left. She found him on the porch of his cabin, assembling a small bicycle. Pio hovered over him holding a wrench. Pio looked up, and Tess immediately caught the animosity on his face. Nevertheless, she gave him a bright smile. "Hi. I'll bet you're happy to be out of school this week," she said.

Pio shrugged, turned and went into the cabin, shutting the door. Zak looked at the closed door, a frown on his face. He had no idea what to do about

Pio's continued resentment of Tess. She'd certainly given him no reason to dislike her.

Tess glanced around at a tire hanging on a long rope from a tree and a huge cardboard carton with a diagram of a child's slide. "Pio didn't exactly look overjoyed to see me."

Zak leaned the bike frame against the cabin. "He just needs more time. Once he's here for the summer, when he'll be seeing lots more of you, I'm sure he'll come around." He led her around the side of the cabin and pulled her into his arms. Tess snuggled against him, savoring the woodsy smell of his skin.

Zak slipped his hands under her jacket and around her midriff. He studied her for a moment, noting the discontent in her eyes. "You look worried," he said. "Is anything wrong?"

Tess sighed. "I can't find Ezzie. He wasn't at camp to fix breakfast this morning, and I've looked all over town."

"Everyone's entitled to an off day," Zak said. "Maybe he just lost track of the time." He bent down and lightly touched his lips to hers. "Come on," he said, reaching for her hand and pulling her behind a thicket of rhododendron.

Tess pressed her hands against his chest. "I really have to get back to camp," she told him. "Lunch, you know. If I start now maybe I'll have enough food cooked by noon to fill that bunch."

Zak only drew her closer. "Lunch can wait," he murmured, his lips moving to her forehead, her cheek, her ear, where the tip of his tongue darted inside. She gasped and tangled her fingers in his hair, drawing his head toward hers until their lips joined.

As they kissed, Zak backed her beneath an ivy-covered overhang that smelled of forest moss, rich humus and decomposing wood—much like the Grotto. Tess wrapped her arms around his neck and snuggled against him. "You feel so good," she said.

Zak unzipped her jacket and slipped his hands inside, resting them on the bare skin beneath her shirt.

"Zak!" Tess yelped, feeling his cold hands. She was shivering from the crisp morning air but warmed by her awakening desire. Now, though, with Pio soon moving into the cabin, she wondered when she and Zak would find time to be alone.

Zak pressed her hips against him. "You have no idea what you're doing to me," he whispered.

Tess felt the hardness of him as his hands pushed against her spine, his hips moving sensuously. "Yes, I have, but there's nothing we can do about it," she whispered back, wishing they could make uninhibited unrestrained love as they had in the night.

Zak moaned. "Unfortunately you're right," he said in a husky voice, his lips moving to the curve of her neck. Tess rested her head against his chest—and was startled by the crackle of limbs from behind him. She looked over his shoulder. Standing a short distance away and watching with a scowl on his face was Pio. Tess jerked her hands away from Zak, pulled her jacket around her and backed out of his arms. Zak's head whipped around, but before he could speak, Pio had turned and fled toward the cabin.

Tess tugged at the zipper on her jacket. "It's just not going to work," she said. "Pio has no intention of sharing you with anyone, especially me."

Zak glanced back at the spot where Pio had stood. He knew Tess was right. Pio didn't want to share him with her. But she had to be wrong about things working out. "I told you," he said, "he just needs more time."

"You didn't see the look on his face. I don't think time will change things." It seemed impossible to rebuild a relationship with Zak when his son continued to come between them. Not only was Pio's attitude toward her a wedge, but she sensed that she and Zak were divided in their philosophies of child-raising, as well.

Zak, too, could feel invisible forces tugging them apart. Could they ever be a real family? What if Pio never accepted Tess? And what about his father's resolve that Basque marry Basque? The subject seemed to be an issue of late.

"Well, nothing's going to be resolved this afternoon," Tess said, "and I have to get back."

Zak rested his hands on her shoulders. "We'll work out something when I return," he promised.

Tess looked into his eyes. "I wish life were that simple," she replied. "For now, just be careful climbing trees." She glanced apprehensively at the cabin, kissed him quickly and headed quickly down the trail to her Jeep.

Five minutes later, she pulled into the clearing beside the cookshack and jumped down. As she walked toward the building, the sound of clattering metal in concert with the roar of an approaching vehicle made her turn her head. Ezzie's old yellow truck, trailing several strings of tin cans, rattled to a stop. Scrawled across the door in big white letters were the words "Just Married." Ezzie stepped from the truck as the men gathered around him. Tess couldn't contain her wide grin when she saw Ezzie wearing a gray pin-striped suit with a white bow tie and a pink flower in the lapel.

She rushed over to the truck. "Ez!" she exclaimed, as he climbed down. She reached out to give Ezzie a hug. "And you must be Becky." She moved around the truck to hug Ezzie's bride through the window. Becky's face was as bright as Ezzie's. She wore a pink dress with tiny white flowers embroidered around the collar. "You look beautiful," Tess said. "When did all this happen?"

"About thirty minutes ago," Becky responded.

Ezzie wiggled his eyebrows up and down. "She was a hard woman to convince, but last week she said yes—and I don't like long engagements. As pretty as she is, she could've been snatched up by someone else."

Becky blushed and said nothing.

Ezzie turned to Tess. "I'm really sorry, TJ," he said. "I guess I sort of lost track of time."

Tess smiled at Ezzie. How could she possibly be angry with someone who looked so happy? "You're forgiven this time," she said. "What are your plans now?"

Ezzie's face sobered, then he looked at Becky, winked and gave Tess a sheepish grin. "Could I maybe have tomorrow off so's I could add it to the weekend for our honeymoon?'' he said. "I promised Becky I'd take her to Crater Lake.''

"Sure you can,'' Tess found herself saying, knowing she'd probably regret the words come dinnertime. She hoped Curt would keep things moving in the pole-timber area while she was busy in the cookshack.

Ezzie called out his thanks as he climbed back into the truck. Then he waved to the crowd of amused lumberjacks as the truck rattled and banged across the clearing and down the dirt road. Tess smiled until they were out of sight. Her smile faded when she turned toward the cookshack.

At lunch she was no more organized than she'd been at breakfast. Even though she started preparations almost an hour before, it was practically a repeat of the previous meal. She managed to get the biscuits baked and on the table, but the water for the green beans refused to boil on the old wood stove, and by the time she'd stoked the fire again the men were already sitting expectantly around the table.

She looked at the somber faces as she cradled the huge bowl of potatoes in the crook of her arm and whipped with quick agitated strokes. The lumps defied her. She slapped the potato whipper down and plunked the bowl on the table. "That's the best I can do.''

Herring scooped out a wad of lumpy potatoes and looked at Tess. "You got any gravy, TJ?''

"Gravy! Damn!'' Tess rushed to the stove as the smell of scorching gravy wafted through the cookshack. With a dishcloth, she grabbed the handle of the big iron skillet and headed for the sink, but before she could get there, the wet dishcloth became too hot to hold and she dropped the skillet, splattering the gravy on the floor.

Tears of frustration stung her eyes. She turned away from the men and took several deep breaths to quell her growing despair. Her eyes focused on the iron skillet and the thick splashes of gravy on the floor. With a shaky hand, she picked up the skillet and set it in the sink. She had no idea how Ezzie did it, but she couldn't handle the job alone, nor would the men be satisfied with a meager plate of lumpy potatoes.

As she made one last trip to the storage shed to get what remained on the shelves, she was both pleased and surprised to see Zak's truck pull in. She'd assumed he'd left by now.

Zak jumped out, leaving Pio in the truck, and walked toward her. "I'm really in a bind."

Tess noted the strained look on his face and the worry in his eyes. "What's the problem?"

"I can't find Becky, and she was supposed to look after Pio for me."

"Becky from the Blue Ox?"

"How did you know?"

"A lucky guess," Tess said. "You missed her by about two hours. She and Ezzie were here before lunch."

"Here?" Zak said, incredulously. "Becky was here?"

"On their way to Crater Lake—for their honeymoon."

"Honeymoon?" Zak stared at Tess for a moment. Then he combed his fingers through his hair. "I knew I should have called and reminded her," he said. "I can't take Pio with me—that area's too rugged. And with Becky gone..." He paused, shifting his gaze to Pio while considering the options. He looked back at Tess. It was only for two nights—one full day. And maybe if she and Pio had time alone...

"Could you," he said, "that is, would you consider keeping him? It's only for two days."

Tess glanced at Pio, then at the expectant look in Zak's eyes and said softly, "You know how he feels about me. And besides, I've never looked after a six-year-old before."

"He doesn't take much looking after. He's really very little trouble," Zak said. "And he's worked in a kitchen before. His mother ran a pub, so he grew up helping her do just what you're doing."

Tess wasn't sure she could cope with a young boy for two days alone, particularly one who so openly disliked her. She'd never done much baby-sitting and had little experience with children. But she knew Zak would not have asked her if there was any other way. She looked at Zak and sighed. "Okay, but if he misbehaves, you'll have to let me discipline him the best way I see fit."

Zak smiled his relief. "He won't give you any trouble, I promise." He retrieved Pio and the boy's small overnight bag from the truck.

Tess looked at Pio's quiet face and large gray eyes. Maybe it would be a chance for them to get to know each other. After all, if she and Zak were ever to get their lives together, his son's acceptance of her would have to come first. She knew how important Pio's welfare was to Zak. She gave the boy an apprehensive smile. "I'm very glad you'll be staying with me, Pio," she said. "We'll try to do something special tonight." She extended her hand.

Pio backed away. "I don't want to stay here." He looked at Zak. "I want to go with you."

Zak set Pio's overnight bag beside Tess, then crouched and pulled the boy toward him. "I can't take you with me. I already explained that to you. If I could, I would, but it's not possible this time. I love you, son, and I'll be back in two days." He hugged Pio, then nudged him toward Tess.

Pio walked over to her with obvious reluctance.

Zak gave Tess a light kiss. "Thanks, honey. I'll make it up to you when I get back," he whispered.

Tess took Pio's hand and held it while Zak climbed into his truck, waved and drove off. As the truck rounded a curve, Tess looked down at Pio and smiled.

Pio stared up at her with narrowed resentful eyes, jerked his hand from hers and ran toward the bunkhouse.

CHAPTER TEN

THE NEXT DAY, as Pio stood on a stool in the cook-shack stirring the huge pot of beans bubbling on the stove, Tess eyed him dubiously. So far today there had been no major incidents. But the evening before, Pio had tested her patience by stuffing toilet paper into the bowl and flushing it until the water rose and welled over the edge. She had held her temper but resolved to discuss the incident with Zak. She had no idea how to handle the boy.

Pio looked around, caught her watching and glared at her. Tess willed herself to be patient, repeating silently that Pio's behavior was the result of being confronted with the prospect of a new mother when he still hadn't let go of the one he'd lost.

He'd been a model child with the men while they'd waited for breakfast earlier. They'd ruffled his hair and tussled playfully with him, and he'd responded with gleeful laughter. But when he was alone with Tess again, he resumed his sullen manner.

Tess piled biscuits onto a platter. "Okay, Pio," she said with a tentative smile, "you can put these on the table." She handed the platter to him, then reached around to lift a pitcher of milk from the counter. When she turned with the pitcher, it collided with Pio, who hadn't moved. She let out a yelp as the pitcher flew from her grip, spewing milk everywhere as it tumbled to the floor. Pio watched, horrified, as the empty pitcher spun slowly at his feet like a top winding down. As Tess gathered towels and aprons to sop up the mess, Pio ran out of the cookshack. Tess rushed out of the building and after him. "Pio, wait," she called, as he scrambled up the stairs of the bunkhouse and disappeared inside.

Tess peered into the long shadowy room, but Pio was nowhere in sight. "Pio, it's okay," she said in a firm voice. Knowing she couldn't go into the men's bunkhouse, she backed onto the porch and waited. A few moments later Pio walked out of the shadows and stood in the doorway. Tears streamed down his face. Tess sensed that the boy wanted to come to her but wouldn't. She crouched and extended her hand. "It's all right, Pio. Will you come back with me?" she asked, pointing to the cookshack.

Pio looked at her outstretched palm, started to place his hand in hers, then withdrew.

Tess reached for his wrist and gently pulled him to her. "It's fine, really. We have lots more milk. Now, come on back and let's finish feeding those hungry men, okay?" She dropped his arm and motioned for him to come with her. Pio hesitated, then stepped forward, following her back to the cookshack.

During the afternoon, Tess sensed Pio's tenuous approval, detecting a greater willingness to help. Yet he still kept his distance. Could it be that he felt disloyal to his dead mother, that he thought he was in some way betraying her by accepting another woman in his life? Tess remembered having the same feelings when Aunt Ruth first moved in and started taking over her mother's duties.

That evening, after Pio had gone to bed, Tess couldn't help feeling disappointed. She'd hoped he would have warmed to her by now, but instead he seemed more aloof. However, he didn't show the outward resentment he had before. Maybe tomorrow would be better. She'd sent Harv Dempsey to town with a few dollars to pick up some playthings for him.

Late the next morning Zak returned. When Pio heard his truck, he raced out of the cookshack to meet him, a bright smile on his face. Zak caught Pio in a midair leap and the boy wrapped his arms around his father's neck. Tess stood at the door of the cookshack shaking soap bubbles from her hands.

Zak looked past Pio to Tess and winked. "Thanks for stepping in for me," he said. "How did you two get on?"

Tess walked out to where Zak stood with Pio and smiled. "We did just fine. And I'll have you know your son is a champion bubble blower."

Zak looked from Tess to Pio, pleased to see smiles on both faces. Perhaps leaving them alone together had been a good idea, after all. "I have big plans for us," he announced.

Tess looked at him curiously. "What kind of plans?"

"Tomorrow is the Taureau de Feu festival," Zak said, "and I plan to take Pio to see it—he used to go to the one in France. I want you to go, too."

Tess glanced around. The men were preparing to leave for the Memorial Day weekend and Ezzie was expected back when they returned on Tuesday. Now that Pio was beginning to accept her, maybe a relaxing day would give him a chance to adjust to her and Zak together. "When would we get back?" she asked.

"Tomorrow night," Zak replied.

Tess looked at Zak. His face shone in anticipation. "I suppose it would be all right to leave this place for the day," she said, feeling a sudden urge to get away from logs, grease guns and heavy machines.

Zak grinned and rumpled Pio's hair. "Now I have some surprises for you both," he said. He reached into the truck and brought out four large boxes, handing two to Tess and two to Pio. "Go ahead," he said to Pio, "take a look inside."

Pio raised the lid of one box. His eyes grew round as he lifted a pair of new black boots from the box. The wide smile he gave Zak was all the thanks Zak needed.

"Go on," said Zak. "Put them on."

Pio flopped down on the ground, set the other box beside him and yanked off his tennis shoes. He pulled on the boots and wiggled his feet, smiling up at his father with sparkling eyes.

Zak motioned to the other box. "Go ahead," he said. "See what's in that one."

Pio opened the second box and folded back the tissue. When he saw the contents—a homespun shirt, a pair of baggy blue trousers and a small beret—his smile spread into a broad grin. "Wow!"

"You'll make a fine young shepherd at the festival," Zak told him, a gleam of humor in his eyes. He crouched, lifted the beret from the box and placed it on Pio's head. "The shepherd and his beret should never part. Wear it like this—" he made a hump with the crown of the beret and plopped it back on Pio's head "—and rain won't run down your nose." He trailed a finger down Pio's nose.

Pio giggled.

Zak stood. "In the orchard, it's handy for gathering filberts." He whisked the beret from Pio's head, scooped up some pinecones and flopped it on his own head. It bulged with pinecones.

Pio and Tess laughed.

Zak shook out the cones and settled the beret on his head again, tipping it back. "If a shepherd wears it like this, he's content. If he wears it low on his forehead like this—" he pulled the beret down and scowled "—he's sullen."

Pio laughed again, his eyes dancing.

Zak tipped the hat to one side. "Like this, he's a rogue and women should beware." He strutted about, his chest out, a rakish grin on his face. "But if he wears it like this—" he flattened the beret and staggered around, the hat sitting like a pancake on top of his head "—he's drunk!"

Pio whooped in childish laughter.

Zak swooped the hat off and plopped it back on Pio's head, then turned to Tess. "Now, take a look in your boxes."

While Zak held the box, Tess lifted the lid. Resting on top was a black-lace camisole—the fitted vest worn by Basque women on festival day. And beneath, she found a white blouse with billowing sleeves. She smiled, remembering how much she'd wanted just such an outfit when she was sixteen—and an excuse to wear it for Zak.

"You'll look beautiful," Zak said.

She folded back the camisole and blouse and found beneath them a black apron and a red-and-black skirt.

Zak beamed. "I've waited a long time for this. I'll have to keep my eyes on you so no boisterous young troubadour steals you away from me."

"And what do I wear on my feet? Tennis shoes or work boots?" she teased.

Zak pointed. "Look in that box."

Tess opened the lid and stared at the white stockings and black dancing shoes with long black leg laces. She smiled. For one day, she'd be a Basque woman and satisfy a curiosity that had tickled her imagination for years. "When do I assume my new role?" she asked.

"When we get to Navarre. We'll change into our costumes there," Zak replied. "We'd better get an early start in the morning, though. The snake begins at nine."

"Snake?"

"Everyone holds hands and snakes through the streets. You'll see." Zak handed the boxes to her. "Just get a good night's sleep. We have a big day coming." He placed his hand behind Pio's neck and led him toward the truck. When Pio looked back at Tess, he smiled a sincere spontaneous smile. Tess felt a warmth creep up her cheeks, and she winked and smiled back.

EARLY THE NEXT MORNING, Zak eased the truck to a halt in the middle of the road to Navarre, then waited while a flock of long-haired sheep crossed the highway and dashed up the embankment to the accompaniment of tinkling bells. An elderly shepherd, wearing a beret, baggy pants and a short pleated cloak, brandished a polished walking stick and marched behind the sheep, urging them on.

Zak leaned forward and said to Pio, who sat by the window, "Tell Tess in Basque what the man's holding."

Pio looked up at Tess, his eyes no longer holding the sparks of laughter she's seen the day before. Reluctantly he responded to Zak's prodding. *"Makhilaks,"* he said sullenly.

"Oh," Tess said. She gave Pio a polite smile.

Pio pressed his mouth into a slash and smiled back. But there was no smile in his eyes.

Tess looked away, suspecting the reason behind Pio's negative behavior had something to do with Zak's insistence, forty-five minutes earlier when they left Bakers Creek, that Pio sit by the window with her between him and his father. From that moment, she had felt the boy's silent resentment.

Zak caught the troubled look on Tess's face. He was still baffled by Pio's behavior. Did the boy specifically resent Tess, or would he feel threatened by anyone who might come between them?

He glanced out the window at slopes covered with pine forests and laced with cascades of flashing water. A mist filled the high mountain valley like a white sea, partially obscuring Navarre. "If you look closely," he said to Tess, pointing in the distance, "you can see the steeple of the church built by the original families who founded Navarre. My grandfather was among them," he added, placing his palm on Tess's knee.

Tess slid her hand over Zak's and held it. Aware that Pio's eyes had noted the gesture with disapproval, Zak returned his hand to the steering wheel. "Oh, well," he said. "Rome wasn't built in a day."

Tess nudged Pio. "May I sit by the window?" she asked.

Pio nodded. His face brightened and he moved forward, allowing Tess to slide under him. He settled against Zak, a wide grin spreading across his face.

Zak winked at Tess. "But eventually," he said, "Rome did get built." Tess laughed, Zak laughed and Pio laughed, even though he had no idea what Zak meant.

The mist lifted like a veil, and when they entered Navarre they found a village gleaming with moisture. They passed a sign reading WELCOME TO NAVARRE: POPULATION 2130, and within minutes they were near the center of town, passing the small white wooden church they'd seen from the mountain.

Already the town was a hum of activity. In front of a bakery, Zak swerved to the curb and tooted his horn. A woman standing in the doorway, dressed in a long skirt, black apron and head scarf, looked up. Recognizing Zak, her face creased into a web of crinkles. She walked over and peered through Tess's window. "Zak," she said, looking around Tess and Pio. She began to talk to Zak in Basque. Zak replied with words Tess couldn't understand. As he did, he gestured, smiled and spoke with obvious enthusiasm. Then the woman nodded to Tess, said something to Pio that made him smile and backed away, waving.

"Who was that?" Tess asked as they drove away.

"A neighbor," Zak replied.

Tess gave him a quizzical glance. "Doesn't she speak English?"

"She doesn't need to," Zak replied. "She has no intention of ever leaving Navarre, and most of the older people here still speak Basque. To them it's important that the language be preserved, and I agree. Basque is unrelated to any other language. I hope Pio never loses it, that he passes it on to his children." He looked down at Pio and patted his leg. Pio smiled up at him.

Zak turned onto a tree-lined street of modest well-kept homes and pulled the truck in front of a small white house. "We'll change here," he said.

"Then your parents are still at the wine conference?" Tess asked, relieved that she wouldn't see them on this particular visit.

"No," Zak replied. "They're back, but their home is a few miles out of town, so we'll stop by after the festival. Come on and meet Saveur and Marie."

Tess climbed out of the truck and looked at the humble white wood dwelling. A clematis vine spiraled along the overhang of the porch, and above the front door, she saw the words "Mata Baita" neatly painted on a polished board.

Zak noticed Tess studying the sign. "It's like a house number," he said. "Navarreans prefer to name their houses rather than number them."

"What does it mean?" Tess asked.

"Marie lives here," he replied. Then he shrugged and smiled. "It's only logical. Marie does live here."

Tess's eyes moved from the sign to a small garden on one side of the house, then to another on the opposite side. She noticed that one garden was ornamental, with roses and tulips, the other nurturing, with vegetables and melons.

Zak walked over to stand beside her. "As you can see, Marie takes great pride in her gardens."

"They're lovely," Tess replied. The scene of the small house with the clematis vine and gardens brought back memories of the small home and sheep ranch she and Zak had once talked of having, and suddenly she was filled with a nameless melancholy. She caught Zak watching her discerningly, and she had the eerie feeling he shared her thoughts.

"All that's missing is a flock of sheep," Zak said. Without waiting for a response, he turned from Tess and called to his son. Pio scurried from the garden and followed them up the steps onto the porch.

Marie met them at the door. A woman of perhaps thirty-six or -seven with long auburn hair fashioned into a braid down her back, she was wearing the traditional festival dress of a Basque woman. In the crook of her arm she held a mixing bowl. Although she wore no makeup, her face looked fresh and young.

"Ah, Zak," she said. "I've been expecting you." She reached down to stroke Pio's hair.

Zak introduced Tess, and after Marie extended her a warm welcome, she ushered them into the living room, where the sound of rock music reverberated through the wall. Marie banged on the closed door. "Monique!" she called.

A muffled response came from inside the room. "I know, I know." The music died.

Zak walked to the door and said, "Monique, you have a visitor."

The door swept open and a willowy young woman of about sixteen appeared. "Zak!" she squealed, before composing herself and leaning casually against the doorjamb. She wore her dark hair cropped close to her scalp, except for a long shock falling over one eye. Large red hoops hung from her ears and her lips were curved in a cool smile.

Zak looked at Monique's cutoff shirt, snug jeans and white boots. "Aren't you going to the festival?" he asked.

"Sure," she replied, shifting her gum to the other side of her mouth.

Zak eyed her with amusement. "Well, you'd better get ready. They're lining up to start the snake."

"I am ready."

"Come on, Monique," Zak said. "I know you better than that. You've always looked forward to wearing the traditional dress."

Monique looked from Zak to her mother then back at Zak. "You gotta be kidding," she said. "I'd rather die first." She turned and slipped into the bedroom, shutting the door. The rock music clicked on again, this time softer.

Zak looked at Marie, and Marie shrugged. "Times are changing, Zak. We can't live their lives for them." She picked up her bowl of batter and began beating once again. "I'd better get this into the oven and you'd better get ready yourselves if you plan to join the snake."

Marie sent Zak and Pio to the master bedroom to change into their Basque outfits. Tess, she said, could use Monique's room.

While Tess braided her hair and slipped into the white blouse and bright skirt Zak had given her, Monique sat cross-legged on the bed reading a rock magazine. She looked up at Tess. "Are you Basque?" she asked.

"No," Tess replied, tucking the blouse into the skirt.

"Then why are you dressing up?"

Tess slipped the camisole over her blouse. "I want to," she said simply.

Monique stopped chewing her gum. "You're kidding. Whatever for?"

Tess drew in the laces of the camisole, pulling it snugly around her slender midriff. "Maybe just to get a taste of your world," she said, finding the thought of being a Basque woman for a day intriguing.

"It's really pretty boring," Monique told her. "There's nothing to do around here."

Tess laughed. "All teenagers think that wherever they are is the most boring place in the world. I know I did."

Monique pursed her lips. "You weren't stuck in a place like Navarre."

"You're right," Tess said. "I was stuck in a logging camp." She thanked Monique for the use of her room and left.

When she stepped into the living room she found Zak and Pio alone. Zak wore the garb of a shepherd—a wide beret, homespun white shirt with a multicolored sash and baggy blue pants stuffed into high black boots. And Pio stood beside him, a miniature of his father. Tess saw the admiration in Zak's gaze. "Will I do?" she asked, smiling. She spun around, sending her dark pigtail flying and the red-and-black skirt billowing around slender white-stockinged legs laced in black ties.

Zak grinned and jiggled Pio's shoulder. "What do you think?" he asked. "Shall we show her off today?"

Pio's smile faded. He glared at Tess and spat in Basque, "Mama was prettier." Moving toward the door, he ran from the house and climbed into the truck.

"What was that all about?" Tess asked.

"He just misses his mother," Zak replied. "It's his first festival without her." He glanced out the window at Pio, who was sitting in the truck.

Marie entered the room and smiled at Tess. "You look lovely," she said. She turned to Zak. "I'm sorry you missed Saveur. He'll be disappointed he didn't see you."

"I'm sorry, too," Zak replied.

Marie saw them to the front door. "You three have a nice time," she called after them, "and look for me at the *piperade* booth."

When they left Marie's house, wispy clouds had begun to gather, threatening to obscure the sun. "Did you bring a jacket for Pio?" Tess asked as they walked toward the truck.

"Of course," Zak replied. "I haven't been away from Oregon that long. I always take jackets and rain boots along wherever I go."

Tess climbed into the truck and reached for the sweater she'd decided at the last minute to bring, knowing how often Oregon's sunny spring mornings could fade into cold dismal afternoons.

By the time they parked the truck, the town was cloaked in gray. In spite of the impending bad weather, Navarre buzzed with activity. People gathered and began forming into long chains for the snake dance. Pio brightened when he saw the papier-mâché effigies of bulls being carried by shepherds dressed much the same as he.

The crowd began to join hands and Zak reached for Pio. "Hold on tight," he said, grabbing his hand and sandwiching the boy between Tess and himself.

The snake took form, winding through the streets toward the town square. They moved with the string, zigzagging through switchbacks of people. A kaleidoscope of faces and forms whirled by, first in one direction, then the other: square and solid farm women with round faces and ruddy skin; willowy young girls with bright eyes and braided hair; trim herdsmen with lean faces and high-bridged noses. The string of people twisted and wound like a serpent, then uncoiled in the town square, the papier-mâché bulls exploding in a crescent of brilliant fireworks.

When the crowd had dispersed, Pio's eyes moved to the group of people gathered in a vacant lot. "Papa," he squealed, pointing. "The rams."

"Come on," Zak said, holding Pio's hand and reaching for Tess's arm. "It's the ram-butting contest." Above the drone of the festivities came the resounding crack of clashing horns. Within the circle of spectators, two shepherds pitted their rams in a bout of brute power, each eyeing the other's animal for signs of weakness as wagers flew back and forth.

Tess groaned as the big shaggy animals repeatedly butted heads. "When does it end?" she asked. "I'm getting a headache just watching."

Zak laughed. "When one of them refuses to fight, which could be quite a while—they're stubborn creatures." He grinned. "But then, they're Basque."

While they stood watching, Tess felt a small hand slip into hers. She looked down. Pio watched the rams intently, apparently unaware that he'd taken her hand. As she studied his face, the warmth of his hand in hers filled her with a strange wistfulness. Suddenly Pio's head snapped around and his eyes focused on their clasped hands. He looked up. His face sobered and he jerked his hand from hers.

"It's okay, Pio," she said, holding her hand out to him, hoping he'd take it again. Pio stared at her for a moment, then reached for Zak's hand, instead. Tess looked at Zak and shrugged off her disappointment.

Although the soft distant rumble of thunder could be heard and dark clouds obscured the sun, the revelry continued, with high-spirited singing and dancing. By noon, appetites were hearty. "Come on, you two," Zak said. "Let's find Marie."

They wound their way through crowds gathered at the concession stands, passing booths that displayed loaves of crisp French bread, huge wedges of cheese, and blood sausages boiling in cauldrons. They found Marie standing behind a counter heaped with paper plates, napkins and plastic forks. Her *piperade* omelet bubbled on a griddle, and the aroma of bacon, tomatoes and spices rose with the steam curling from the eggs as they cooked.

Pio looked expectantly at Marie, who smiled and lifted a wedge of omelet from the griddle. She slipped it onto a plate. "Here you are," she said, handing it to him.

She turned to Zak. "Why don't you leave Pio with me and take Tess to the Palombiere for lunch."

"Palombiere?" Tess said.

"Place of the Doves," Zak explained. "The pub." He looked at Pio, who sat on the curb eating his omelet a short distance away. "If you really don't mind," he said, "we'd like that."

Marie smiled. "I don't mind. And since I have to see your parents later, I'll drop Pio off there when we're done," she added. "Now you two go on."

Zak crouched in front of Pio and explained what Marie had suggested. Pio looked at Marie and smiled at the crispy pastry she held up for him, then nodded his approval.

At the Palombiere, a group of men gathered under the wooden sign displaying a white dove and hanging over the entrance. When Zak and Tess approached, heads turned toward them. "Hey, Zak! De Neuville! Yo, Zak!" voices called out in greeting.

Zak nodded to his friends and nudged Tess through the door into the quaint old pub. They wove past scarred wooden tables and slid onto a long bench. Zak turned to acknowledge someone who clapped him on the shoulder, then waved to another who called to him across the room.

"You're a popular figure around here," Tess said, feeling like an outsider.

"I grew up in Navarre," Zak replied, "and so did most of the people here."

Tess sensed a strong camaraderie among the people. She also felt a cultural separation.

Zak touched her arm. "Ready to order?"

"Uh-huh," she said, looking around for a menu.

Zak chuckled. "Don't worry about menus," he said. "There are none. The selection is always the same—mutton, pork or *salmis de palombe*."

"*Salmis...*"

"Doves simmered for three days in wine, garlic, vinegar and spices. With it you get soup, salad, *piperade,* French bread, cheese and either coffee with brandy or wine."

"Why don't you order for me," Tess suggested. She looked around at the gathering of people. Smoke curled upward as men with berets tipped back from their weathered faces swapped stories in Basque.

While Zak ordered their meals, the door to the tavern swept open and Tess recognized Vince, Zak's brother. He stood in the doorway for a moment, his eyes flicking over the tables. Then he spotted them. Weaving his way through the crowd, he approached and straddled a bench opposite them. He nodded to Tess and smiled at Zak.

Zak smiled back, surprised to see Vince, knowing he rarely frequented places as traditional as the Palombiere. "What brings you here?" he asked, noting that Vince was wearing a navy blue windbreaker instead of his usual leather jacket.

Vince's eyes followed a young waitress zigzagging her way between tables. "The food's pretty good," he replied.

"Then go ahead and order," said Zak. "It's on me." He looked at the young woman who seemed to have captured his brother's attention, then at Vince. "Where's your friend Dede?"

Vince shrugged. "She split. Took off with a punk from Eugene." He shifted his gaze to the waitress again.

Zak arched a brow. "Anyone you know?"

"Who?"

"The waitress."

"Oh, you mean Kit Butler?" he said with a nonchalant wave of his hand. "Her father's my boss—owns the video store."

Zak contemplated the woman's long dark braid and Basque costume. "Butler?"

"To answer your unasked question—" Vince swung his leg around and settled on the bench "—no, she's not Basque. Her family moved here from Portland because they wanted to live in a small town."

Zak curved his arm around Tess, then looked across the table at Vince and asked, "Why is she working here instead of for her father?"

Vince gave Zak a wry smile. "She's not into arcades and videos. Claims they're not her thing. She's sort of a back-to-the-land health nut, if you know what I mean."

"You'd better be careful of that kind," Zak said, looking at Tess and winking.

One corner of Vince's mouth tipped up. "Oh, I don't know. Some of what she says makes sense."

A few minutes later an arm reached over Vince's head as the young waitress placed a basket of sliced French bread and a steaming tureen of thick soup with vegetables in front of Zak. "Hi," she said, smiling at Vince. "I thought you were an antifestival hamburger freak." She set three heavy china bowls and an assortment of silverware beside the tureen.

Vince gave her a dubious smile. "I needed someplace to get out of the rain."

"A likely story," she kidded.

"What's that supposed to mean?" Vince asked.

She set a platter of *piperade* on the table. "That I don't believe you're really a junk-food junkie, but rather, a closet *piperadie*." Before Vince could reply, she pressed her way through the crowd and disappeared into the kitchen.

Zak ladled soup into a bowl and handed it to Tess, then filled one for Vince. "I think she's got your number," he said.

Vince smiled, his eyes on the swinging door to the kitchen. "I can live with that."

Zak slipped his arm around Tess and gave her a little squeeze. "Just remember, little brother, there's nothing like a good woman to settle a man down fast."

Vince's eyes shifted from Zak to Tess. "Don't wish that on me yet," he said. "I still have a few more years of browsing."

Zak laughed. "At least you're browsing in greener pastures."

As they finished their meal, wine began to flow, and soon the shrill flutters of a flute rose above the other sounds in the room. Men shoved tables against the wall and the crowd fanned out, then someone placed a goblet of wine in the center of the floor.

Vince stood up. "This is where I split," he said. "See you two at home later. Thanks for the lunch."

"Glad to do it," Zak replied.

After Vince left, Zak leaned close to Tess's ear. "They're building up to the *zamalzain*—the dance of good against evil," he said. "It's a very difficult dance. In order to do it right, the dancer has to start learning it when he's very young."

A dancer dressed in rags and wearing a grotesque mask staggered onto the floor as if drunk. Moving with exaggerated motions, his feet shuffled to the music of the flute and the rhythm of a drum.

"He represents evil," Zak explained to Tess. "When he dances, watch the wine goblet. If it spills, evil is vanquished and goodwill reigns. Now the crowd will pick someone to represent good."

As Zak spoke he heard his name called out. "Come on, de Neuville!" He looked around and shook his head, making a negative gesture with his hand. "De Neuville!" someone else cried out. A man tugged on his arm and the crowd began to clap and shout in unison, "De Neuville, de Neuville, de Neuville!" Several men dragged Zak from the bench, then set a second wine goblet on the floor, in front of Zak. He smiled, nodded his head in resignation and approached the other dancer.

Zak faced the masked dancer across the filled wine goblets, his upper body erect and rigid. Only his legs moved in time with the shrill music of the flute. He brushed the rim of the glass with his foot before executing intricate steps around it, then backed away. The masked dancer approached, his feet moving above and around his glass so closely it trembled. The crowd gasped.

As Tess watched Zak dance, she realized how deeply the Basque culture was ingrained in him. She saw it in the proud way he held his head as he performed the complicated steps, and she sensed it in his regard for the traditions, his resolve to hold on to their unique language, his strong alliance to family.

Voices rose as the dance reached a climax. Then Zak suddenly leapt into the air, alighting on the rim of his goblet and as quickly soaring away. The glass rocked precariously but didn't spill. The dancer representing evil took his turn. His sandals landed firmly on the rim of his glass, but when he leapt away the goblet rocked and tumbled onto its side, spilling its contents.

The room reverberated with cheers and wild shouts. Zak bowed to the crowd, flopped down on the bench beside Tess and took a long drink of beer. He mopped his brow with a wet towel someone passed to him. "That used to be easier," he said, swabbing the towel across his face. "I think I'll teach Pio and let him take over from here." He glanced at Tess and smiled. "So, how did I do?"

"You were great," Tess replied, knowing she'd always hold the scene in her mind, and in her heart. After a pause she ventured, "Do you want to stay in Navarre always?" The words had been hovering on her tongue, but until now she couldn't bring herself to say them.

"Maybe not always," Zak replied, "but it's where I want to raise Pio—" he reached out and took Tess's hand, gazing into her eyes "—and have a family."

Tess considered Zak's gesture, sensing what he was saying. She looked beyond him to the huddle of men in berets at the next table, the group of old women in head scarves, the cloaked shepherd standing by the door.

If she were to share a life with Zak and Pio, would she ever fit into this world or be accepted by these people? More important, would she ever be accepted by Zak's parents?

CHAPTER ELEVEN

A DARKENED AFTERNOON SKY greeted Tess and Zak as they left the Palombiere. Zak put his arm around Tess and drew her close, feeling her shivering in her light costume. "Maybe we'd better head for my parents' house," he said. "We can change there."

Tess slipped her arm around Zak's waist and they darted for the truck. "Are you sure it's a good idea—stopping by your folks' place?" she asked. "I *am* the daughter of Gib O'Reilly, which I'm sure won't make your father's day."

"Don't worry. You'll have him wrapped around your little finger before he knows what happened—just the way you've done with me," Zak assured her. "Besides, we have to pick up Pio."

Fifteen minutes later, when they turned into the long drive leading to Zak's parents' home, Tess stared at the huge house looming like a gray stone fortress. Two wings flanked the main section of the two-story building, and chimneys rose from the end walls of each wing. Zak had described his home years before, but somehow Tess had never imagined that it was so massive. With the dark clouds gathering above, it looked almost foreboding. "It's so big," she said.

Zak laughed. "My grandfather built it in stages. The wings are separate living quarters for two families and many descendants—the eldest child marrying, remaining with the family and eventually taking over."

Tess hesitated before asking, "Then you're expected to keep up the tradition?"

"Yes," Zak said, dismissing the subject as he opened the truck door and hopped out.

Tess climbed down and looked at the stately home. An ancient wisteria vine wound its way above a window and over the arched entry, breaking the plain stone facade. The wind whipped its lacy leaves, tossing them aside, revealing a nameplate over the door. Tess stepped to the entry and squinted to read the words.

The front door swept open. Gratianne de Neuville appeared holding a bottle with a large rubber nipple. Under her arm a newborn lamb wiggled to be free. She saw Tess looking at the sign and smiled. "It means 'Sweet Promised Land,'" she said.

Gratianne's words had the odd effect of making Tess's throat constrict and her eyes mist, although she couldn't think why. She blinked and looked back at Zak, who was approaching with one bag tucked under his arm and the other clutched in his hand.

Gratianne's gaze shifted to Zak, then back to Tess, taking in her costume. "Please come in," she said, her mouth spreading into an uncertain smile.

Tess caught the questioning look Zak's mother gave him and wondered if Zak had even told his parents they'd be visiting. When they stepped inside, Zak looked around. "Did Vince and Pio get back yet?" he asked.

"Yes," Gratianne replied. "They've been back for a while. Pio's out back watching Vince work on his car, no doubt asking him a thousand questions." The lamb squirmed in Gratianne's arms.

"May I?" Tess asked, holding out her hands. Gratianne passed the wriggling little animal to Tess, then gave her the bottle. The lamb grabbed the nipple and sucked eagerly. "There you are," Tess said. "You're an impatient one."

Gratianne's clear blue eyes rested on Tess. "You've handled animals before," she stated. "I can tell."

Tess smiled. "My grandfather always gave me the bummer lambs to care for," she replied, upending the now empty bottle. The lamb bumped his nose against the nipple. "You poor little waif. With no mother, you'll have to wait until tomorrow for more." She held the lamb against her. He nibbled her collar, then rested his head on her shoulder.

Gratianne looked at Zak, who was setting the bags down. "I'm afraid your father's busy working on his books—taking inventory of the stock."

"Sheep?" Tess inquired.

"Wine," Gratianne replied. "Come on into the kitchen. We'll have cheese and wine. Jean-Pierre will put down his books for good Roquefort." Gratianne took the lamb from Tess and handed it to Zak. "Take him to his box—next to the hot-water heater," she said. "And son," she added as Zak was leaving the room, "there's a piece of fleece by the box. Put it next to him."

Zak smiled at his mother, then turned to Tess. "I do believe she'd take the little beggar to bed with her if Father would allow it."

"Oh, go on with you," Gratianne said. "You're worse than I am." She motioned for Tess to sit at the long table, then she placed a board with a fresh wheel of cheese before her. On the counter Tess recognized two cheese molds, with wooden hoops and drawstrings. Gratianne saw her looking at the hoops. "Does your family make cheese?" she asked.

"My grandmother did," Tess replied. "She used to let me squeeze out the whey, then she'd give it to me to drink."

"And you found that a special treat?" Gratianne asked.

Tess laughed. "No, I hated it, but I never told Grandma because I didn't want to lose out on squeezing the cheese."

Gratianne smiled. "We all have our little tricks to get what we want," she said. "I use many with Jean-Pierre."

Tess looked around the spacious kitchen. A magnificent ham wrapped in an immaculate white cloth, with the gleaming ball of a joint showing, hung from one ax-hewn oak beam. The aromas from ropes of sausages, strings of red peppers, wreaths of garlic and various herbs and spices filled the kitchen.

A massive stone fireplace stood open on three sides, with the face of each opening trimmed in hand-painted tiles. "The tiles came from France," Gratianne commented, noticing Tess's interest.

"They're lovely," Tess said. She looked at the mantel, where pewter candlesticks and copper trays rested on a strip of crisp white linen embroidered with threads of red and blue. "Tell me about the house."

Gratianne's eyes brightened. "Jean-Pierre's father built it in 1928, shortly after he brought his family to America," she said, placing a tray of crackers on the table. "The stones came from the property, but he sent to Portland for the red roof tiles and to France for the hearth tiles." She cut a wedge from the cheese. "Go ahead." She handed Tess a small flat knife.

Tess helped herself to a cracker and spread it with the soft cheese. "What did Mr. de Neuville's father do before coming to America?"

Gratianne sat across from Tess and reached for a cracker. "They had a winery, but since Jean-Pierre's father was not the firstborn, he wasn't entitled to any of the property, so he decided to come to America and start his own winery. All of the vines here were started from rootstock he brought with him from France."

Voices came from the living room. Tess turned and saw Zak with his father. "So," Gratianne said to her husband, "you could smell the cheese." She looked at Tess. "Jean-Pierre has a nose like a rabbit when it comes to sniffing out Roquefort."

Jean-Pierre's eyes rested on Tess, his dark gaze moving from her face, down her dress and back up to her eyes. "Miss O'Reilly," he said in a reserved voice, a polite smile on his lips. "Did you enjoy the festival?"

"Yes, thank you," Tess replied, feeling the older man's assessing gaze.

"Your dress is lovely," Gratianne said. "Did you buy it just for the festival?"

"Zak bought it for me," Tess replied, smiling at Zak.

Zak reached over and squeezed her hand. "Honey, why don't you change so I can take you on a tour? I want you to see the winery."

Tess gave Gratianne a quick smile. "Do you mind?"

"No," Gratianne replied. "Please, make yourself comfortable."

Tess nodded to Jean-Pierre and left with Zak to get her bag. In the hall, just outside the door to the powder room, Zak took her in his arms and kissed her. She slumped against him and stayed there, relishing the strength of his arms. Then she looked up at him. "Your father disapproves," she said.

"Give him time," Zak replied. "He sees his world changing and knows he must eventually change, too, but he still can't accept it. But that has no bearing on us." He gazed into her eyes. "I love you," he whispered.

Tess held his gaze. "And I love you, too, but it won't work. Your parents will never accept me, and I doubt if Gib will ever accept you."

Zak crooked a finger under her chin. "It's our life, not theirs. They just need more time." He kissed her and left her standing in the hall.

She reached for her bag, then stepped into the powder room and closed the door. Slipping out of her outfit, she folded it and placed it in her small canvas bag. Then she pulled on her jeans and her flannel shirt.

As she stared at her reflection in the mirror while combing her hair, Jean-Pierre de Neuville's hushed voice drifted down the hall, his words low and impatient. "Exactly what are your intentions with this woman?" she heard him say.

"Shush," Gratianne warned. The voices became subdued. Tess opened the door slightly and listened, but all she could catch were sentence fragments.

"...old-world values," Jean-Pierre was saying.

"...could never understand Pio and his culture as a Basque woman would," Gratianne added.

Tess shut the door and pressed her back to it, her eyes fixed straight ahead. Although she was inside Gratianne and Jean-Pierre de Neuville's stone fortress, she felt as if she was on the outside, with the wall of stone separating them. The same wall that would always come between her and Zak.

She turned to the mirror and fussed with her hair and refreshed her makeup for an unnecessarily long time. She wasn't anxious to face Zak's parents again, or even to remain in this house where she was an outsider.

After a few minutes she heard a knock on the door. "It's me," Zak called in an anxious voice. "Are you all right?"

Tess drew in a long breath and opened the door. "I want to leave, Zak. Now."

Zak's eyes flashed with alarm. "You heard?"

"Yes, I heard." She reached for her bag. "It won't work. I'm just not a part of your culture and never will be. I don't belong here."

"I don't think you can be the judge of that right now."

"Then who can be? Your mother? You heard what she said, and she was right. I could never understand Pio the way a Basque woman could. And there's Pio himself—we both know what his feelings are. Then there's your father."

"Okay, we'll leave. But first, I want to show you the place where I grew up."

"That won't change anything."

"I'm not expecting it to change anything," Zak said. "But I do want you to see it. Now, come on." He extended his hand and led her into the kitchen.

"Where is everyone?" Tess asked, relieved to find the room empty.

"Father's back in the wine cellar taking inventory, and Mother went to pen up the new lambs before the rain starts."

Tess looked out the window toward the garden. A sod path led to a stone building, which she assumed was the winery. Beside the structure she saw a mixed orchard of fruit trees—plums, cherries and apples. And on the hillside beyond the winery stretched rows of grapevines gnarled with age and heavy with leaves. As lovely as the place was, Tess felt anxious to complete the tour and return to Bakers Creek. Slipping on her jacket against the cold damp air, she followed Zak into the garden.

"There's Teodoro by the winery," Zak said, taking Tess's hand. "Come on, I want you to meet him."

Tess looked up the sod path. An old man sat beside the stone building, carving a piece of wood. He seemed unaware of their approach.

"Teodoro!" Zak said, touching the man's thin shoulder.

Teodoro raised his head, revealing a bronzed face creased with lines etched by wind and sun. "Ah, Zak."

"This is Tess," Zak said.

Teodoro looked at Tess and turned to smile at Zak. He uttered a string of Basque words, then sat back with a broad grin on his face.

Zak laughed and nodded in agreement.

"All right," Tess said, finding herself smiling with them. "What was that all about?"

"He says, 'Women and linen should only be chosen by daylight,'" Zak replied. "It's an old Basque proverb."

Tess cocked her head. "Should I be flattered?"

"Of course. He also said that I must have chosen you in bright light, meaning you're very beautiful."

Tess grinned at Teodoro and the old man nodded his head and grinned back. "You will see the winery, yes?" he asked her.

Zak smiled at Tess. "He used to be in charge of the winery and he's very proud of it. He's been with our family since Father was a boy, although he's retired now."

"Why does he stay here?"

Zak looked surprised. "It's his home," he replied. "He'll always be cared for here."

The sky rumbled and heavy drops of rain began to plink against the tin roof of the winery. Tess zipped her jacket and pulled the collar around her ears, feeling a bite in the air. They entered the building and were at once greeted by the musty smell of fermenting grapes.

When Tess's eyes adjusted to the darkness, she saw three huge vats and a row of casks. She felt comfortable in this dark dingy place. The cavernous room with its stone walls, oak beams and familiar smell reminded her of her grandfather's root cellar and the happy times she'd spent skimming fermenting fruit, corking bottles and occasionally tasting his fragrant homemade wines.

She slipped her hand into the crook of Zak's elbow. "Do you plan to continue this tradition?"

Zak covered her hand with his. "Yes," he said. "Family traditions are meant to be passed on. I'd like Pio to be a part of it, too."

Tess couldn't help admiring Zak's strong sense of duty toward his son. She squeezed his arm and looked up at him. "I think Pio's a very lucky little boy."

Zak smiled, "Perhaps," he said, "but he also needs a mother. I can't take care of all of his—"

"Zak!" Vince's voice echoed through the building. "It's Pio! He's gone!"

The color drained from Zak's face. "What do you mean, gone?"

"I mean he's nowhere around," Vince said. "He was with me, playing with a coil of rope and watching me work on my car. Then he just disappeared. I found this—" he held up Pio's jacket "—near the woods."

"Damn, Pio wouldn't!" Zak said. "Come on—both of you." He rushed out of the building, Tess and Vince close behind.

"Where are we going?" Tess called after him.

"My old tree house—over near the river," Zak said, angry with himself for neglecting to tear out the old ladder and platform. He quickened his pace.

"Jeez!" Vince yelled. "The floor's half-rotted. He could fall. I don't know how the hell he got away without me seeing him."

"Don't blame yourself," Zak said. "I should have taken down the ladder."

Cold rain pelted against their faces as they raced between rows of grapevines, and by the time they crossed the vineyards and reached the forest, the rain was falling in sheets.

Tess stopped to pull the ties on her hood, gathering it close around her face. "How far to the river?" she shouted.

"It's right below us," Zak shouted back as he waited for her to catch up, "and it's deep down there."

"He's so little to be out here alone," Tess said, alarmed.

"He's not supposed to be out here alone, and he knows it," Zak replied. "I've told him a dozen times not to wander down here—"

"What's that?" Vince pointed toward the river where something red flopped in the wind. He and Zak broke into an all-out run and Tess stumbled along behind. Reaching the edge of the embankment high above the river, they found Pio's hat snagged on a limb. Zak looked over the sharp drop-off to the river

below. "Oh, no! He's fallen over the side!" He
snatched the small rain-soaked hat from the branch
and rushed to the edge of the embankment. "He could
never survive down there," he yelled, peering through
the rain at the river swirling below.

Vince squinted as the rain swept across his face. "I
don't see how he could go over the side," he cried.
"That brush is mostly blackberries. And even without thorns it's too dense to get through."

"I hope you're right," said Zak. He shielded his
eyes against the downpour and looked around. "We'd
better find him soon. His clothes must be soaked clear
through." He pointed to where the trail forked and
said to Vince, "Just in case he didn't head for the tree
house, you go that way and check along the river.
We'll go this way."

Vince headed down the narrow path, and Tess and
Zak continued toward the tree house. As they ran
along the uneven trail, Tess shoved tendrils of wet hair
from her face, feeling a shiver race through her as the
icy rain pelted against her skin. When they stopped
momentarily to look around, Tess felt as if her legs
were about to buckle under her. Suddenly a sharp
crack exploded above them. Flinching, Tess looked
up. Before she could see what was happening, Zak
hurled her to the ground and threw himself on top of
her. Moments later, a huge limb crashed to the
ground, inches from where they lay.

Zak pulled her into his arms. "That was too damn
close," he said, looking at the gnarled oak limb lying
beside them. "Let's get to the tree house and get out
of here."

They scrambled up a small rise and made their way down the opposite side, ducking under low limbs heavy with moisture and shoving back branches that blocked the trail. A short distance from a giant oak tree, Zak looked up and cried, "There it is! He's there!"

Tess's gaze moved up the massive trunk to a platform high above the ground. "You're right. I see his hand."

"Pio!" Zak yelled. He got no response. "I'm going up." He started up the ladder made of weathered wooden boards nailed to the tree, but when he put his weight on the third step, the board splintered and ripped from the tree, sending him tumbling to the ground.

Tess reached for him. "You'll never make it. You're too heavy," she said. "I'll go up."

"No, those boards are rotten. I'll have to go back to get a ladder and some ropes. You wait here and make sure Pio stays put." Without waiting for a response, he turned and raced back toward the house.

Tess saw Pio's hand move. "Pio!" she yelled up. "Stay still." Pio shifted dangerously near the edge of the platform but didn't seem to hear her. "Pio!" she yelled again, but there was no response.

Without hesitation, Tess grabbed one of the boards nailed to the tree and began to climb gingerly past the broken board and up, feeling the weathered slats twist and creak with her weight. By the time she reached the crude structure and pulled herself onto the platform, her forehead stung from the cold rain and her cheeks were numb. She looked at Pio's small form curled up and drenched to the skin, his face drained of color, his lips a deep purple.

"Pio!" she cried, pulling him from the edge of the platform. She took him by the shoulders and shook him. "Pio!" she repeated, feeling alarmed when he didn't respond. She shook him again.

Pio's eyelids fluttered and opened. He looked at Tess but gave no sign of recognition. "Mama?"

"No, Pio. It's Tess."

Pio grabbed Tess and wrapped his arms around her neck. "Mama," he repeated, then began to whimper.

Tess cradled him in her arms, feeling his cold face against hers. "You poor little thing. You're freezing," she whispered, rubbing him briskly.

Looking down, she knew the frail ladder would never hold both of them; she'd have to wait for Zak. She lay Pio against the platform, took off her jacket and wrapped it around him. He reached for her and she held him close. "It's all right, Pio," she said, stroking his head. She could hear his soft sobbing and see his little body jerking pitifully. "It's okay, Pio. It's okay," she repeated.

She lifted Pio onto her lap. Feeling him shivering inside the jacket, she rubbed his back briskly as she rocked him. Gradually his sobs abated and she sensed he was drifting off.

When Zak arrived with a rope and ladder and looked up, a heaviness settled in his chest. High in the giant oak, Tess huddled with Pio on the rotted platform as the limbs beneath them yawned and creaked in the blustery wind. "Stay there until I get this rope up to you," he called, his voice shaky. He could see that Tess was no longer wearing her jacket and knew her flannel shirt must be soaked through.

"Hurry," Tess yelled, her teeth chattering. "Pio's so cold."

"All I could find was an eight-foot ladder," Zak said. "I hope it's tall enough to get the rope to you." He propped the ladder against the tree. "Is he okay?"

"Yes," Tess replied, "but he's sleeping."

"Sleeping!" Zak cried. "He's probably got hypothermia. Wake him up and keep his circulation going or he'll go into shock."

Tess shook Pio. "Come on, Pio. Wake up!" Pio opened his eyes momentarily, then they closed and his head slumped against Tess. "Pio!" she shouted. "Pio! Wake up!" Again he opened his eyes, then shut them again almost at once. Tess looked over the side. "I can't get him to stay awake. Throw the rope up here so I can make a harness and lower him." As she scooted to the edge of the platform and looked over, she realized how far down it was to Zak.

Zak stood at the top of the ladder and tossed the rope toward her. It caught on a limb, then slipped away and fell back down. He heaved it again. As it sailed toward the platform, Tess leaned over, holding on to Pio with one hand and reaching for the rope with the other. She felt the platform give and jerked her arm back. The rope dropped away, but when she looked down, she saw it had caught on the top rung of the tree ladder. Gripping the edge of the platform, she stretched toward the rope, grabbed it and pulled it up.

"I hope this works," she mumbled, tossing the end of the rope over a sturdy limb above her. Pio lay limp as she threaded the rope under his arms, around his waist and between his legs to make a harness, her fingers clumsy from the cold. She jerked on the knot that held the harness in place, then stood with one hand gripping the rope and the other holding a thick branch for balance.

"He's ready," she called to Zak. "I'm going to lower him. Take up the slack and loop your end of the rope around something down there." Her stomach lurched as she looked over the edge.

"I'm ready," Zak said, his anxious voice rising from below. "For God's sake, be careful."

The mossy rain-soaked boards creaked as Tess stepped cautiously to the edge in order to lower Pio. "Hold the rope tight. I'm going to ease him off the platform," she said. The rope burned her cold hands as she lowered Pio over the edge. When the rope tightened against the supporting limb, she shifted her weight.

The platform cracked.

"Zak!" she shrieked as the board gave way and a piece of the platform sailed to the ground. Frantically she reached back to regain her balance, grabbing a limb for support.

"To the right!" Zak shouted as he held the rope with Pio hanging in midair. "Move your foot to the right!"

Tess shifted her foot until it came to rest on the solid stub of a broken limb, then she braced herself. When Zak at last yelled, "I've got him!" she took a deep breath, relieved. She wasn't sure she had any strength left in her.

"Now we've got to get you down," said Zak.

"Don't worry about me," Tess replied. "Just untie Pio and I'll climb down the rope."

Zak released the harness from around Pio while Tess secured the rope to the heavy limb overhead. She entwined her legs with the rope, and backing off the edge of the platform, slowly began to lower herself. When her foot hit the ground, Zak bundled Pio's cold limp body into his arms. "Come on," he said. "Let's get him home."

They moved as quickly as they could manage toward the house. By the time they got there, the numbness Tess had felt on the platform had given way to a cold clammy sweat.

Vince met them in the vineyard, and Gratianne and Jean-Pierre were anxiously waiting at the entrance to the winery.

"How is he?" Gratianne asked unsteadily.

"Not good," Zak replied. "Call the doctor."

"I'll do it," Vince said, rushing ahead.

Zak carried the half-unconscious boy into the house and up the stairs to his room. He laid him on the bed, removed Tess's jacket from his chilled body and started to unbutton his shirt. Tess pushed Zak's hands away. "Here, let me do that," she said. "You get some towels—and throw some in the dryer to warm."

Zak hurried out of the room and moments later tossed some towels onto the bed and ran out again. As Tess stripped off Pio's shirt, he began to stir. "Mama," he wailed, opening his eyes and reaching out.

"It's okay, Pio," Tess said softly as she grabbed one of the towels Zak had brought. She rubbed the boy vigorously. "You're so cold."

Pio looked at her but his eyes didn't appear to focus. "Mama," he cried again, reaching for her.

Tess pulled him against her, then wrapped the comforter around him and held him, rocking him in her arms until Zak returned with the warm towels. Quickly they enfolded Pio in the towels, then wrapped him in the comforter again.

"What did the doctor say?" Tess asked as she held Pio.

Zak looked at his son's pallid face. "He's coming right over. He said we should keep him warm and give him something warm to drink as soon as he's conscious enough to take it."

"He still doesn't know what's going on," Tess said, looking down at Pio. "He just keeps calling for his mother."

"The doctor said not to be surprised if he's confused and has some loss of consciousness," Zak said, reaching out to stroke Pio's face. Pio stirred and began to whimper.

As Tess held him, she felt his helplessness, sensed his anguish as he called for a mother who would never come to him. Her eyes misted and she held him tighter. "It's all right," she kept repeating as he called out. "We're here."

The doctor arrived and verified that Pio was suffering from hypothermia. While he checked Pio, Tess stood with Zak and Vince at the foot of the bed, and

Jean-Pierre paced between the door and the window. Gratianne kept busy warming towels.

The doctor coiled his stethoscope and placed it in his bag. "He's lost so much body heat it may be a while before he fully regains consciousness."

"It just doesn't seem cold enough for him to have such a severe case of hypothermia," said Zak.

"The cold rain is the main factor," the doctor explained. "The lowering of skin temperature by even a few degrees can double the metabolic rate. All you can do now is keep him warm and give him lots of sweetened liquids—not too hot, though. He'll sleep a lot."

"Is that normal?" Tess asked.

"It is for what he went through," the doctor responded. "He had a lot going against him—his age, the wet clothing, the cold rain and the wind, and of course the emotional trauma."

"Emotional trauma?" Zak said.

The doctor looked up at Zak. "Didn't you say the boy had recently lost his mother?"

"Well, yes," Zak replied.

"That's half his battle," the doctor said. "Emotional strain is hard on the body, particularly when it's trying to recover from shock. Stay with him and keep reassuring him that he'll be fine."

"Should he be in the hospital?" Zak asked.

"No, that's not necessary. His color's coming back and his heartbeat's stable and strong. He'll be better once he warms up. The emotional recovery may not be as fast. Call me if there's any change for the worse," the doctor said, closing his bag.

Zak walked the doctor to the door, and Tess sat on the bed, staring at Pio. He seemed so small.

Gratianne stood beside her. "He looks so alone in that big bed," she said, verbalizing Tess's thoughts.

Tess tucked the cover under Pio's chin. As she did, Gratianne reached down and grabbed her wrist. "What have you done to your hand?" She turned Tess's palm up.

Tess looked first at one hand, then the other. Her palms were raw. "I guess I didn't notice," she said, surprised. "It must be rope burns. We were so busy with Pio—"

"We've got to put something on them," Gratianne said. "And you must get out of those wet clothes. I'll get a robe for you and throw your clothes in the dryer."

When Tess started to get up, Pio's head moved. "Mama?" he asked, reaching up.

"It's okay, sweetie," Tess said, reaching out to touch Pio's face. "We're here." Pio opened his eyes, looked at Tess for a moment, then closed them again and rested peacefully.

"I'll be back with a robe," Gratianne said. She smiled, then turned and left the room. As Tess sat with Pio, her eyes moved to a small picture frame on the bedside table. She lifted it and studied the photo. A young woman with a round face, kind eyes and a long braid over her shoulder stood with Pio, her hands resting on his shoulders. They were both smiling. There was nothing particularly striking about the woman, but it was evident that she loved her son.

"That was the last picture of them together," Zak said. The doctor had gone, and he'd been standing in the doorway, watching. He sat on the bed beside Tess.

"She was pretty," Tess replied, setting the picture back on the bedside stand, "and she looks very nice."

"She was a good woman," said Zak, "and a good mother. Pio loved her very much."

Tess brushed the hair from Pio's forehead, then rested her hand there. "He feels much warmer now," she whispered. When she glanced toward the door, she saw Jean-Pierre and Gratianne standing there but had no idea how long they'd been watching. She looked down at Pio. On his lips was the trace of a smile, although he was still asleep.

Gratianne draped a woolly robe on the foot of the bed and handed her a tube of ointment. "Go soak in a hot bath, then put this on your hands. Afterward, come to the kitchen and have some soup and hot spiced wine. Pio will probably sleep for a while now."

Tess tucked the comforter under Pio's chin. When she looked down at his peaceful face, she felt a strange bond with him, even though she was aware he'd been calling for another woman. "Thank you, Mrs. de Neuville."

"Please, it's Gratianne," she said, smiling.

Tess saw acceptance in Gratianne's eyes. "Gratianne," she repeated.

Scurrying to the bath, she peeled off the wet clothes, immersed herself in the soothing water and soaked until she felt warm again. She toweled herself dry and slipped on the robe. When she stepped out of the room, she met Zak in the hall. He put his hand on her arm and bent to kiss her on the lips. "I'd like to crawl into that robe with you," he said in a low sexy voice, his finger trailing down her neck and resting on the hollow of her throat.

"I'm afraid you'd find a very tired, very hungry woman inside," she murmured.

He smiled. "Mother's waiting for you in the kitchen. Go on in and eat." He kissed her again, then continued toward Pio's room.

In the kitchen, Gratianne poured Tess a mug of hot wine, then placed a bowl of steaming soup and two large slices of warm crusty bread in front of her. Tess glanced around. "Where is Mr. de Neuville?" she asked.

"Back in the winery," Gratianne replied. "I sometimes think that's his real love, not me."

Tess laughed and looked toward the dark window, surprised that it was so late. While she finished her supper, Gratianne left for the laundry room, assuring her that she'd have her clothes back to her shortly.

Tess returned to Pio's room and found Zak straightening the covers. "He's sleeping," he said. "He woke up and had something to drink while you were gone, and he asked where you were."

Tess stared at Zak. "He knew I'd been here?"

"He seemed to," Zak said.

Tess sat on the edge of the bed next to Zak. "Do you think he'll be ready to leave here tomorrow?" she asked.

"The doctor seemed to think he'll be back to normal by then," Zak replied. "But Mother wants to keep him here for the rest of the week, since I still have one more nest to climb." He gave her a sheepish grin. "But before we go, I'm planning a little talk with him, and he's going to learn what it means to be grounded."

"Grounded? What are you going to ground him from?"

"I guess climbing trees—unless you have some better ideas."

Tess grinned. "I think you and Pio are going to be just fine now."

Gratianne brought Tess her warm dry clothes and Tess slipped into the bathroom and dressed. When she returned to Pio's room, the lights were dimmed and Zak had dragged two chairs over beside the bed. "I just want to sit here for a little while—until he's sleeping soundly," he said. He held out his hand to her. "Will you stay, too?"

Tess squeezed his hand, curled in one of the chairs and watched Pio by the glow of a night-light. After a while her eyelids felt heavy. Zak's voice began to drift away, then return. She blinked and rested her head back....

Some time later—minutes? hours?—Tess thought she heard a voice saying her name. "Tess?" came a small voice again. She opened her eyes and found Pio looking at her. *"Ez utzi."*

"He says, 'Don't leave me.'" The words were from Zak, but his voice seemed distant.

Tess closed her eyes again, not certain if she was dreaming and not caring. All she felt now was a need to rest.

CHAPTER TWELVE

TESS AWOKE to a rapping noise. Disoriented, she looked around at the unfamiliar room. Eerie gray light filtered through opaque curtains, drawn against a dismal overcast sky. As she lay beneath a puffy quilt listening for the sound again, she heard only the hoarse sigh of the wind rustling through the trees. The last thing she remembered was seeing Pio and hearing Zak's voice—or had that been a dream? She had obviously fallen asleep in her clothes, but she had no idea how, or when, she'd gotten to this room.

The rapping came again. She blinked and looked toward the door. "Tess? It's Gratianne. May I come in?"

Tess smoothed her hair and raised herself to a sitting position against the pillow. "Yes," she said, hoping her hair wasn't too disheveled.

Gratianne peeked around the door and smiled. "You had a very long night."

Tess ran her hand over her hair again. "Does it show?"

Gratianne laughed. "Only on Zak's worried face. He's concerned about you."

"Where is he?"

"With Pio and the doctor." Gratianne sat on the edge of the bed, her body angled toward Tess. "Zak insisted the doctor come by and take another look at Pio, but I think Pio would rather see you."

Tess tilted her head and looked at Gratianne. "Me?"

Gratianne smiled. "Does that surprise you?"

"Yes, very much," Tess answered, a smile playing about her lips. "He's not his father's son when it comes to me, I'm afraid. I guess Zak told you."

Gratianne's quiet blue eyes rested on Tess. "Zak said there had been problems, but what I saw last night didn't give that impression. I saw a woman reach out and a boy accept and return her love." Her eyes brightened. "You've filled a void for Pio."

Gratianne's words made Tess feel warm. "If I have," Tess said, "I'm grateful."

"Well, you have," Gratianne reaffirmed. Then the brightness in her eyes faded. "Now, Jean-Pierre wants to see you. Do you mind?"

Tess looked toward the door. The thought of facing Jean-Pierre de Neuville this particular morning made her heart race. His words the previous day still chafed. She plucked at the quilt. "No, I suppose not."

Gratianne went to the door and poked her head out. "Jean-Pierre," she called down the hall. She moved to sit on the bed once again.

Jean-Pierre entered the room, his expression stoic, and when he spoke, Tess felt tension crackle in the air. "Miss O'Reilly," he said, "I want to thank you for rescuing my grandson."

Tess looked directly at him. "I only did what anyone would have done."

"No," he said, softening somewhat, "that's not true. You did what only someone who cared would do."

Tess saw the sincerity in his eyes. "Zak's son is very special," she said, "and I care about Zak."

"I can see that now." Jean-Pierre moved to gaze out the window, his form a dark silhouette against the mournful gray sky. "I can also see that Zak cares a great deal about you." He turned halfway around, the light from the window illuminating his white hair and accentuating his strong features. "But you must understand," he said, "my son and grandson are also Basque."

Tess moistened her dry lips with a nervous flick of her tongue. "Your son and grandson are American, Mr. de Neuville," she stated.

Jean-Pierre's eyes narrowed as he faced her. "But in their veins runs Basque blood. And if Basque blood continues to be mixed, our ancient race will die."

Gratianne shifted on the bed and faced her husband. "It's inevitable that all civilizations be assimilated," she said in a firm voice.

Jean-Pierre looked at Gratianne and raised his chin. "And when the Basque are assimilated, the most ancient of European languages will be forgotten."

Gratianne's eyes flared, then fixed on his. "We preserve what we can, Jean-Pierre, but we can't force the next generation to follow."

"But we don't have to accept what they're doing." Jean-Pierre's gaze sharpened. "The only reason the Basque have survived is because they've ignored their invaders." His eyes rested on Tess.

Zak appeared in the doorway. "It's also the reason they've learned so little," he said. "It was you, Father, who said that the best sheepdogs we have—the quickest to learn—are Alta and Reb, both crossbreeds. Cultures also learn from their invaders." He bent to kiss Tess. "How are you feeling, sweetheart?"

Tess smiled up at him. "Like I wouldn't care to take a hike in the rain. How's Pio doing?"

"See for yourself," Zak said. "Pio!"

Pio appeared in the doorway but said nothing. He moved to Zak's side and stared at Tess much as he had the first time she met him, but his eyes were no longer resentful. She extended her hand. Pio looked up at Zak, and when Zak nudged him he scurried over to the bed and took Tess's hand. "Come on up," she said, patting the bed.

Pio smiled a wide bright smile and crawled up beside her. She wrapped her arm around him and pulled him to her, and Pio's smile spread into a wide grin. "You gave us quite a scare, young man," she said.

Pio looked up at her and patted her cheek. *"Zuk laminak,"* he teased.

"Oh, no," Tess replied. "I'm not going to be one of your little people who cleans the house." She smiled, remembering the Basque story Zak had told her about the *laminaks*—little people who live in caves in the mountains and come into the house during the night, when the family is sleeping, to polish the copper and brass and sweep the floors.

Zak laughed. "He doesn't want you to clean the house. He wants you to be his own *laminak*. He's a regular chip off the old block. I do believe he has a crush on you."

Tess looked at Pio's smiling face and saw flickers of mischief in his bright eyes. "Maybe I'll just wait for him to grow up, instead," she said, rumpling his hair.

"Oh, no, you won't," Zak replied. "I've waited long enough already."

Without speaking, Jean-Pierre left the room. Tess glanced toward the door. "Whatever it is you're waiting for," she said, "it won't be with your father's blessing."

"We'll see," Zak said, undaunted. "Meanwhile, he's waiting to give Pio a chess lesson, and I'm starving, so I'll meet you in the kitchen for breakfast." He motioned for Pio to follow. Tess was left alone with Gratianne.

Tess slipped from under the quilt and started to fold it. Gratianne reached for one corner. "It was much different for me," she said as they lapped the quilt over. "When I married Jean-Pierre I was only sixteen and it was our parents' choice, but I've never regretted it. We lived here with Jean-Pierre's mother and father, working alongside them to make it our home, knowing the place would eventually be ours. And someday it will belong to Zak and his family."

Tess looked across the bed at Gratianne, wondering if the feelings she'd expressed the day before—that only a Basque woman could understand Pio—still held. Her lips darted into a brief smile. "What about Vince?" she asked. "Don't you think he might eventually want to live here?"

"Even if he did," Gratianne replied, "it's not his choice. Zak has birthright."

Tess looked away, her eyes flickering with impatience. "So I heard," she said. "If he marries a Basque woman."

Gratianne looked at her. "Times are changing for us, and even Jean-Pierre has to face the inevitable. He likes you. He just needs time."

"And how do you feel?" Tess asked pointedly.

Gratianne shrugged. "Zak's my son. What I want most for him is his happiness. If the two of you decide to spend your lives together, what can I say but—" she raised her eyes to meet Tess's and smiled "—welcome to our family." Then she added, "And I also know Jean-Pierre. He will eventually welcome you, too."

Tess looked into Gratianne's eyes, thankful for her reassurance but realizing Jean-Pierre's acceptance of her could still be a long way off. "Zak and I aren't even discussing marriage," she said, draping the quilt across the foot of the bed. "There are too many obstacles right now."

"Obstacles between the two of you?" Gratianne asked, surprised.

Tess smoothed the quilt, feeling at ease with Zak's mother. "No, not really between us," she replied. "More like . . . surrounding us."

"Fathers?"

"Fathers . . . logging camps . . . property disputes. I've often felt that Zak and I are just not meant to have a life together."

Gratianne sat on the bed and motioned for Tess to sit beside her. Gratianne hesitated. "I want to tell you something I've never told anyone," she said at last.

"Don't tell me anything you might regr—"

Gratianne raised a hand to hush her. "It's not a deep dark secret, just something I thought you should hear," she said. "When I was fifteen my father told me I would be marrying Jean-Pierre de Neuville as soon as I turned sixteen. I was outraged. At the time I thought I was in love with a boy who lived down the road from me—we'd even planned to marry some-day. But suddenly that choice was taken away. I felt like everyone was running my life, that I had no con-trol of my own destiny. I even thought about running away."

Tess considered what Gratianne had said, then ventured, "How old was Mr. de Neuville when you married?"

Gratianne held her gaze. "Twenty-five."

Tess's fingers nervously toyed with the corner of the quilt folded beside her. She turned to Gratianne, her eyes probing. "What would the families have done if Mr. de Neuville had chosen to marry a woman who wasn't Basque?"

Gratianne shifted restlessly on the bed. "I suppose they would have sent him away, but fortunately Jean-Pierre didn't object."

Tess looked at her curiously. "I thought you didn't want to marry him."

Gratianne smiled. "I didn't at first," she said. "But when I saw him, well, things changed."

"How long did it take you to fall in love with him?"

Gratianne's eyes grew brilliant. "About two minutes. He was a few years older and he'd been away in France learning to be a vintner, so I'd never met him—or at least, didn't remember him. But from the first time I set eyes on him I couldn't get him out of my mind. He was very handsome, much like Zak. And after we'd married, as our relationship began to grow and he returned my love, I began to wonder, what if Jean-Pierre had been the one I'd loved before and I was forced to give him up for someone else?"

Tess looked at her intently. "What would you have done then?" she asked.

Gratianne met her direct gaze. "I would have run away with Jean-Pierre if that's the only way I could have had him." Her blue eyes flashed. "Fortunately, I didn't have to make that choice—and no one ever tried to separate us." She paused for a moment, then asked, "Do you love Zak?"

Tess looked at Gratianne with a start, shaken by her question. "Yes," she admitted, "I do."

Gratianne stood up and shoved back the curtains, allowing light from the overcast day to brighten the room. "Then don't let a couple of mulish dogmatic men come between you." She smiled warmly at Tess. "Now, come join Zak in the kitchen for breakfast."

When Gratianne left the room, Tess reached for her small overnight bag, which she found beside her bed, and went into the adjoining bathroom. After brushing her hair, she pulled it back and gathered it with a leather thong, then she applied a light coat of lipstick. Still feeling the warmth of Gratianne's words she left the bedroom to join Zak.

Zak noticed the light in Tess's eyes as soon as she entered the kitchen. As he seated her, he leaned over, his lips close to her ear. "You look beautiful, and very happy," he whispered, wondering what had passed between Tess and his mother—who'd looked like the Cheshire cat when she'd come to the kitchen a few minutes earlier. "I'm sorry about what happened... what Father said. But I suspect Mother made things right."

Tess glanced at Gratianne, who hummed softly as she poured eggs from a ceramic bowl onto a griddle. "Your mother is very perceptive," she said, listening to the eggs sizzle in melted butter.

Zak arched a brow. "Most women are, which is why we men have to toe the line."

Tess nudged him and looked over at Gratianne. "Is there anything I can do to help?"

"No," said Gratianne. "We're just having *piperade*. I hope you like omelets."

Tess grinned. "If it's what I saw on Marie's griddle yesterday, I know I'll like it." She looked around, then asked Zak, "Where's Pio?"

"Setting up the chessboard," Zak replied. "Father takes his chess seriously. He even beat Erik Szabo, the Hungarian grand master, in an exhibition tournament several years ago. He has hopes that Pio will someday offer him a challenge."

Gratianne slid wedges of spicy omelet onto two dishes and set them in front of Tess and Zak, then she placed a platter of toast on the table. "I ate earlier with Jean-Pierre," she said. "If you two will excuse me, I have to feed my baby." She lifted a bottle of milk capped with a large rubber nipple from a pot of warm water on the stove and left the room.

Zak stole the moment to pull Tess onto his lap and kiss her soundly.

Gratianne's voice startled them. "Oh, I almost forgot..."

Zak opened his eyes and drew his lips from Tess's, but continued to hold her when she tried to pull away. "Yes?" he said, catching his mother's wink.

"Vince said to tell you both goodbye. He mentioned something about stopping by the Palombiere before going to work. I still can't figure out what the attraction is there. I thought all he ate was hamburgers."

Zak grinned at Tess. "He may have reacquired his taste for *piperade*."

"Mmm," said Gratianne, unconvinced. She disappeared into the shadows of the hallway again, leaving Zak to continue where he'd left off.

After Zak and Tess finished breakfast, they wandered into the large living room where Jean-Pierre and

Pio were sitting opposite each other at the chess table, the game already under way. Pio squirmed restlessly in his chair, turning to catch Zak's smile.

Jean-Pierre looked at the boy sharply. "Pio, pay attention."

Pio quickly moved his king's knight, his eyes resting on the chessboard momentarily, then shifting to the window where bright sun now peeked through the clouds.

Jean-Pierre moved his bishop. "You must keep your mind on the game," he said. "See what I've done? By placing my king's bishop in this position, I'm able to pin your knight."

Pio's feet moved up and down under the table, and his eyes darted to the window, then to Zak. Zak winked at his son. "Father, I don't think your pupil is with you this morning. It seems our Oregon weather has let you down."

Jean-Pierre looked toward the window, where a blaze of light illuminated the polished wood floor and the buff wool rug. He smiled across the table at Pio. "All right, son, go on."

Pio scampered away before his grandfather could change his mind. Jean-Pierre looked up at Tess as he set up the board again. "You say you play?"

Tess shrugged. "A little."

Jean-Pierre arranged the board, positioning the black pieces in front of himself. "Feel like sitting down and showing me what you can do?"

Tess smiled politely. "I'm afraid I wouldn't be any match for you."

"How can you tell unless you try?"

Zak nudged Tess and smiled, urging her to play. Tess reluctantly slipped into the straight-back chair while Zak pulled another chair up to the side of the board. "I must warn you, Father, this woman is full of surprises."

A hint of a smile played about Jean-Pierre's lips.

Tess opened by sliding the king's pawn forward, and Jean-Pierre responded in kind. Then, as if each had been energized by some unseen force, they took turns in a series of seven quickly executed moves, each of them slapping their pieces smartly on the board. Tess paused momentarily, then moved again.

Jean-Pierre sat motionless, studying the board intently. Then he looked up at Tess, and when their eyes met she saw the mask of aloofness fall away, replaced, she thought, by respect. "You know the opening well," he said.

"The Ruy Lopez is my father's favorite," she replied. "We've played it a lot."

"That's evident," said Jean-Pierre.

Zak watched Tess with a pleased expression. It appeared that she could at least make the old master cringe a little.

After several more deliberate moves, Jean-Pierre captured a king's pawn, sacrificing a knight in the process. He sat upright without moving his eyes from the board, a complacent look on his face. "This is the Breslau Variation of the open defense," he said. "I'm afraid it gives me a rather strong attack."

"Mmm," Tess said absently, staring at the board.

An hour later, after a long series of studied moves, Tess reached for her king, gently lay the piece on its side and resigned. She knew it was only a matter of time and careful execution before Jean-Pierre would win.

Jean-Pierre looked up. "That's the best game I've played in a long time. You say your father taught you?" he asked, pulling out the small drawer in the chess table and putting the pieces inside.

"Yes," Tess replied, placing her pieces in the felt-lined drawer in front of her. "We played often when I was growing up."

Jean-Pierre studied her for a moment, then asked, "Is he a rated player?"

"He was, years ago," Tess said, "but I don't think he's played in any tournaments lately, so I have no idea what his rating would be now."

Jean-Pierre sat back in his chair, one finger lightly tapping the table. Zak glanced at his father and saw the dark look of challenge on his face. The man wouldn't dare be thinking what Zak suspected he was thinking. He wouldn't take on Gib O'Reilly in chess, would he? The idea made Zak feel extremely uncomfortable. They'd kill each other before the first play. Zak got to his feet. "I think we'd better be getting back to Bakers Creek, Father," he said. "I still have some work to complete at the park—"

"Over fifteen hundred?" Jean-Pierre asked, his eyes fixed on Tess.

Tess looked up.

"Your father's rating. Was it over fifteen hundred?" Jean-Pierre repeated.

"Oh, yes," Tess said. "I'm sure it was much higher than that, but I can't remember what it was." She turned to Zak, then shoved her chair back and stood. "I enjoyed the game, Mr. de Neuville."

Jean-Pierre rose slowly. "We'll...have to do it again sometime," he said tentatively.

Zak looked at his father. Jean-Pierre de Neuville, he realized, was not a man who could admit too quickly that he'd been wrong about something—or someone. His admission would have to come with time. But in his eyes, Zak saw a new respect for Tess.

Zak extended his hand toward his father. "Thanks for everything, Father. I'll be back for Pio on Friday. Don't let him pull anything else like he did yesterday," he said.

Jean-Pierre clasped Zak's hand. "He's just a curious growing boy," he said. "He has to try his wings."

Zak's eyes flashed. "But I distinctly told him not to climb to the tree house."

"A young boy forgets easily."

"Then he should be disciplined," Zak insisted. "Besides, if we don't insist he stay within the bounds we set for him, he won't believe anyone cares about him." Zak took Tess's arm and they left to find his mother and Pio and tell them goodbye.

LATE THE NEXT AFTERNOON, Tess pulled up in front of Gib's house and waved to Mr. Wadley, who was washing his car. "Are you and Mrs. Wadley going anywhere today?" she called across the quiet street.

"Nope," Mr. Wadley replied. "We make it a point to stay home on Memorial Day—we don't want to end up as statistics. How about you? You and your folks going anywhere?"

Tess smiled. "Not if I can help it," she said. She bounded up the stairs to the porch, and when she stepped into the living room, the aroma of ham baking in the oven tickled her nostrils. "Aunt Ruth! Gib!"

"In the bedroom, sweetie," Aunt Ruth called back.

Tess giggled when she caught sight of Gib sitting on the floor with pins between his lips, turning up the hem of the dress Aunt Ruth was making. "We'll be with you in a minute," Aunt Ruth said from her perch on a low stool.

Tess caught Aunt Ruth's glare and forced her face to sober.

"Don't you say a damn word," Gib said out of the corner of his mouth while continuing to hold the pins between pressed lips.

Tess looked down at her father, then winked at Aunt Ruth. "I'd offer to help, but it looks like you've already got him trained. I'll be in the kitchen setting the table." She turned toward the hall, laughing lightly.

"Tess," Aunt Ruth called after her. "Your catalog came—the one from the university. It's out there on the buffet."

Tess scanned the catalog eagerly. She wasn't sure how college fit into her future now that Zak was so much a part of it, but she could still think about it. As she looked over the various business courses, Aunt Ruth called to her again. "Honey, would you please check the ham and baste the yams with some of the syrup on the counter?"

"Consider it done." Tess closed the catalog and went into the kitchen. She peeked in the oven and saw a glazed ham, trimmed with pineapple and maraschino cherries, on one rack, and a bubbling casserole of candied yams on the rack below. She reached for the yams and placed them on the counter, then spooned on more syrup before returning them to the oven. In a steamer on top of the stove she found fresh asparagus. Replacing the lid, she turned to set the table.

A few minutes later Gib wandered into the room, followed shortly by Aunt Ruth, who immediately scurried about dishing up the food and putting it on the table. They took their places eagerly. Gib carved the ham and passed the platter of sliced meat around the table.

As Aunt Ruth placed a thick slice on her plate, she commented, "I sure don't like Tess being out there alone with those men—especially with all that's been going on. Really, Gib, it's not a job for a young woman. It's beyond me why you don't just sell the company and be done with it." She cut her ham in short quick strokes. "Carl Yaeger's offer might not be what you want, but it is an offer."

Tess looked at Aunt Ruth. "Carl Yaeger made an offer? A real offer on paper?"

Aunt Ruth glanced at Tess. "Yes."

"Gib, why didn't you say anything?" Tess asked.

"Because I haven't made up my mind one way or another yet," he replied.

Tess speared a slice of ham. "But you *are* thinking about it," she said. "You could at least fill me in, you know."

Gib glared at Aunt Ruth, then shifted impatient eyes to Tess. "When and if I decide to sell," he said in a firm voice, "you'll be the first to know. I don't want pressure from either of you to sell before I'm ready. And I'm not ready to throw in the towel yet."

Aunt Ruth raised her chin. "You won't be ready to sell until you drop in your tracks out there," she said. "Meanwhile, your daughter's working with men like that Jed Swenson when she should be thinking about a home and family."

Tess gave Aunt Ruth a warning glance.

Aunt Ruth looked at Gib long and hard, then smiled at Tess and tried to change the subject. "What did you do yesterday, sweetie?" she said.

Tess felt the blood suddenly rush from her face.

"Honey, are you all right," Aunt Ruth asked in alarm.

Tess dabbed her mouth nervously with her napkin. "I'm fine," she said. "Just a little tired from the job."

"That's exactly what I'm talking about, Gib." Aunt Ruth's voice grew shrill. "She's doing work that should be done by a man twice her size and—"

"Aunt Ruth," Tess interrupted, "I'm not tired from the job. I was in Navarre—with Zak and his family."

No one spoke. All that could be heard was the sound of utensils clinking against china.

Tess looked at Aunt Ruth, whose face had paled, then at Gib, who continued eating as if nothing had been said. After a few minutes Gib looked up. His eyes focused on Aunt Ruth. "This is one hell of a meal!" he said, raising a slice of succulent ham to his lips.

Tess glanced from Gib to Aunt Ruth, catching the older woman's startled look before seeing her face break into a wreath of happy crinkles. Tess covered her mouth with a napkin and burst out laughing. Gib looked from one to the other. "What the devil's wrong with you two women?"

Tess got to her feet and walked over to her father. She bent over and kissed him soundly on the cheek. "You," she replied. Then she whispered in his ear, "I love you, Dad."

He flushed. "How about passing the yams?"

"Sure." Tess winked at Aunt Ruth, served herself, then passed the bowl to her father.

Gib spooned some yams onto his dish and passed the bowl on to Aunt Ruth. "Northwest Tire called. Looks like the skidder tire's been shot with a high-powered rifle," he said. "They were able to fix it, though. The shot didn't damage the sidewall."

Tess speared asparagus from the platter and placed them on her plate. "I'll call the police when I get back to camp," she said. "No doubt they'll want to talk to me. I just hope they nail Swenson."

"What makes you so sure he's the one doing everything?" Aunt Ruth asked. "They seem like pretty drastic steps to take just because a person's mad."

"I'm sure he's behind it all," Tess insisted. "I don't think it's coincidental that everything started happening right after I fired him—especially since we already know he has a hot temper. I hope he also has a big savings account, because he'll need it to pay for everything. Pass the butter please, Gib."

Gib reached for the butter. "I tend to agree with you, since I can't think of anyone else with a motive," he said. "Better tell Zak to keep an eye on him."

Tess smiled inwardly at Gib's casual reference to Zak. Had he, after all these years, finally accepted him? She split open a roll and slipped a pat of butter inside. "How about a game of chess after dinner, Gib?"

Her father smiled, sparks of challenge in his eyes. "Kiddo, you're on."

Three hours later Tess conceded the game to Gib. "You'll get your comeuppance next time," she said, grinning. "It's all starting to come back now."

Gib sat back in his chair and studied Tess. After a few moments he said in a solemn voice, "Just don't stay away too long, baby, okay?"

Tess smiled into her father's anxious eyes. "Don't worry. I'm through running away."

After a few minutes she thanked Aunt Ruth for dinner, hugged Gib and left. She'd had a wonderful afternoon, but she was eager to tell Zak that Gib had come to terms with their relationship. She wasn't sure where things would go from there, but at least one monumental obstacle was out of the way.

When she arrived at Zak's, she found no one home. Disappointed, she returned to her cabin. Restlessly she paced the floor, shoving idle fingers through her hair. She checked his place again around ten, but he still hadn't returned. She gave up the idea of seeing him until after work the following day.

Logging operations resumed after the Memorial Day weekend, and Tuesday passed without incident. Ezzie showed up as promised, a smile on his face, sparks dancing in his eyes. And it was obvious to everyone he was in love.

After work Tess stopped by Zak's cabin, but he still hadn't returned. She checked again later but found the cabin dark. She couldn't imagine where he'd been for the past two days, but assumed it had something to do with the nest climbs and the wildlife park. Feeling depressed, she returned to her cabin, soaked in a hot bath and slipped into her robe.

Her arms wrapped around her to hold her robe closed, she glanced out the window, toying with the idea of dressing and stopping by Zak's cabin once more before going to bed. As she stood there, lights from a car turning onto the dirt road flashed against the window. She backed away, but then recognized the sound of Zak's truck. She dashed to the door and pulled it open just as Zak bounded onto the porch.

He caught Tess in his arms, kissing her long and hard. Still holding her he kicked the door shut. "God, you feel good in my arms," he said, inhaling the fragrance of pine-scented soap and spicy shampoo, feeling the warmth of her radiating against him. He needed her love desperately. He wanted to strip the robe from her eager body and make wild passionate love to her, but his urgency was tempered by thoughts of what he must tell her—what he'd learned on the ridge.

CHAPTER THIRTEEN

TESS CURLED HER FINGERS in Zak's hair and looked up at him, consumed with curiosity. "Where have you been for the past two days?" she asked, her fingers making tiny little patterns on his neck.

Zak stroked her sides, his thumbs tracing the swell of her breasts pressed against him. He moved his hands down, along her back, over the curve of her spine. "I was up on the ridge—" he kissed her on the forehead, the tip of her nose, her lips "—and in Bakers Creek." His hands moved lower to cup her buttocks, pulling her against him.

Tess reached around to grasp Zak's hand, and she pulled him over to sit on the sofa. "Why on the ridge? And what's going on in Bakers Creek?" she asked, determined to get some answers.

Zak settled into the cushions, then inhaled deeply to steady his breathing. "After I dropped you off on Sunday," he said, "I was hiking around near the north end of the property, looking for perch trees—and Jed Swenson showed up."

Tess's eyes narrowed with suspicion. "What was he doing there?"

"He brought in a backhoe to divert the water from Saturday's rain before the road washed out again,"

Zak replied. "He's getting ready to put in the culvert."

Tess bit her bottom lip. "I'd like to know what he was doing up there when he *wasn't* diverting the water," she said. "No doubt I'll find out in the next few days."

Zak's mouth tipped up at one corner. "Maybe, maybe not. Anyway, I decided it would be a good time to ask a few questions—in a conversational sort of way."

"Sounds like a stimulating afternoon," Tess said with a wry grin. "Sorry I wasn't along."

Zak smiled. "Just wait. It may be more stimulating than you think. Anyway, while I was talking with him—I was fishing for information on his background, specifically if he'd had any military experience or knew anything about explosives—I found out he'd been in the marines."

"Considering his hang-up about taking orders, I find that surprising," Tess said.

"I doubt his company commander was a woman. Anyway, he was very reluctant to talk about it, but he did mention that he'd been discharged early, then he changed the subject. I got suspicious—thought maybe he'd been given a dishonorable discharge—so I did some checking in Bakers Creek."

Tess raised a hand. "Wait, let me guess," she said. "You found out he was discharged for accidentally blowing up the barracks while tossing a grenade to a friend."

Zak smiled. "Not quite, but I managed to pry out of him that he'd been released in July, 1970 and that he'd come back to Bakers Creek as soon as he was released. So I checked through the *Bakers Creek Gazette* about that time and I found this." Zak slipped a paper from his shirt pocket and unfolded it. "I think you might find it interesting," he said, straightening the paper.

Tess leaned toward Zak and followed along as he read:

"On the morning of April 2, 1970, while serving as Platoon Sergeant of Company G, Second Battalion, Fifth Marine Division, Sergeant Jedidiah Swenson was severely wounded while evacuating a fallen comrade when the unit came under heavy automatic-weapons fire from enemy forces. Despite his wounds, Sergeant Swenson ran across a fire-swept range, completely exposed to view, and delivered a hail of machine-gun fire against the enemy. Fighting pain, weakness and loss of blood, he braved the concentrated fire and charged an estimated twenty-five enemy soldiers advancing to attack, continuing to fire until the enemy ran for cover. For courageous and inspired performance in the face of overwhelming odds, Sergeant Jedidiah Swenson has been awarded the Congressional Medal of Honor...."

"Let me see this," Tess said, taking the paper from Zak's hand. She reread the citation, unable to believe her eyes. But the words were there. She scanned the article again. "I can't believe this!" she said. "Swenson actually received a Congressional Medal of Honor?"

"And, of course, a Purple Heart for his wounds. But that's not all. After I got the information from Swenson about his being in the marines, I asked him what the problem had been at Timber West and he just said he wouldn't work for a woman, so I prodded some more. Now get this." Zak couldn't repress a grin. "Apparently Swenson was raised by six women—his mother, grandmother and four older sisters. I think he's just had his fill of women telling him what to do. I also think you'd better take another look at Curt Broderick. Swenson has stuck to his story that Curt cut the tree, and I, for one, believe him."

"But that doesn't make any sense at all," Tess said. "What would Curt have to gain by doing all those things? He's already woods boss, so he can't go any higher."

"I asked Swenson that, too."

"And?"

Zak shrugged. "He said he didn't know either. All he knew was what he'd seen—Broderick cutting the tree."

"Well, I'm not saying Swenson's off the hook yet." Tess's eyes moved back to the paper in her hand. "But I will keep an eye on Curt—at least see where he goes during his spare time, find out who he hangs around with."

"You might ask him if he was in the service, and if so, what he did. Maybe he's our explosives expert. The job on the ridge road was done by someone who knew explosives."

"That's what Herring said," Tess replied. "Now that I think about it, Curt really didn't have much to say about the whole thing. He just sort of avoided the issue. But still, there's no reason for him to do all those things—blowing up the road, cutting the tree, shooting out the skidder tire. And incidentally, the tire *was* shot."

"Considering everything else that's happened," Zak said, "that doesn't surprise me." He curved his arm behind Tess and rested his hand on her hip. "You know, Swenson's really not a bad guy. He's a hell of a worker. If you need a new woods boss, you might give him another chance."

Tess snuggled against Zak. "He doesn't work for women, remember?" she reminded him, enjoying the little patterns Zak's finger made on her hip—patterns that seemed to draw the gown up and the robe open, exposing her thigh.

"Mmm." Zak's eyes shifted to the satiny skin he was exposing. He rested his hand on Tess's bare thigh, desperately wanting to feel her naked body pressed against his, but apprehensive because he hadn't told her about what he'd found on the ridge....

"I'm glad you're here," Tess whispered, enjoying the sensations Zak's hand was creating and the tingles caused by his teasing fingers.

"So am I." Zak's lips came down on hers, snatching her breath away. His tongue slowly filled her mouth, searching, tasting, thrusting deeply and intimately.

When at last they parted for air, Tess was the first to speak. "I have some good news," she said. "At least I think you'll like it."

Zak looked at her with curiosity. "What?"

"Gib's not objecting to us—you and me," Tess said. She explained Gib's reaction to her announcement about being in Navarre.

Zak smiled. "Well, that's one bullheaded old cuss out of the way. Now, we only have one to go—and I think you've just about got him wrapped around your little chess finger."

"Do you really think so?" Tess asked, eager to hear more. "Did your mother say something?"

"No, she didn't have to. Anyone who'll be Father's chess buddy is *in*," Zak said. "So I guess our only problem now is keeping the two old goats from butting heads."

Tess sighed. "I don't think that's possible. Gib never has a good word to say about your father, and I'm sure it's the same for your father."

"You're right," Zak said, wondering if the two men could ever come to terms with being in-laws. If they didn't, they'd eventually become an effective wedge between him and Tess. It had happened more than once—the fathers clashed and he and Tess became defensive, forced into taking sides. But now he had to consider Pio. The boy had been torn between them all,

and he didn't want him to end up in the middle of a
feud, as well. He'd had enough unhappiness for one
little person.

Zak bent over and kissed Tess lightly. "I hate to
break this up, honey, but I have to leave for Portland
early in the morning to deliver the chicks to the air-
port, and I need to discuss something with you before
I go."

Tess looked up at him. "You act so serious."

"I'm afraid this *is* kind of serious," he said, "and
I wish I could put it off, but I can't."

Tess noted a muscle in Zak's jaw tense. The subject
was serious. She saw it in his eyes, the furrows in his
forehead and the lines about his mouth. She reached
out to smooth away his tension. "You're okay?" she
asked, feeling a moment of panic at the thought of
something happening to him. "Pio? Your job? What
is it?"

Zak looked into her apprehensive eyes, aware that
she felt no concern for herself, only for him. Could he
sacrifice his integrity? Compromise his values? He
drew a long breath...

"Zak?" Tess's voice broke into his thoughts. "Tell
me. If there's something wrong, I need to know."

Zak ran nervous fingers through his hair. "You have
to stop logging near the ridge," he stated. "You're
working in the primary zone of a perch tree."

Tess stared at him in disbelief. "You can't be serious," she said. "A perch tree? No chicks—just an
empty nest?"

"It's also an alternate nest tree."

"But you told me perch trees were nests that have been abandoned for years. Besides, we never planned to cut that particular tree, only the pole timber."

"It still could disturb the birds."

"How can you do this, Zak? We're trying to get our lives together. Gib's finally accepting you...." She pushed her hair away from her face in agitation. "Do you have any idea what this will do?"

"I'm sorry about that," he said, aware of her rising anger, "but I can't let your father run my life—or dictate how I do my job."

"Fine." Tess jumped to her feet and paced the floor, her steps short and rapid. "But you'd better understand one thing," she said, her fingers drumming against her folded arms. "If Gib wants to keep cutting, we'll keep cutting, and the only way you'll stop us is to have me arrested—unless, of course, you want to arrest a sick old man." She looked directly at him. "And I thought I was naive at sixteen."

Zak's eyes narrowed. "Don't put me in this position," he warned. "No one needs to be arrested."

"Then don't shut down Timber West," Tess pleaded.

Zak drew in an exasperated breath. "I'm not shutting down Timber West. I'm only asking you to stop logging within six hundred feet of the perch tree."

"That's more than twenty acres!" Tess said, flailing a hand in the air.

Zak saw the heightened color in her face and the quiet rage in her eyes. He felt backed into a corner.

"You have other timber, and other areas where you can log."

"The pole timber happens to be what's keeping us going right now," Tess said in a strained voice. "We've just wiped out the last of our working capital in order to make our quarterly tax payment, and in ten days we have a loan payment due. And that's just for starters. We owe money for skidder tires, busted equipment and wages—which might possibly be paid if we harvest pole timber." She paused to settle her erratic breathing.

"I know you're struggling financially, and I'm very sorry about it, really I am," Zak said, "but you'll still have to stop logging near the tree."

"I'll do whatever Gib decides."

Zak glared at her. "Then you might end up in jail," he said. "Your father's as ornery as hell. You know what he'll decide."

"Yes, I know what he'll decide. So I suggest you stay clear of Gib after today. You won't be very popular with him—again."

Zak held her unwavering gaze for a long silent moment. When she offered nothing more, he waved a dismissive hand and said, "All right, have it your way, but it's out of my hands now—the report's already gone in." He turned and threw the door open, sending it crashing against the wall, and stormed out. Tires spun, spitting mud as the truck lurched forward and sped off into the darkness.

Tess slammed the door and stared at it, her heart racing, blood rushing to her face. Zak's crusade was very noble, but he was carrying things too far. She refused to stop logging because of an empty nest! Certainly Zak wouldn't have her arrested and sent to jail, would he?

THE NEXT DAY, Tess stood on a rise at the edge of the forest, looking across the clearing to where logs were being stacked on the landing. In the distance she heard the buzz of chain saws cutting trees and the whine of the skidder hauling logs. Beneath her feet the ground vibrated with the rumble of the bulldozer. She was so weary that the noise from the machines grated on her nerves.

Zak's parting words hung heavy on her mind. If they were forced to abandon logging the pole timber, she could only speculate about Gib's reaction when he learned Zak was behind it. Meanwhile, the more timber she could get down, the less she'd hear from Gib, when and if that time came.

She watched Curt lower the blade of the Cat, shoving limbs onto a burning pile. During her wakeful night, she'd pondered Curt's reactions to the various incidents, wondering now if he actually was the one behind it all in spite of the fact that there seemed to be no logical reason for him to sabotage his own job. She'd also gone over in her mind what she'd say to him today, how she'd draw him out. But in the clear light of day, as she watched Curt operating the bulldozer, she questioned her reasoning. She wanted to point a finger at someone, and before last night that person had been Swenson. Now, she realized, it was time to

start asking new questions—beginning with Curt
Broderick.

While she waited for Curt to finish moving brush,
she saw Gib's truck lurch up the rough road. When he
pulled into the clearing, she noted that he was wearing his hard hat and work boots. She wasn't anxious
to broach the subject of the perch tree, but she did
want to tell him what she'd learned about Swenson.

Gib approached. "I just got word that the price of
pole timber went up again, and this stand is top grade.
It might just keep us in business."

Tess's mouth curved in a smile, but inside she felt
the sting of Zak's ultimatum the night before about
logging the pole-timber area. "We should be done here
in less than three weeks," she said, noticing her father's hard hat and work clothes.

"Any problems?"

"I was just about to ask Curt some questions," Tess
replied.

Gib eyed her curiously. "What kind of questions?"

"Mainly about his past. Who he worked for. I'm
beginning to think he may have something to do with
everything that's been happening around here." She
explained what she'd learned about Swenson, then
offered her reasons for suspecting Curt. "He was the
first to discover the landslide—he's woods boss, so
he's first on the job. He was also the first to discover
the skidder tire, which he claimed ran over a spike.
Now we find out it was shot out with a high-powered

rifle, and he just happens to keep one on a rack in his truck.''

"So do lots of people."

"And Swenson says he actually saw Curt cutting the tree Jean-Pierre de Neuville claims was on his property. Regardless of whose property it's on, you didn't order it cut, I didn't order it cut, and neither did Mr. de Neuville."

"That may all be true, but the fact remains that Curt has no damn reason, so why would he do it?"

"That's what I hope to find out."

"Well, you'd better keep him on here until we get this timber down. Without it, all the men might be looking for new jobs."

"That's another thing I wanted to talk to you about," Tess said in a tight voice, approaching the next subject with trepidation. "There are some old-growth firs among the pole timber, and one of them has an eagle's nest in it."

Gib eyed her suspiciously. "So?"

Tess gave him a quick nervous smile. "We're not supposed to log within six hundred feet of the tree."

"That may be, but I've seen that nest and it's been inactive for years."

"Yes, but the eagles are still using it for a perch—roosting at night."

"Then they'll have to find another place to perch. There's no way in hell I'll stop the logging just because of an empty nest."

"What if we're . . . ordered to stop?"

"Then send whoever does the ordering to me—and you just keep logging. No one's going to order me to stop cutting my own timber because of an empty bird's nest!"

"We do have other areas where we could log—"

"We have pole timber right here that needs cutting while the price is high. Now, I'll be on my way home," he said, dismissing the subject.

As Tess watched her father's truck pitch and plunge down the crude road, she desperately hoped Zak would not carry out his threat. She looked toward the creaking bulldozer and saw it lumber to a halt. Curt jumped down to toss scattered limbs onto the pile.

"Curt!" she yelled, motioning to him.

Curt walked over to where she stood. "About two and a half weeks and we should have this area cleared," he said as he approached.

Tess smiled. "Good. Gib's thinking about putting this area into grass and leasing it for pasture, so as soon as the timber's down, we'll need to do something about these stumps."

Curt rested his hands on his hips and surveyed the area. "We can grub 'em out with the Cat," he said.

"I thought about that," Tess replied, "but we'll be needing the Cat to log a piece of land we just contracted. The quickest way would be to blast them out, but Swenson's the only man around who knows how to handle explosives—and we're not likely to hire him to do it." She gave Curt time for her words to sink in, then added, "I don't suppose you've ever done anything like that, have you?"

Curt looked at her quickly, then his gaze shifted away. "No," he said. "I've never handled dynamite, and I don't think I'd like to start now."

Tess's eyebrows went up. "I guess I don't blame you." After a moment, she asked, "Were you ever in the service?"

Curt looked at her with a start. "No, why?"

Tess shrugged. "I want to sort of pool skills around here, and I figure the men who've been in the service might have learned skills we can use. Have you done any other type of work besides logging?" she asked.

"Some construction work," Curt answered hesitantly.

"Where?"

"In Portland."

"Who did you work for?"

Caught by surprise, Curt replied, "Maddox," then paused a moment before adding, "Construction."

Tess noticed that Curt seemed a bit ill at ease. "What type of construction? Light, industrial?" she pressed.

Curt drew in a long breath. "Both."

"Dozer work?"

"No...well, yes. We did some...tearing down."

One glance at Curt's strained face told Tess he wanted out of this conversation. She made a mental note to check on Maddox Construction in Portland and see what she could learn about Curt Broderick. "Was that before or after you logged in Montana?" she asked.

"Before," Curt replied, his eyes moving restlessly about the clearing.

"Well, if you hear of anyone who can blast out these stumps, let me know," she said, giving Curt a brief smile.

Curt nodded. "I'd better get back to the Cat now," he said, shifting his weight to leave.

Tess was aware that Curt was unusually anxious to go back to work. As she watched him skillfully operate the bulldozer, she hoped something would turn up that would prove her suspicions about him wrong, but she didn't hold out a lot of hope.

Two days later, as the men were shutting down for the night, a plain brown sedan pulled in next to the skidder, where Tess stood talking to Herring. An officious-looking man in a business suit stepped out. "I'm looking for Teslyn O'Reilly," he said.

Tess stepped forward. "I'm Teslyn O'Reilly."

"Ms. O'Reilly," the man said, holding up a small folder with an identification card, "I'm Special Agent Richard Keightly, and I'm with the U.S. Department of the Interior—Fish and Wildlife. It's been brought to our attention that you're clear-cutting within the primary zone of a bald-eagle nest and I must ask you to cease and desist all operations in this area immediately."

"The nest has been abandoned for years," she said, "and we don't plan to cut any timber close to the tree. Besides, how can you be certain we're actually cutting in the primary zone?"

"The tree and the restricted zone have been plotted on an aerial photo."

"Could we continue just for a few more days, until we get this timber—"

"I'm sorry, no. You must stop now. Today." Agent Keightly reached into his inside breast pocket and withdrew a paper. "This is for you."

Tess looked at the paper. "What is this supposed to mean?"

"It's a court order."

Tess felt the blood drain from her face as she studied the document. She looked at Agent Keightly. "Will you be coming back?"

"No," he replied. "Not unless we have reason to believe you're still logging." He climbed into his car.

Tess peered down at the paper and before he closed the door said, "Well, I suppose we have no other choice but to move our operation to another area."

"We appreciate your cooperation, Ms. O'Reilly," Agent Keightly replied. With one final glance around the clearing, he drove off.

Tess stared after the car until it was out of sight, then she turned to the men who had gathered in the clearing. "Get busy," she said. "We still have trees to cut." She'd leave a good stand of timber near the nest and only harvest the pole timber on the lower area. Maybe there would still be enough board feet to pull Timber West out of hock.

Every day for the next week they worked from first light till dark. Gradually the stack of logs rose high on the landing. Tess had just returned to the cutting site after calling and notifying the truckers to start loading when the plain brown sedan returned, accompanied by an Oregon State Police car. Two officers stepped out of the police car and flanked Agent Keightly. As they approached Tess, one of the officers stepped forward. "Teslyn O'Reilly?"

"Yes."

"Before we ask you any questions, you must understand your rights. You have the right to remain silent. Anything you say may be used against you . . ."

CHAPTER FOURTEEN

THE CELL DOOR clanged shut. Tess looked around. It was a four-bunk cell shared by three women. One inmate, scarcely more than a girl, lay curled up on one cot and facing the wall. The other, an Amazon of a woman with a hawklike nose, stepped forward. Her face was as hard as the concrete floor. Tess's lips darted into a smile, then she sat on the empty lower bunk, wondering where Gib had been when she'd called.

The big woman towered above her like an ominous Statue of Liberty. "That bunk you're on there's mine, honey," she said in a gruff voice.

Without speaking, Tess jumped up and climbed onto the upper bunk. She might take on Jed Swenson, but she had no intention of quibbling with this formidable hulk. The woman settled herself beneath where Tess lay, and Tess felt the entire frame of the metal structure give under her weight. The woman grunted and spoke again. "Whatcha in for, honey?"

In a voice unfamiliar even to her own ears, Tess squeaked, "Disturbing a bird's nest."

The woman droned, "You're pretty frail-lookin' to be a smart ass, honey. Now, I asked ya. Whatcha in for?"

"I'm really not kidding. I was logging in an area where there's an eagle's nest—"

"You were what?" The woman sat up, whacking her head on the bottom of Tess's bunk and letting out a string of colorful expletives.

Somehow, in this bare gloomy cube of space that caged them, Tess saw the humor of the situation and she snickered. "That does sound a bit ridiculous, doesn't it, but that's it. I'm booked for disturbing an eagle's nest."

The woman sent a bellow of laughter ringing through the corridor and bouncing off the walls. "Now, don't that beat all? There're rapists and murderers and child molesters out roamin' the streets, and what do those twits do? They arrest a snip of a woman for disturbin' a bird's nest. Well, don't that beat all." The woman rose to her feet, grinning broadly.

As Tess looked at her, she found something warm about her puffy eyes. She sat up on her bunk and smiled back. "I'm Tess O'Reilly" she said, extending her hand.

The woman crunched Tess's hand. "I'm Rita Clatsop. You wanna know what I'm in for?"

Tess wasn't sure she did, but if Rita Clatsop wanted to tell her, she'd definitely listen.

"I'm in here for walkin'."

Tess tilted her head as she tried to figure out what "walkin'" was.

A twinkle shone in Rita's eyes. "You know, streetwalkin'. Well, not me—my girls."

Tess swallowed. "Oh."

"Those twits around here won't even let a lady make a livin'—lockin' me up for what I do best. Me and my girls can't make a decent livin' doing nothin' else. Now they're gonna reeducate us. How do ya like that?" Before Tess could respond, Rita continued. "You ever been out on the street?"

"Well, no, I, uh—"

"Well, before I started my own business, I'd worked my way up to the top," she said. "The very top. I even took on some fancy dudes high up in big business, if you know what I mean...with the suits and ties and all. But since I moved my business to Bakers Creek, the girls don't get those high-class kind anymore. But they say the boys around here are a lot more fun."

Tess swallowed. "Bakers Creek?"

"Yeah, south end of town—Crossbuck Tavern. It's my place, ya know. You say you're in loggin'?"

Tess cleared her throat. "Well, yes. I manage Timber West Logging."

"Oh sure," Rita said. "I know quite a few of the boys. Nice bunch."

Tess's eyes grew wide. "Which ones...I mean, who do you know from Timber West?" she asked, trying to imagine which of the men would visit the Crossbuck.

"Sean Herring," Rita replied. "Comes to see Rosie. Nice fella. Real quiet, though. And Mac Royer. Jennie always makes him take a bath first. But I'm sort of thinkin' about sellin' the place. Kinda got me a boyfriend. Jeddy wants me to quit."

"Jeddy?"

"Big fella who used to work for ya—Jed Swenson."

Somewhere in Tess's throat was a voice box, but for the moment she was unable to find it.

Rita continued undaunted. "He's different from the other fellas I've known. Always brings me somethin', ya know? Flowers, a kitten—even brought me a tree once."

"A tree?"

"I said I needed some firewood, so Christmas Day he came haulin' in this tree and chopped it up right in my front yard. Got me through last winter, though. Never had no one treat me like a lady the way Jeddy does."

"He doesn't mind if you call him . . . Jeddy?"

"Well, I don't call him that to his face because that's what his sisters call him and he's kinda sensitive about it. He's usually just plain 'honey.' Anyway, we have this sort of understandin'. He treats me like a lady, and I just let him sort of do what he wants. Jeddy don't like me tellin' him what to do, so I don't. He's a cutie, though. Makes up for it in other ways."

Tess caught the distant wistful light in Rita's eyes. "Then you know about him in Vietnam?"

Rita nodded. "You mean about his leg?"

"Leg?"

"Losin' half his leg. You didn't know he's got a wooden leg?"

"Well, no," Tess replied. "He never mentioned that."

"Wooden from the knee down. He got it shot up pretty bad fightin' off forty men. Got a Congressional Medal of Honor for doin' it, though. But he only mentioned it once. He don't like to talk about it, so I never bring it up. That leg's a real touchy subject."

Tess looked at Rita. "What about Curt Broderick?" she ventured. "Do you...I mean, has he..."

"Curt's been in once or twice. Not a bad fella, but since he's been hangin' around Carl Yaeger he's different. I never did like Carl. Pretty rough about takin' what he wants from the girls, then leavin' fast."

Tess's eyes narrowed. "How long has Curt been hanging around with Carl Yaeger?"

"I don't know. A month, maybe two."

Tess thought about what Rita had just told her. Carl Yaeger had recently made a firm offer to buy Timber West—convenient timing, just after all the problems started. Could there be a connection? She found that curious. She looked up at Rita. "What will they be teaching you to do after you leave here?"

"Sewin'," Rita replied, "just sittin' on some factory bench sewin', for half the pay I'm gettin' doin' what I like to do most. But if Jeddy wants to get married—and he's mentioned it a few times—I just might tie the knot and settle down."

Before Tess could pursue the topic of Rita marrying Jed Swenson, a guard unlocked the cell door. "Your bail's been posted, Miss O'Reilly. You're free to go."

Tess stepped into the corridor. "What do you mean my bail's been posted? I wasn't able to reach my father. How did he know?"

"I don't know who your father is, miss, but a Mr. de Neuville's here. He posted bail for you. You'll be notified about the hearing."

Tess stiffened. "Hold it a minute. If Zak de Neuville posted my bail, you can just unpost it. I have no intention of leaving with him." She stepped back into the cell and crossed her arms. "And you can tell Mr. de Neuville I'll sit in here and rot before I leave on his bail money."

"Miss, I'm not sure you can do that. I'll have to check and let you know," the guard said, locking the cell door.

Tess gripped the bars and called after the guard as he walked away. "I know my rights and I *can* do that. I don't have to accept charity, and I have no intention of paying the bail money back to Zak de Neuville."

Scratching his head, the guard walked away. Moments later, footsteps rang through the corridor. "This way, Mr. de Neuville," she heard the guard saying.

Zak marched in long angry strides toward Tess's cell. "Come on, Tess, you're going with me," he stated.

"Oh, no, I'm not," she replied.

Zak rested his hands on his hips and glared at her. "This is ridiculous."

Tess tilted her head. "Ridiculous? Isn't it what you wanted? I was under the impression that you're the one who put me here."

Zak looked at Rita Clatsop, who stared at him from behind Tess, then his eyes shifted back to Tess. "I don't intend to argue with you here," he said, lowering his voice. "Just come with me and we'll talk about it outside."

Tess held the bars and peered between them. "I don't seem to be getting through to you, Zak. Read my lips. No." She enunciated with an exaggerated movement of her lips. "N-o—"

"Atta girl, honey," Rita interjected.

"I'm sorry, sir," the guard said. "I guess you'll have to leave."

Zak took a long breath, his eyes fixed on Tess. "This is your last chance..."

Rita walked around to stand by Tess, her big hand draped over Tess's shoulder. "The little lady said no."

Zak's gaze darted to Rita, then back to Tess. "This is just great," he muttered. He scowled at Tess for a moment, then waved his arm in resignation. "Fine! Have it your way." As the guard led Zak back along the corridor, Tess climbed onto the top bunk, stretched out and smiled.

Her first night in the county jail wasn't too bad. The young woman was released and Tess was left alone with Rita Clatsop. Rita talked freely about her childhood and the circumstances leading to her life on the street, and Tess liked her. She found Rita to be a compassionate and understanding person and hoped she'd find what she wanted with Jed Swenson.

The next day, Tess was released. Although she wasn't given details, she learned that the charges had been dropped because Gib agreed to shut down logging operations in the pole-timber area. Gib came to pick her up, and as he pulled the truck onto the highway, she turned to him. "Well, I hope you're satisfied. I kept logging like you said," she spat angrily.

"I told you to come to me if someone threatened to shut us down," he replied. "Why didn't you?"

Tess stared blankly out the window. "I didn't think you'd be too receptive, especially since Zak was behind it. You do know he's the one who reported the nest, don't you?"

"He told me," Gib replied. "He also said he told you to stop, and you refused."

"Of course I refused," Tess said with exasperation, "because I knew that's what you'd do!" She heaved a sigh. "That *is* what you'd have done, isn't it?"

Gib looked at her. "Probably. A man has to do what he has to do."

"I don't understand," Tess said. "You don't seem particularly mad at Zak."

Gib shrugged. "Like I said, a man has to do what he has to do." He smiled. "At least he stands by his convictions. I like that in a man."

Tess settled against the seat. "I tried to call you yesterday. Where were you?"

"Probably out pacing off the property," Gib said. "Jean-Pierre de Neuville's slapped us with papers—suing us for cutting trees on my own land." He drew in a heavy breath. "Maybe it's time to sell."

"Do you mean that?"

"With all the equipment repairs and no pole timber to bail us out, I may have to accept Yaeger's offer."

"No, you don't," Tess said. "Jean-Pierre de Neuville would buy the land in a minute."

Gib scowled. "Before I'd sell it to de Neuville, I'd give it to Yaeger."

"Well, don't go signing any papers yet," Tess said. "I just learned that Yaeger and Broderick are friends. Yaeger could have planted Curt to sabotage our operation in order to force us to sell."

"I've known Carl Yaeger for years."

"That doesn't mean he wouldn't do something like this," Tess said. "I've heard he's pulled some pretty shady deals."

"He's a good businessman," Gib countered. "Moves in when the time is right."

"Sure," Tess snapped. "But he's the one who *makes* the time right. Just don't do anything until I have a chance to find out a few things about Curt, like precisely what he did at Maddox Construction in Portland."

Gib looked thoughtfully out the window. Then he turned to Tess. "Don't you mean Maddox Demolition?"

"Maddox Demolition?" Tess stared at her father.

"In Portland—biggest demolition company in the northwest."

Tess blinked several times. "If that's so, it *has* to be Curt behind everything." She'd definitely keep an eye on him. If he was involved with Carl Yaeger, they might make another move. "The police sure are slow to take action around here," she said, weary with the prospects of more trouble. "Except, of course, when you threaten a bird's nest," she added ruefully.

After Gib dropped her off at the cabin, Tess headed for Zak's. In her mind she saw his face peering into her jail cell the day before when he'd come to post bail. She'd acted childishly and she owed him an apology. The whole jail episode should never have happened. She should support Zak's efforts to preserve the eagles, not thwart them. With luck, she'd be able to set everything straight, so that they could get on with their lives.

She stepped onto the porch and raised a tentative hand to the door, then knocked lightly. When there was no response, she walked around to the back. She'd seen Zak's truck in the parking area, but he was nowhere around. For a few moments she listened while scanning the surroundings, and gradually she caught the unmistakable sound of woodchopping. Following a well-worn trail into the forest, she hiked between tall fir and cedar, moving in eager strides toward the sound.

She reached a small clearing, and paused to gaze across to where Zak stood, stripped to the waist and brandishing an ax. For a moment she just stared at the play of muscles across his shoulders and down his back. Over and over the blade cracked into upright logs, splitting them cleanly. He rested the ax against a stump, mopped the perspiration from his brow, then grasped the ax once more.

Tess stepped into the clearing. "Hey, mister," she called out. "You're not holding that ax right."

Zak turned abruptly, then smiled. "The name's not mister," he said, releasing the ax and moving slowly toward her. "It's Zak—Zakhra Bertsolari de..." His voice trailed off, and for a moment he stood looking at her across the clearing. When he opened his arms, Tess rushed to him and he crushed her in his embrace. She kissed him with fervent intensity, then looked into his eyes. "Is there any place in your life for a stubborn bullheaded woman who loves you?"

Zak smiled down at her. "There's always room in my life for a stubborn bullheaded woman," he replied, "if she'll have a headstrong obstinate man who loves her, too." Then his face sobered. "I'm sorry about what happened, forcing you to shut down logging on the ridge."

"No," Tess said, "I'm the one who's sorry. I should never have listened to Gib. And I should never have acted so childishly when you came to bail me out, but I was still angry."

"I put you in an awkward position," Zak said. "Believe me, honey, it was one of the hardest things I've ever had to do. Am I forgiven?"

Tess looked up. "Yes, you're forgiven." A thoughtful smile spread across her face. "Actually, I'm not sorry I spent the night in jail," she said. "Rita was an interesting cellmate."

Zak arched a cynical brow. "She looked fascinating."

Tess laughed. "No, really. She told me Jed Swenson's courting her—"

"Swenson courting?" Zak looked amazed. "Well, from what I saw of the woman, he'd better not step out of line."

"I don't think he wants to. He's a real Romeo. Brings Rita flowers and all. He's even talking marriage—"

Zak pulled her tightly against him and kissed her again, stifling her words. Then he reached for his denim shirt and pulled it on. "I know of a more appropriate place to continue this," he said, tucking the shirt into his jeans.

Tess looked at him with curiosity. "Where?"

"The Grotto." He pulled her along behind him and headed for the ravine. Tess followed eagerly. It had been years since they'd made love on a bed of cool soft moss in the shadowy twilight of the forest.

As they reached the edge of the ravine, Tess pulled Zak to a halt. "That's Jed Swenson's truck," she stated, looking through the trees to where the ridge road cut an opening in the forest.

Zak turned and saw Swenson's drab tan vehicle. "He's probably finishing the road. There's still some grading to do at the north end."

"Then why is he parked down here?" Tess asked.

Zak shrugged. "Maybe he's checking his handiwork, seeing how the road's draining since he put in the culvert."

"I suppose," Tess said, feeling uneasy but not knowing why. They turned away from the truck, but when they started to descend the fern-covered slope, a muffled explosion from above made them snap their heads around. "What was that?" she yelped.

"Let's go," Zak urged. "It sounded like it came from the direction of the ridge."

They scrambled up the embankment and pressed their way between boughs of cedar and fir, emerging on the freshly graveled logging road a short distance from Jed Swenson's truck. "If Swenson's blowing up his own road, it doesn't make a hell of a lot of sense," Tess said, quickening her pace to keep up with Zak.

Zak glanced over his shoulder. "Well, he's obviously blowing up something," he replied, "and it isn't far from here—"

"There he is!" Tess pointed ahead.

"Swenson!" Zak yelled. "Hold it there!"

Jed Swenson looked back briefly, then dashed through the dust still hovering in the air and scrambled into the large concrete culvert under the road.

As Zak raced toward the culvert, Tess rushed to catch up and grabbed his arm. "You're no match for Swenson," she said, frightened.

"I don't know what the hell he's doing," Zak said, shrugging off Tess's hand, "but match or no match, I'm going in after him."

"Zak, no!" she shrieked, "Please don't!"

Suddenly Curt Broderick burst out of the opposite end of the culvert, grabbed a backpack lying beside the road and took off toward the woods. Swenson shot out of the culvert after him, then tripped and fell.

"Get him!" he yelled to Zak. "He tried to blow up the culvert."

Zak glanced at Swenson, then chased Curt. Lunging for him, he managed to grab him by the legs as he headed into the woods. Curt fell to the ground and Zak threw himself on top, but Curt heaved Zak off his back, sending him sprawling to the ground. Zak jumped to his feet and crouched forward. "You're not going anywhere, Broderick," he said.

Curt sprang to his feet and glared at Zak, his face red, veins bulging in his temples. "Don't try to stop me," he said, rushing at Zak with fists raised.

Zak blocked Curt's blow with his forearm, then grabbed Curt's arm, jerking him off balance. As Curt fell to his knees, Swenson raced up and pinned his arm behind him in a hammerlock.

"Now you're gonna talk," Swenson said.

"Not to you, Swenson."

Swenson tightened his grip and lifted the arm higher. "You were tryin' to blow up the culvert, weren't you?"

Curt winced but said nothing.

"Weren't you?" Swenson bellowed, pushing the pinned arm even higher. "And you were tryin' to put the blame on me."

"Take it easy, Swenson," said Tess. "Don't break his arm. Just hold him while we check out the culvert."

She and Zak walked over and crawled into the culvert. "If he was planning to blow it up, he didn't make it," Zak said.

Tess noticed several jagged cracks in the curved concrete surface above them. "He may not have been trying to blow it up—just fracture it so the first loaded truck would collapse it."

"Sounds logical," Zak agreed as they emerged. "Why don't we see what Curt has to say?" They walked over to where Swenson held Curt Broderick in his powerful grip.

Tess looked down at Curt. "You worked for Maddox Demolition," she stated. "And you also set the charge that caused the landslide, didn't you?"

Curt's eyes flared in anger, then he looked away, saying nothing.

"Fine," Tess said. "But if you don't want to talk here, they'll get it out of you at the sheriff's office. I suspect they'll also learn you shot out the skidder tire and cut the hydraulic line on the Cat—"

"I'm not taking the blame for Carl Yaeger," Curt snarled.

"So it was Yaeger," Tess said. "Whatever he offered you must have been pretty damn good."

Curt struggled against Swenson's grip for a moment, then gave up, grimacing, as Swenson tightened the hammerlock. "He said he'd give me part interest in his operation and make me foreman if I got you to sell out to him. He's the one who planned it all—the landslide, the skidder tire, the culvert..."

"And the tree?" Swenson added.

Curt glared at Swenson, then nodded.

Zak reached for the pack Curt had dropped, unzipped it and rummaged inside. "This is interesting," he said, drawing out a taped packet of half-sticks of dynamite. He shoved them back into the pack and turned to Tess. "We'd better call the sheriff."

Tess looked at Swenson. "Can you manage him till the police get here?" she asked.

"Sure. He's not going anywhere," Swenson replied, confident. "We'll be right here."

Tess smiled at Swenson. "Thanks," she said. "I guess I owe you an apology. Maybe we can't work together, but I think you're a good man."

Swenson crooked his neck and spat a wad of tobacco into the dirt, then smiled. "Just doin' my job."

CHAPTER FIFTEEN

TESS LEANED FORWARD, intently studying the chessboard resting on the coffee table in her cabin. After a moment, she moved her pawn. "All along I thought there was something familiar about the name Maddox," she said. "I guess Curt worked there for about six years."

Gib's bushy brows drew together in concentration. He moved his queen, then responded, "I still can't get over Yaeger putting him up to it, though."

"Well, I'm not surprised," Tess said, sliding her rook across the board.

"Pay attention," Gib said. "That's not a very good move. You can take it back if you want."

Tess contemplated the board for a minute, then rolled her eyes. "That *was* pretty dumb, wasn't it?" She moved the rook back two rows.

Gib grinned. "That's better." He advanced a pawn.

"What do you think's going to happen now?" Tess asked.

Gib studied the board. "They're looking at conspiracy and several felony charges," he replied. "And by the time I collect damages, Yaeger won't be too anxious to pull anything like that again."

Tess looked up. "You really plan to hit them hard?"

"Hell, yes," he said. "Timber West was doing pretty damn good before they started their dirty dealings. We might not even have had to depend on the pole timber if they hadn't caused all those problems. If we can collect damages, we might end up sitting pretty."

"Then would you still want to try and make a go of it here?" Tess asked, in a weary voice.

Gib studied his daughter, then sighed. "I think I'm about ready to bail out. I guess I just don't have the fight I used to have to keep this place going."

Tess eyed her father, a wry smile on her lips. "Don't worry about fight. You still have plenty of it. You'll be blowing off steam till your dying day. I can just hear you at your funeral—'don't jerk the casket...the hole's not deep enough...who the hell sent all the flowers...'"

Gib laughed. "Am I that bad?"

"You're impossible." Tess's eyes shifted to Gib's fingers. "You're also going to lose your bishop!"

"What!"

"Pay attention, Gib."

As he studied the board, there was the sound of footsteps on the porch. Tess got up off the sofa and opened the door. "Zak!" Her eyes shifted nervously from Zak to Jean-Pierre de Neuville, who stood beside him. "Hello, Mr. de Neuville. Uh, please come in," she said in an uncertain voice. She gave Zak a questioning look and stepped back.

Jean-Pierre nodded a polite greeting. "It's nice to see you again, Miss O'Reilly." A hint of a smile touched his lips.

Gib stared intently at the chessboard, obviously ignoring their guests.

"Gib?" Tess said.

Gib raised his eyes to Jean-Pierre. "If you're here to settle out of court, you've wasted a trip. I'm not about to give up anything that's rightfully mine."

Jean-Pierre moved to stand above the chessboard. "I didn't come to talk about the hearing, but I do want to discuss another deal with you," he said, his eyes moving over the board studying the positions of the pieces.

Zak reached for Tess's arm. "I want to talk to you, too," he said softly, pulling her toward the door.

"Now?" Tess whispered, incredulous. She glanced at the two older men. "We can't go now," she said in a hushed voice. "They'll kill each other."

Zak's lips spread in a slow smile. "Then our problems will be over, won't they?" he said. "Come on. They're grown men."

"I really don't think we should leave them."

"Father?" Zak called. "Why don't you sit down and finish the game for Tess. We're taking a little walk."

Jean-Pierre looked from Zak to the chessboard, then his eyes rested on Gib.

Gib glanced up and shrugged. "You play?" he asked.

"Some," Jean-Pierre replied, lowering himself to the sofa.

Zak nudged Tess onto the porch, drawing the door closed behind them.

"They'll be fine—at least for the duration of the game," he said.

Tess sighed in resignation. "I suppose."

Zak took Tess's hand and they scurried across the dirt road and into the woods. Under a canopy of trees, he pulled her into his arms and kissed her soundly. When at last they drew apart, she looked into eyes that told her she was loved, and admired, and cherished.

Zak trailed a finger along her cheek. "I have something for you." He reached into his pocket and took out a small velvet box. "You have to promise me one thing, though," he said, cradling the box in his hand.

"Yes?" Tess's eyes glistened with excitement. "What do you want me to promise?"

Zak opened the box. "That you'll never bury this again."

Tess looked at the small gold band. "Zak!" she exclaimed. "How did you ever find it?"

"I had to perform surgery on our tree," he replied, "but the ring was still in the bottle where you'd left it."

Tess took the ring with a shaky hand, then tipped it so it would catch the light. "*Eskualdun fededun*—the Basque is faithful," she murmured, reading the familiar inscription.

Zak took the ring and reached for her hand. "Will you marry me?"

"Oh, yes!" she cried, holding her hand out for the ring. Zak slipped it on her finger and she looked up at him with curious eyes. "When did you go back for it?"

"Last week," he replied. "But I didn't want to put it on your finger through bars, so I decided to wait."

"I wish I could show it to Rita," said Tess, holding out her hand and gazing in wonder at the ring she never thought she'd see again. "We talked about you that night. She thought it would be best for me to find someone else. She said she knew some really nice fellows."

Zak gave her a knavish grin. "Well, if you want to reconsider..."

Tess moved her hand so that the ring glittered in the sunlight. It seemed so natural to have it on her finger again. "You just name the date," she said, reaching up to kiss him.

Zak kissed her gently on the forehead. "Very—" he moved to the tip of her nose and pecked it lightly "—very soon." He punctuated his statement by kissing her firmly on the lips.

For a few moments Tess savored the luxury of Zak's lips on hers, then she reluctantly pulled away. "Where will we live?" she asked.

"Here."

Tess glanced around. "Here?"

"Well, in my cabin for a while. The way I figure it, we can add a bedroom for Pio and maybe a small family room. That way we'd have plenty of room for now—at least until I finish with the cheetah program and our family starts to grow.''

Tess couldn't contain a wide grin at the prospect of having Zak's children. "And when the family starts to grow, would we move to Navarre?'' she asked.

Zak shrugged. "That depends.''

"On what? I thought you wanted to move there and take over the winery.''

A frown creased Zak's brow. "Would you be comfortable living there?''

"Comfortable?'' Tess said. "You say that as if living in that huge house would be a hardship.''

Zak smiled, his hands gliding up and down her sides. "We'd have the south wing to ourselves—it faces the vineyards. And since Mother and Father want to start traveling as soon as they have someone to take over, we'd be alone quite a bit and—''

"Zak!'' Tess pressed her fingers to his lips to silence him. "I'd love it, but . . .'' She paused.

Zak looked at her, worried. "But what? What's wrong?''

Tess sighed. "I really want to start college this fall.''

"College?''

"I told you that before. Why does everyone just shrug it off? That's the same reaction I got from Gib and Aunt Ruth the first time I mentioned it. Is it so unbelievable that—''

"Honey,'' Zak interrupted, "you can do whatever you want. I just haven't given it any thought since you mentioned it.''

"That's my point. No one believes me. I could commute to Eugene. I've looked over the catalog and I'd like to study marketing."

"Marketing?" Zak considered the ramifications. "I think that's great. We could use a marketing expert at the winery."

"I'm not going to be an expert," Tess said, "just your average run-of-the-mill college graduate."

Zak looked at her lovingly. "I doubt that. You'll never be run-of-the-mill anything."

Tess smiled. "But what about Pio? Won't he need a mom in the house when he comes home from school?"

"No problem," Zak assured her. "He'll be getting off the bus at the wildlife park each day. He's got a regular round of chores there. His mom can just concentrate on studying and going to school."

Tess tickled Zak's cheek with her finger. "You can't take up all of Pio's after-school time, though," she said. "He and I have a project planned." She saw the question in Zak's eyes and smiled. "Pio's new tree house. The way I see it, we'll build a two-story house with a shake roof and a balcony and—"

"Planned?" Zak said, his brows gathering. "You've already planned this?"

"Of course," Tess replied, her finger trailing along his bottom lip. "Pio's expecting it."

"So that's what you were telling him just before we left Navarre. I wondered what that was all about."

"It was a bribe," Tess admitted. "You have to do that with kids sometimes, you know. I told him I'd build him a new tree house if he promised he'd never, ever, climb up to the old one again. So, he promised." Her mouth quirked. "It'll be tricky staying one step ahead of my new son, but I think I can manage."

Zak looked puzzled. "You've never been a mother before," he said. "Where did you get all the experience?"

Tess raised a delicate brow. "Being Gib O'Reilly's daughter."

Zak laughed. He reached for her hand, pulling her along. "Now I have something else to show you."

"Where are you taking me?"

"To the Grotto."

Tess stopped, tugging Zak to a halt. "You're not serious!" she exclaimed. "Right in the middle of the day? We might get caught."

Zak laughed. "I see what's on your mind, but that's not what I planned—at least not until later. Come on." He pulled her into the woods and they followed a deer trail toward the hollow where their Adam-and-Eve tree stood. After they climbed down the steep embankment of the ravine, Tess paused for a moment to absorb the quiet beauty of the cavernlike mossy hollow.

Deep in the shadowy twilight of the forest, boughs of giant cedars hovered protectively overhead, blocking the light but not the mist sifting through the evergreens. All around, moss and lacy ferns covered the forest floor, twists of ivy climbed the embankment, and ropes of oak vines clung to trees. Although some timber in the area had been cut, the Grotto was untouched.

Tess looked at the big oak tree and squinted. The words "Adam loves Eve" were almost obscured by years of growth. She released Zak's hand and walked over to the tree. The hollow where she'd left the ring so many years before gaped open, tool marks scarring the edges.

Zak stood beside her and slipped his arm around her waist. "I didn't want to do that," he said, "but the hole had almost closed completely."

"Is this what you wanted to show me?" Tess asked, staring at the unsightly hole in their tree.

Zak drew a small flashlight from his pocket and clicked it on. "No," he replied. "What I want to show you is inside the hole. Take a look."

Tess stooped down and peered into the opening as Zak flashed the light inside. "What am I supposed to see?"

The beam of light caught several pieces of rusty wire that groped out from the core of the tree. "That's old barbed wire," he said. "While I was rooting around inside for the bottle with your ring, I snagged my hand on it, so I dug some of it loose. Look at it closely. There are several strands embedded in the tree, and each one has a different kind of barb. They were apparently part of an old fence that was nailed to the tree. Do you realize the significance of it?"

Tess studied the wires. "Well, I'm not sure."

"They show that a fence used to run through this area for a very long time—eighty years or more." Zak directed the light to one of the wires. "The flat twisted barb on that wire closest to the core of the tree dates back to the early 1900s. The next—that one with the S-shaped barb—goes back to about 1915. And the one closest to the outside, with the double-wire barb, is relatively modern."

"The tree's actually grown around them," Tess said, staring at the three sets of barbed wire.

"Yep," Zak replied. "I checked in the county records and found the old survey map and property description. When my father had the place surveyed recently, there was no way to tell where the old fence line ran, and it looks like the surveyor was off by about fifty feet."

"Then Gib has been right all along?"

"That's right. This tree is even described on the old survey as a line marker. I explained it to my father and showed him the tree and the old property descriptions, and he agreed I was right."

"Then he's dropping the suit?"

Zak shrugged and smiled. "He can't sue a man for cutting trees on his own land. I'm afraid Father and I have misjudged your father."

Tess looked at Zak's happy face. "How can you look so pleased when you know your father's going to have to eat crow?"

"I'm not pleased about that. I'm just glad they're running out of things to feud about."

"I'm sure they'll find something," Tess said. "When is your father planning to tell Gib about the property line?"

"About the same time he makes an offer on your place. He needs more grazing land, and since there's also a perch tree where Jed Swenson was logging, he can't clear the land up there, either."

"You shut your father down, too?" Tess's lips parted in disbelief.

Zak gave her a bland smile. "Mmm. I don't think I'm very popular around her. Anyway, Father wants to make an offer on the tract Timber West sits on. There's probably about sixty acres of cleared land—"

"Seventy," Tess corrected, "and almost fifty acres of timberland left—not counting the ridge." She pursed her lips. "But I can't imagine those two ever agreeing on anything long enough to make a deal." She took Zak's hand, tugging him around. "And talk about agreeing," she said, feeling apprehension churning in her stomach again, "we'd better get back before the game's over and all hell breaks loose."

Zak sighed. "I guess you're right."

They followed the trail back to the cabin. As they approached, loud angry voices could be heard. Tess's heart hammered. "I told you we shouldn't have left them alone," she scolded, breaking into a run.

"They were only playing a game of chess," Zak replied, lengthening his strides.

They bounded onto the porch. When Zak hurled the door open and Tess crashed to a halt behind him, Jean-Pierre and Gib turned in their direction.

"What the hell's going on?" Gib demanded, staring at Zak.

Jean-Pierre rose to his feet, impatient eyes also on Zak. "Is that any way to come into a house?"

Zak looked from his father to Gib. "We heard yelling and thought—"

"Hardly a reason to knock down a door," Jean-Pierre said.

"We just thought . . ." Zak looked at the two older men and realized that neither looked particularly angry. "What was all the yelling about just before we came in?"

Jean-Pierre squared his shoulders and glanced at Gib. "We were just discussing a business deal."

Tess eyed Gib uneasily. "What kind of business deal?"

Gib looked into his daughter's suspicious eyes. "We were discussing the sale price of Timber West. I don't intend to get robbed blind—"

"Robbed blind!" Jean-Pierre bellowed. "You got this place for a song. And that dead horse you call a bulldozer isn't worth the cost of hauling it away!"

"Dead horse, is it?!" Gib shouted back. "Then why are you so anxious to buy it?"

Zak stepped between the men. "Hold it there," he said, raising a hand. "Tess and I have an announcement to make. Then you two can continue your. . .discussion." He wrapped his arm around Tess and pulled her against him. "Like it or not, Tess and I are getting married."

When neither Gib nor Jean-Pierre spoke, Zak continued, "The two of you have been feuding for years. You've meddled in our lives and tried to keep us apart—but not anymore. We love each other and we won't let either of you come between us again.''

"And furthermore,'' Tess added, "someday you'll both be grandfathers to our children and they'll be your heirs, so think about *that* during your business discussion.''

For a moment Jean-Pierre said nothing. He stood motionless, looking at Zak and Tess. Then he turned to Gib. "I guess we should recognize when we're defeated,'' he said, a smile cracking his face. He extended his hand.

Gib's eyes rested on Jean-Pierre's hand, and for an instant Tess thought he wasn't going to take it. Then Gib smiled, too, and clasped Jean-Pierre's outstretched hand. "That boy of yours is damned persistent,'' he said, "but he got himself a helluva woman.'' He winked at Tess. "I just hope he can handle her.''

Zak gave Tess a squeeze and looked at Gib. "I'll do my best.''

"Good.'' Gib turned to Jean-Pierre. "Now about this land...''

"Your asking price is completely unreasonable,'' Jean-Pierre continued.

"Unreasonable!'' Gib's eyes flashed. "There's over two million board feet of marketable timber left on this land. We're talking seventy- to eighty-year-old second-growth timber—''

"Only if there aren't any eagles' nests around!''

"Wait!'' Zak broke in. He looked from his father to Gib. "Why don't you two settle the whole thing there?'' He pointed to the chessboard. "First winner of two games gets his price."

Jean-Pierre's mouth turned up in a confident smile. "I'm game," he said.

Gib shrugged. "Why not?"

Tess looked at her father, then at Jean-Pierre. "Incidentally," she said, "who won the last game?"

Jean-Pierre pursed his lips and motioned with his head toward Gib. "He did," he mumbled. "But not easily."

"Not easily! You left yourself wide open. All I had to do was move in—"

"It wasn't my game to start with—"

"Stop!" Tess cried. "Just sit down and get this over with."

Gib and Jean-Pierre moved around the table and sat opposite each other. Tess saw the eagerness on both faces as they arranged the pieces. "Now, if you two won't kill each other," she said, "Zak and I have some unfinished business." She looked at Zak and nodded toward the door. Zak took her hand and they left the cabin.

After they'd stepped onto the porch and closed the door, Tess looked up, arching a brow. "It should be an interesting game."

Zak gave her a quizzical look. "You never said exactly what your father's chess rating was. You do remember, don't you?"

"Of course," Tess replied.

"Well?"

Tess smiled. "Nineteen hundred—" she gave him a wry grin "—that is, the last time he was rated."

Zak let out a sharp whistle. "It's going to be close," he said, gathering her into his arms.

Tess raised herself on tiptoes to kiss Zak. As he pulled her close, she whispered, "Adam, why don't we continue this at the Grotto—now that our fathers will be occupied for a while."

Zak grinned. "I like that idea, Eve."

As they stepped from the porch, Jean-Pierre's voice rose. "Scrap that old equipment and the place would make a helluva wedding gift, wouldn't it Gib?"

"You said it, JP," Gib replied. "A helluva gift. Your play..."

Zak shook his head. "As I've said before, the only time I ever heard my father use profanity was when your father was involved—but this time it's music to my ears." He draped his arm across Tess's shoulders and drew her to him. "Mrs. Zakhra de Neuville," he said. "I like the sound of that."

Tess wrapped her arm around Zak's waist and looked up at him, her eyes filled with love and eager anticipation for the life they'd at last be sharing. "So do I," she replied. "So do I."

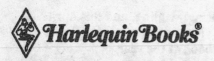 **Harlequin Books®**

GREAT NEWS...
HARLEQUIN UNVEILS NEW SHIPPING PLANS

For the convenience of customers, Harlequin has announced that Harlequin romances will now be available in stores at these convenient times each month*:

Harlequin Presents, American Romance, Historical, Intrigue:

> May titles: April 10
> June titles: May 8
> July titles: June 5
> August titles: July 10

Harlequin Romance, Superromance, Temptation, Regency Romance:

> May titles: April 24
> June titles: May 22
> July titles: June 19
> August titles: July 24

We hope this new schedule is convenient for you.

With only two trips each month to your local bookseller, you'll never miss any of your favorite authors!

*Please note: There may be slight variations in on-sale dates in your area due to differences in shipping and handling.

HDATES-R

This April, don't miss #449, CHANCE OF A LIFETIME, Barbara Kaye's third and last book in the Harlequin Superromance miniseries

Hamilton
H·O·U·S·E

A powerful restaurant conglomerate draws the best and brightest to its executive ranks. Now almost eighty years old, Vanessa Hamilton, the founder of Hamilton House, must choose a successor. Who will it be?

Matt Logan: He's always been the company man, the quintessential team player. But tragedy in his daughter's life and a passionate love affair made him make some hard choices....

Paula Steele: Thoroughly accomplished, with a sharp mind, perfect breeding and looks to die for, Paula thrives on challenges and wants to have it all...but is this right for her?

Grady O'Connor: Working for Hamilton House was his salvation after Vietnam. The war had messed him up but good and had killed his storybook marriage. He's been given a second chance—only he doesn't know what the hell he's supposed to do with it....

Harlequin Superromance invites you to enjoy Barbara Kaye's dramatic and emotionally resonant miniseries about mature men and women making life-changing decisions.

HARLEQUIN
American Romance®

THE ROMANCE THAT STARTED IT ALL!

For Diane Bauer and Nick Granatelli, the walk down the aisle was a rocky road....

Don't miss the romantic prequel to WITH THIS RING—

I THEE WED
BY ANNE McALLISTER

Harlequin American Romance #387

Let Anne McAllister take you to Cambridge, Massachusetts, to the night when an innocent blind date brought a reluctant Diane Bauer and Nick Granatelli together. For Diane, a smoldering attraction like theirs had only one fate, one future—marriage. The hard part, she learned, was convincing her intended....

Watch for Anne McAllister's I THEE WED, available *now* from Harlequin American Romance.

ITW